Alaska State Troopers:

GEEZER SQUAD

Ron Walden
Alaska True to Life Crime Writer

ISBN 978-1-95-726336-6
eBook 978-1-95-726337-3

Library of Congress Catalog Card Number: 2022918821

Manufactured in the United States of America.

FORWARD

Anyone involved professionally in the criminal justice system isn't likely to have the same sense of humor or personal character as regular folks. We can't talk about our jobs or the people we deal with daily, like most working people.

Those daily things are confidential. We're not allowed to discuss them outside the office, and even then, with no one except a few other law enforcement people. This restriction is what makes cops seem standoffish and unfriendly. They're not really. They're like any other person you meet. That's also why cops hang out with cops. In reality, we can be rowdy, uncouth people at times, I suppose.

There's a group of us, all retired law enforcement, that gather at my house most mornings for coffee. Our group has been tossed out of about every cafe in the vicinity, not for behavior, but for staying too long. Now we meet at my kitchen table for our daily gab session and coffee, of course.

I've used the personalities of these retired officers to create characters in this book. The characters and story are fiction, but the personalities are real. They're a great bunch of friends and loyal companions.

I'm proud to be part of the **"Alaska State Troopers: GEEZER SQUAD"**.

CHAPTER ONE

"911 operator, what is the nature of your emergency?"

"Uh, hello. This is Nicholas North. There's a pickup truck at the end of my driveway. Still running, but the driver looks dead. I think he was shot."

"What's your location, Mr. North?"

"Smith Way, off Ciechanski Road."

"Please hold while I get an officer headed to your location." The line went dead for several seconds, then the operator was back.

"Mr. North, unless the victim needs your medical assistance, I want you to return to your vehicle to wait for the officer. This is to protect the scene. The officer should be with you in about three minutes. Please stay on the line until he arrives."

"OK, Ma'am. I'll wait in my truck," said the caller.

"While we wait, can you tell me how you came to find the victim?"

"I'm Nick North and I own the auto repair shop at the "Y" in Soldotna. I worked late and was coming home when I found the truck parked on the road with no one around it. It was and still is running. I never touched anything. Just looked inside and saw the driver laying on the front seat. It looks like he was shot three times."

"The officer just turned onto Smith Way." She reported.

"Yeah, I see his lights flashing."

"You can hang up as soon as the officer reaches you. He'll give you further instructions. And there are two more officers on the way."

Nick was standing in front of his truck when the trooper climbed out of his patrol car. He waved at Nick but went directly to the victim's vehicle and looked inside before speaking to Nick. He took a small camera from inside his vest and snapped several pictures before reporting by radio.

"The victim is obviously deceased. There are what appear to be three bullet holes visible in the body. Two in the chest, one in the forehead." The trooper reached inside the truck and turned off the engine.

Two more patrol cars arrived as the first trooper walked over to speak with Nick North.

"Hello," he said as he approached, "I'm Trooper Ericson. Did you report the body?"

"Yes, I'm Nick North. We've met before at my repair shop in town."

"I remember you," said the trooper. "You live nearby, don't you?"

"Yes, at the end of this drive. That truck was there when I came home from work. I could see the driver was dead as soon as I got close to the window. I called it in." North dropped his cigarette butt on the ground and stepped on it with a heavy sole boot.

"I'd like for you to go home and remain there until I contact you. It'll take several hours to process the crime scene. You might as well get some sleep while you can," the trooper suggested.

"I'll be at the house. Just come down there when you finish." North understood the process and climbed into his truck to go to his house.

Ericson turned to speak with approaching investigators. It was near midnight on June 24th. The days now provided more than nineteen hours of daylight on the Kenai Peninsula. It wouldn't be necessary to order artificial lighting to investigate this crime scene.

As with any crime scene, it's important to ensure the investigation doesn't destroy any evidence. The entire area would have to be photographed with a great deal care with attention to detail given to footprints, tire tracks, shell casings and any items found at the scene and inside of the vehicle. It would be hauled to the Alaska State Trooper garage in Soldotna and a search warrant obtained before the inside could be searched. As Nick North had said, it was obvious the driver was deceased, but a professional medical opinion would be needed for that. A call was made requesting a medic come to the scene for that opinion and pronouncement while troopers continued the investigative process. These three men had worked many scenes as a team and had a consistent system for investigating crime scenes, with each trooper covering a different facet of the search. One did photography, one did tracks and fingerprinting while the third searched the area surrounding the vehicle. They were accustomed to using this proven team approach.

Dispatch notified the Detachment Commander of the apparent homicide. The captain gave orders to call back for any further assistance or advice. He'd be in the office early in the morning.

An hour later, a large flatbed tow truck arrived to load the victim's vehicle for delivery to the trooper office and to secure it in their garage. One of the investigating officers, Trooper Oats, followed the wrecker, keeping the evidence in sight. He helped the driver offload the vehicle and move it inside the garage for secure storage until the search warrant was obtained.

Trooper Ericson finished his notes and asked Trooper Donald to remain at the scene until he returned. "I'm going down to North's place to interview him. When you finish you can wait in your car until I get back. I shouldn't be more than an hour. I'll get a statement and have him come to the office in the morning."

Ericson drove the short distance down the drive to the home of Nick

North. It was a nice chalet-style log home surrounded by a dense spruce forest. The grass in the front yard was neatly trimmed and maintained. The trooper stepped onto the front porch and knocked on the door. North must have been sitting in the living room and answered the knock within seconds.

"Come inside, George, I've been waiting for you."

"Despite the circumstances it's good to see you again too, Nick. How are you holding up?"

"I'm OK, but I'm not used to finding dead folks in my driveway. Did you recognize the dead guy?"

"Yes," replied Ericson, "It's Lee Woods. He's a patrolman on the Soldotna Police Department."

"I saw it was him right away. He lives up the road a couple of hundred yards past my drive." North was staring at the floor and shaking his head. "We weren't good friends, but we did have a neighborly beer from time to time. We both work weird hours and didn't socialize much."

"I'm going to need some information from you, Nick. I'll do a short interview and if you OK it, I'll record it. I would like you to come to the office in the morning and make a formal statement. Is that alright with you?"

"Sure," replied North, "I'll have to go to the shop and open up first, but the office girl can pacify customers until I get back."

The trooper took a recorder from his pocket and placed it on the table between them. "For the record, please state your full name and date of birth." He continued to ask about the events of the evening, double checking many details of the discovery of the scene. The interview went on for nearly an hour.

"I think that'll do it for tonight, Nick." Ericson handed North a business card with the Trooper office phone number on it. "Call me when you get opened up in the morning." He stood to leave, but turned and asked, "Do you have any questions for me tonight?"

"Nothing that can't wait until morning," said North, but he paused and looked up at the trooper. "There is one thing I'm curious about. Did you notice anything strange about the wounds?" he asked.

"Do you mean the placement of the shots on the body?" replied Ericson.

"Yeah, I do. Whoever shot him must have been another cop or military person. I was a Ranger in the military and those shots indicate an execution, at least to me." North leaned back in his recliner.

Ericson smiled with a wry grin, "I'm not willing to commit to any conclusions just yet, but you make a very good point. I'll see you in the morning at the office."

It was now just after 2:00 a.m. and Nick was exhausted. He had put in a long summer day at his shop with another day like it ahead tomorrow. Now he would have to take a couple of hours to make his statement to the troopers. It was time to get some rest.

The following morning Ericson was in the office early, as was Captain Phil Bradshaw. Ericson tapped on the office door. The captain looked up and motioned for him to enter.

"Good morning, George," he began. "I know you had a late-night last night, but I have an idea to run by you. With that unrest going on out in Bristol Bay, I was ordered to send my men to help in King Salmon and Naknek. We're really shorthanded in this office. What do you think of my idea of getting some retired troopers with investigative experience to take over your dead body case?"

"I think it would be a great idea if you can talk the colonel into it. We don't have enough troopers to handle daily business of this office, let alone personnel to investigate a probable murder case. Do you have anyone in mind?"

"I thought I'd try to talk Bill Koogan into heading the investigation. He has the experience and a reputation for solving difficult cases. He retired as a lieutenant, and I think he stays in contact with some of his old investigators. Bill lives locally and, if you agree with the idea, I'll call him and see if he'll take the job. If he does, I will try to sell the idea to the colonel."

"I think it's a great idea," said Trooper Ericson. In fact, the next item on his list of things to ask the captain this morning was the manpower shortage. This plan would certainly help a great deal with that problem. "I'll get out of here and let you get to the task. I have a lot of details to check on right now."

"Go ahead, George. I'll let you know how I do with Bill and the colonel." The captain began to look through his phone index for Koogan's number.

An hour later, Bill Koogan was escorted to Captain Bradshaw's office where the matter was discussed, and a contract rate agreed upon. "Give me a few minutes to get approval from the colonel, Bill. Meanwhile I'll have the secretary assign you an office to use. She'll be assigned to you for calls, transcription, and such. How many investigators do you think you'll need?" asked the captain.

Bill Koogan scratched his head and thought a moment, "Since we have a lot of evidence to search, I think we should start with me and three investigators. Depending on the outcome of the initial investigation I'd say three should do the job. That may change, depending on the complexity of the case."

Captain Bradshaw punched the intercom button and asked Trooper Ericson to come to the office. When he appeared at the office door Bradshaw ordered, "Introduce Bill to Shirley and assign her to his investigators. Get him a secure room to use to inspect the evidence you gathered and then find any supplies he may need. Shirley can do the gathering for you. I'm calling the colonel now and I'll let you know how he feels about this plan."

Ericson motioned for Bill to follow. The two men walked down the hall to a large, mostly vacant, office. There was a large conference table and four chairs, a coffee pot, a large safe, a telephone and a small array of office supplies.

"As soon as the captain gets the OK from the colonel, I'll bring you all the pictures and evidence to examine. I'll have Shirley get you anything you need. For now, we'll have to wait for authorization. You can use the phone to round up a crew. My intercom number is 29."

"Thanks, George, I'll start calling my prospective crew while I wait."

Bill drank coffee almost daily with three to five retired troopers and police officers each morning. They were good, trusted friends with whom he had worked many years. It felt good to have responsibilities to occupy his daily life. He was feeling useful again. Rather than waste an hour waiting he sat at the table and dialed the telephone. His first call was to John Ashley to ask if he would be interested in joining the team. He agreed and failed to ask about wages.

Next on his list was Randy Craig. Once one of the best evidence analysts he'd ever known. Again, the offer was accepted without question.

Last, but not least, was Bob Barratt. An outdoorsman, trapper, hunter, and outstanding situation analyst. Bob asked all the questions the others had not, including, "What's the pay?"

He just finished with Bob when Ericson returned to take him to the captain's office. "The colonel gave him the go-ahead, Bill. Bring your coffee and come with me. He needs to brief us on what we can and can't do."

Captain Phil Bradshaw was all smiles when they entered. "The Colonel thought this was a great idea and asked me to welcome you aboard. He also said to ask that you NOT cause him as much headache as you did the last time you worked for him."

All three men laughed at the remark. He'd worked for the colonel when he was a corporal in the Ketchikan office. The current Colonel was then a Corporal and had taught Bill the value of careful investigation. It meant the difference between a long and costly trial or a guilty plea in court.

"As you well know, Bill, we've used retired troopers on cold cases for years. This one is different because it's an active, open case. We'll swear you and your team to a new oath and pay current contract rates to each of you. You will be reinstated as active officers, but not required to do patrol duty nor wear a uniform. You will be plain clothes officers with the rank of detectives. That's something new for us. Congratulations. That is, if you still want the job."

"I've asked three men to join the crew. Myself, John Ashley, Randy Craig and Bob Barratt. When do you want them here for swearing in?"

"I'll try to have all the all the paperwork done by this afternoon. I want to follow up on the investigation as soon as we can. The medical examiner will have his report for me by noon. You and your crew can use the search warrant the judge has promised us today, to search and fingerprint the victim's truck in the garage. I want daily progress reports. Let me know if you need anything."

He turned to Ericson, "George, see to it they have two vehicles: a van and a four-wheel drive SUV. The van should be marked. The SUV should not. Anything else?"

There wasn't. The men stood to return to the new office.

CHAPTER TWO

An hour after the four new investigators signed their contracts with the State of Alaska as temporary employees, they huddled around the conference table examining photos and diagrams done in the middle of the night.

Bill Koogan oversaw the detail and had asked John Ashley to remain in the office with him while Randy Craig and Bob Barratt were sent to the garage to search the inside of the truck for more evidence.

The judge had been prompt with the search warrant, enabling the medical examiner access to the body for transfer to the crime lab in Anchorage. With the body gone the men could continue to search the interior of the truck.

Samples of dirt on the floorboards were taken along with many more photos. Once the tasks were completed, they brought all they found to the little office and added it to the other items already displayed. Barratt and Craig added the results of the fingerprint search inside the cab of the truck.

Koogan assigned the task of cataloging every item on the table, giving each item an evidence number and bagging them for safe keeping. Koogan asked Barratt and Craig to drive to the scene to see if officers had missed anything that night. All four members of the new team were intent on their tasks. Each was experienced, needing no supervision.

George Ericson was summoned to the office when Nick North came in to make his formal written statement. George introduced North to Koogan and Ashley. The men shook hands before Nick was escorted to another small office where he would write his statement. Nick North remained in the little office for more than an hour, handwriting his statement, while a secretary took each sheet he completed and put the words into the computer for later printing. When the document was completed and entered in the computer, it was printed and given back to Nick for approval and signature, as was his hand-written copy..

Ashley and Koogan arranged the photos taken by the troopers the previous night. The photos were shot around midnight when the sun was low in the northwestern sky, giving an exceptional view of the crime scene. The evening light illuminated the tire tracks of each vehicle.

North's pickup had a large lug-type tread making distinctive tracks in the dusty road.

Lee Wood's truck was equipped with Michelin brand tires, again making it easy to distinguish which vehicle made which tracks.

Like the tire tracks, the footprints were easy to identify. North had worn work boots with a distinctive waffle tread. Woods left no prints as he never exited his vehicle.

There were other smaller, less distinguishable tracks in the dust, but it was nearly impossible to tell when they were made. These tracks had a hard leather sole and were most probably a lady's size seven or eight shoe.

The men carefully searched each photo, looking for details telling the movements of the person wearing the shoe, but it was impossible to determine the person's direction of travel.

The movements of the waffle-sole boots were easy to follow. He had moved from the pickup truck to the victim's truck and returned to his own pickup, presumably to call 911. Barratt had found two crushed cigarette butts where North had waited. This seemed to confirm North's story of finding the body.

The four investigators were gathered in the small conference room evaluating the evidence available to them. North had returned to his shop an hour ago.

Barratt rubbed his chin, "You know North was right about this looking like an execution. They could use these photos to teach a class on killing. Heart, lung and brain. It doesn't get more perfect than that. I don't think this guy had any idea what was about to happen. He wasn't in uniform, but they found a weapon on his belt. It appears to me he knew whoever was approaching his truck, rolled down the window to speak to them and was shot before he felt threatened."

"I agree with that assessment," remarked Koogan.

"There's something else that puzzles me, Bill," added Barratt.

"What's that?" asked Koogan.

"Look at the tire tracks. North said he came home and saw the neighbor's truck at the end of his drive and stopped to investigate it. He saw the body and called 911." Barratt was reminding his fellow investigators of the details.

"That's what he claims. What do you see, Bob?"

Barratt moved several photos to the edge of the table. "Take a look at these tire tracks. Tracks of Woods' tire prints go over those made by North turning into his driveway." He picked up two photos showing the lug treads obliterated by the Michelin tire treads where they crossed the lug tire print. We might want to see if North has a motive. Bill, why don't you go to the Soldotna Chief of Police and see if North and Woods had any conflicts."

Koogan nodded agreement and went to the telephone to have dispatch get Chief Bud Griffin of the Soldotna City Police on the telephone. Bud and Bill had been acquainted for many years, and the chief answered with a cheery voice.

"Hello, Bill. What are you up to these days?" he asked.

"Good to hear you, too, Bud. Me and three of my old troopers took a contract to do an investigation. I need to see you in your office, if you have time to see me."

"When do you want to meet, Bill?"

"As soon as possible, Bud. This concerns your officer Lee Woods who was shot yesterday."

"Oh, I didn't know you were handling that investigation. How soon do you want to meet?"

"I'm at the trooper office. If you can work me in I'd like to see you right away."

"Come on over, Bill. I'll have the receptionist bring you to my office when you get here. Do you want some coffee?" asked the chief.

"No, thanks Bud. I've had enough for today, but I'll be right there."

Five minutes later Bill Koogan walked into the Soldotna Police station and was greeted by a girl at the desk behind the glass window. "Good to see you Mr. Koogan. The chief is expecting you." She stood, walked to her side of the locked door and let him in. She led him down the hall to the Chief's office, let him in and returned to her desk.

Chief Griffin stood to shake hands with his old friend. "Have a seat, Bill. I haven't seen the full report on Lee's death. What are you able to tell me at this point?"

"On a professional basis I'll tell you anything we know. That's why I'm here. A local businessman in Soldotna claims he found the body in a pickup at the end of Nick North's driveway. Woods had been shot three times execution style, while he was in his truck. Our evidence doesn't quite match with his story and I'm trying to verify that story. I didn't know Lee Woods. What kind of man was he? Was he a good cop?"

Griffin looked down as he crossed his hands on his desktop. He blew out a long breath. "I'll give you a copy of his employment record. Like most cops he's been reprimanded a few times, but he was a good officer. Hard worker. Everyone in the department liked him."

"OK, Bud, what aren't you telling me?" asked Bill.

Griffin rose from his chair and walked to the door to close it.

"What I'm about to pass on to you is mostly office rumors. Squad room talk is that he was a lady's man and, over the years, had been reported for hitting on some local ladies, not all of whom were single.

Many of the reports were anonymous, but there were quite a few complaints made. There were no accusations of assault or wrong-doing, just unnecessary contact. He had been warned several times, but no charges were ever filed against him. Those reports are in the personnel file."

"Are there names to go with these allegations?" asked Bill,

"Some, but mostly squad room talk. Funny you should mention Nick North. There were rumors he was seeing Nick's wife while Nick was working. Again, this is not fact, but rumor. To my knowledge neither Nick nor his wife ever filed any complaint. I have heard Nicks wife went to visit her parents in Oklahoma and has been gone for a couple of months. Again, rumor and not fact."

"I'm going to let you in on some private information, Bud." Now Bill was staring at his own hands. "Nick North says he found the body in the truck which was still running. He did a report today and it looks close to true, but the facts say differently. The victim was shot three times, Heart, lungs and brain, execution style. North himself noted the placement of the shots and commented on the shot placement. Because of these suspicious circumstances I came looking to see if there was a motive. If Woods was seeing North's wife, we could have a motive. We've only been on the case for one day and already it's getting complicated."

"I've already given you unverified information because it seems pertinent, but I won't violate ethics rules, even for you, Bill."

"I understand and I appreciate what you have given me. I'll make every effort to determine if the rumors are true. I have no wish to embarrass your department. At this point the rumors are between us, and I thank you for the heads up." Bill stood, picked up the personnel file from the desk and reached out to shake his old friend's hand.

"I have a reporter on his way to this office for an interview about the case. Do you mind if I mention your team to the reporter?"

"Go ahead, Bud. It's all going to be public soon enough anyway. See you later."

With that Bill Koogan took the file and left the station to return to the office at the trooper building. Upon his return he spoke with the other members of the team while they scanned Lee Woods' employment record. It was late in the afternoon and near quitting time. They locked the office, securing the evidence inside. On his way to the parking lot Bill stopped to report to Captain Bradshaw.

Upon entering his personal vehicle, he sat and realized how exhausted he had become. "I didn't think I was that old," he told himself.

The following morning, he entered the office and was stopped by Captain Bradshaw. "Have you seen the local newspaper, Bill?" he asked.

"No, why?" The captain handed him a copy of the morning edition.

Koogan read the headlines - "MURDER CASE INVESTIGATED BY ALASKA STATE TROOPER GEEZER SQUAD".

"Bud Griffin," said Koogan in an irritated tone. "He has always liked pranking me."

"I didn't expect your team to start making headlines the first day on the case," commented Bradshaw

CHAPTER THREE

The other three investigators were in the office when Bill Koogan entered carrying a copy of the morning paper. "I guess our team has a new name," reported Koogan, tossing the newspaper on the conference table for all to read.

The three men scanned the article and laughed, "Finally some honest reporting," said John Ashley.

"OK you Geezers, let's get to work. Where do we start this morning?" Koogan was a little irritated with the notoriety.

"In my Geezerly opinion," spoke Bob Barratt, "I think it's time for us to have Mr. Nick North come in for an interview. We need to resolve these discrepancies. Are they just differences of opinions or are they a change of facts? We need to have a motive if we intend to pursue North as a suspect."

"I agree," said Koogan, "and we may have a motive. I saw SPD Chief Bud Griffin last evening and the squad room rumor is Woods was seeing Nick North's wife while he was at work. If that's true we have a motive. We have to be careful, though, this is only rumor. I agree we should get North in here and see if we can learn anything new. When we finish, no matter what we learn, we need to take it to the DA to see if he thinks we have enough to prosecute and get an arrest warrant. I'll call North and ask him to come in to go over his written statement. I want Randy to do the interview. Any objections to my plan?" asked Koogan as he scanned the faces in the room.

"I guess you'll have to take the sap gloves back to the car, John." Bob Barratt was making a joke about the weighted leather gloves some officers once used as an edge in physical confrontations.

"Aw shucks, Bob. I haven't used them since I retired. I was looking forward to it." John Ashley had never been an aggressive officer but could joke with Barratt on a moment's notice.

"OK, Randy. You three make a list of things to go over with him when he arrives. Try not to make this sound accusatory or confrontational. Who do you want with you to do the interview?" asked Bill Koogan.

"I guess Bob would be best. John has to take his sap gloves to his car anyway." The men laughed.

"Try to video the interview if you can. If he refuses, just record the session. I'm going to call the DA to see if there is anything we haven't thought of. I'll have the captain ask Mr. North to come down for the interview."

Koogan stopped at the captain's office to ask him to direct North to an interview room. He then drove the eleven miles to the court building to meet with DA Walker.

The DA agreed with the assessment of the investigators regarding discrepancies in the evidence and the story told by Nick North. Walker provided several questions to be asked during the new interview. The courthouse meeting took less than a half hour. Bill returned to the office to relay the information to Randy and Bob for use during the interview.

"Is he coming for an interview?" asked Bill.

"Yes," replied Randy, "But he can't come before one o'clock when his office girl returns from lunch. We'll be ready."

Bill looked at his wristwatch.

"We have a little time, guys. Let's take the van and go to Froso's Family Restaurant for some lunch while we have the time."

"Good idea, Bill," commented John Ashley, grinning. "That means you're buying! All Right!"

Once the interview room was set up the crew left the office to have lunch. Keeping an eye on the time in order to be ready when the suspect was to arrive, the good-natured sarcasm continued. After lunch Koogan picked up the check, complaining all the while, knowing he would be able to put this on the expense account in place for the investigators. It was shortly before the 1:00 pm when they returned to the office.

"John and I will be in the conference room if you need anything," noted Bill.

It was 1:30p.m. when Captain Bradshaw escorted Nick North to the small office they would use for the interview. A video camera was set up to record the session. North was asked if he objected, but said it would be alright with him.

Randy began the interview, "For the record, please state your full name and date of birth".

With the formalities registered, the men got down to business.

"Mr. North, I want you to relax. We've been over most of this information before, but there are a few things we need to review."

Randy had a notepad on the desk in front of him with a list of items to cover. "Would you like something to drink while we talk?"

"No, I'm fine. I just need to finish with this and get back to my shop," replied North.

And so, the interview began by reviewing and reaffirming the information of the last meeting. Several minutes into the review Randy looked up at Nick North.

"By the way Nick, do you own a .38 caliber Smith and Wesson Air

Weight? You know, the compact revolver.”

"I owned one once, years ago. But I traded it for another handgun a long time ago. Why do you ask?” inquired North.

"We had word from the crime lab the bullets found in Woods’ body were probably fired from such a handgun.” Randy reached up to scratch the top of his head, “Someone said you were quite an outdoorsman and did a lot of reloading. Is that true?”

"I guess it is,” he replied. “I go to the range a lot and do my own reloading. I shoot a lot. I was trained as an Army Ranger and I like to keep my hand in the game.”

"That’s interesting. I reload myself. Would you mind if I came by your loading room and see what you have to work with?” asked Randy, off-handedly.

Randy turned his attention to his notes. “It says here your wife is out of state, is that true?”

"Yes. She is in Oklahoma visiting her family. I’m so busy in the summer and she has nothing to do. It just seemed like a good time for her to make the trip.”

Randy could sense Nick becoming uneasy with the way this was heading. “Oh, OK. I was just curious about her leaving in the summer. Most wives want to leave in the winter. Is everything alright for her?”

"Yeah, she doesn’t fish. I’m gone all the time leaving her with nothing to do, so she thought it would be a good time to see her folks.” Nick looked at his hands for a long time. “Where are we going with this anyway?” he asked.

"I’m sorry if I’m making you uncomfortable, Nick. It’s just that there are some discrepancies between your story and the evidence we’ve gathered. I’m just trying to resolve the differences.”

"Hold it right there, Trooper. If you’re investigating me regarding Woods’ death, I think I should have a lawyer.” North was becoming anxious.

"You have that right,” commented Randy, “If you want to call one right now you can use the phone on the desk. I’ll step out of the room.”

"I think I want to end this interview right now and go to his office and ask him what I should do.” North stood to leave.

"If that’s what you want to do, Mr. North. I’ll have an officer come to escort you to the front door.”

"I think I’d better leave,” demanded Nick.

Randy reached for the telephone and called for John Ashley to escort Mr. North out of the office.

Once Nick North had been escorted from the building, all four team members met in the small office used for the interview. Randy was making some notes when the others arrived.

"I take it this interview didn't go well," commented Bill Koogan.

"He began to get uncomfortable when I asked if he owned a Chief Special. And he stood to leave when I broached the subject of his wife not being in town for some time. It's all on the tape. When I began to ask about his wife, he immediately wanted to lawyer up. I think we should try to get a search warrant to search his home and re-loading room. I'm betting we'd find more of the same bullets found in the body."

"I'll call the DA and see if he can work it out. We need to get there before he can remove any evidence." Bill made the statement while reaching for the telephone.

"Bob. You and John go to the DA's office and get the search warrant as soon as it's signed. North should be working at his shop right now, but if he was frightened enough to want a lawyer he may be suspicious enough to go home to remove any incriminating evidence. We have to beat him to the punch."

"Come on, John. Let's get to the courthouse."

With a small salute Bob and John hurried out of the office while Bill was still on the phone with Walker at the DA's office.

"Randy, take the SUV and try to beat North to the house and stop him from entering until we get the search warrant there." Bill Koogan was spreading his men very thin, but he had to report to the captain before he could join Randy at the home on Smith Way.

He drove away from the trooper office in his private vehicle. He was nearly at the private driveway when word came that his two teammates were on the way with the search warrant. Serving a search warrant is a normal procedure, but in this case the object was to attempt to find evidence in a murder case in the home owned by the suspect. These situations were always dangerous. Bill arrived at the home to find Randy standing in the front yard, waiting. Nick North had not yet arrived. It was assumed he was still meeting with his lawyer. As Bill stepped out of his vehicle, he had an idea.

"Randy, do you have a phone number for Mrs. North?"

His head bobbed in understanding as he reached for his notebook to find the number. "Got it right here."

"Contact her and let her know we intend to search the house and want to know if there's a key hidden out here somewhere. That way we won't have to do any damage to enter. Perhaps she'll agree to that."

Again, Randy nodded and dialed the number. A woman's voice came on the line on the fifth ring.

"Hello," said the voice

"Hello, Mrs. North. This is Trooper Randy Craig. There's been a problem in your neighborhood and we have a search warrant to enter your home. I need to know if you have a key hidden outside the house. It would save us damaging your home."

"Oh, My Lord! What kind of problem is it?" she asked.

"I'd rather not say on the telephone, but it is a serious offense. Please don't be alarmed, but we need to enter the home to search for several specific items. As for the rest, I'll be happy to explain, but it'll have to be a little later today."

"Under the flowerpot on the step. There's a key for the ground floor door. Is everything OK?"

"Yes, everything will be fine. With your permission I'll call my captain and he'll explain everything to you, but we are on the scene right now and don't have the time. May I have him call you?"

"Yes, of course. I'll be waiting for the call."

Randy hung up and lifted the flowerpot to find the key as he dialed the number for Captain Phil Bradshaw. He explained the situation to the captain and asked him to call Mrs. North. He agreed to make the call and tell her as much as he could.

Randy had just closed his call with the captain when Bill waved his arm and pointed down the drive to where John was approaching with the search warrant.

CHAPTER FOUR

While unlocking the front door on the ground level, Bill Koogan instructed Randy Craig and John Ashley to search the upper two floors carefully, to determine if North had hidden the Smith and Wesson Chief Special that the lab had determined was the weapon used in the killing.

"You guys know the drill," he said. "Be sure to photograph the locations of any evidence you find. Bob and I will take the lower level where his reloading bench should be."

"Don't forget North could come home at any time," commented Ashley.

Upon opening the door, it was easy to determine where his reloading room was located. They entered through a laundry room area. The stairwell to the upper levels was located on the rear wall of the large room. There were three doors in the wall to the right. The one near the entry door was open and his reloading room was visible. Bob Barratt immediately began to photograph the entire area. Once he had completed the task, the others entered with Craig and Ashley going to the upper floor via the stairwell.

Bob carried a small satchel filled with evidence gathering tools: plastic and paper bags, fingerprinting supplies, glass and plastic containers and photo supplies. While Bob pulled a pair of blue gloves onto his large hands, Bill checked what was behind each of the other two doors.

The center door was a bathroom, very clean and tidy. The other was small bedroom which looked like a guest room. He gave the two rooms a preliminary search before returning to tug on his own pair of protective gloves. By the time this was done, Bob had finished photographing the entire reloading room.

"I see a gun cabinet containing several long guns over there," said Bob, pointing his thumb toward a spot on the left wall. "I'll start there if you want to check the contents of all the drawers for the gun."

Bill went to the large bench and work area to open the drawers. As he approached, he noticed a quart-size plastic container with what appeared to be .38 caliber rounds with lead bullets of the same type used in the shooting. "Got something here, Bob," he called to his partner.

Bob came to the bench with his camera in hand. "Wow, that looks like the same kind of ammo they dug out of the victim."

"It sure does," mused Bill Koogan. "He didn't appear to me to be someone dumb enough to leave critical evidence laying on his bench, though. Get some photos and we can keep looking around for the gun."

Bob photographed the container and cartridges, then wrote on an evidence tag. He placed the container in a large plastic evidence container and sealed it with the tag attached. This container was placed in his satchel in the center of the room. Bill continued to open and carefully inspect each drawer. The process went on for several hours until Ashley and Craig came down the stairs from the upper floors.

"We're almost finished here," commented Bill. "Did you find anything interesting?"

"Not much. Some shot up targets. Pistol targets. Whoever did the shooting was a pretty good shot. All in the black and mostly in a small group. There was a small stack of these targets indicating this guy does a lot of shooting." It was Craig making the statement. "Other than that, we didn't find anything unusual upstairs. By the looks of the place though, it does look like the wife has been gone for a long time."

"Go ahead and load and go back to the office. We'll be along shortly. We're nearly finished here ourselves. No gun, but we found some ammo that looks like the same bullet type used in the murder. I'm thinking we should clear it with the captain and go to the auto shop to take North into custody for murder. I'm sure the captain will want to clear the arrest with the DA first." Bill kept packing equipment while he spoke.

A half hour later Bill, with coffee cup in hand, entered the office of Captain Phil Bradshaw. It took only a few minutes to pass on the results of the search.

"Bob is packing up the cartridges we found to send them to the crime lab," Bill reported, "But I think we have enough to make an arrest, even though we didn't find the gun. This guy is savvy, and I think he might just decide to run. We made him nervous when we asked him about the evidence from the scene. Can you call the DA and get us an arrest warrant?"

"I can try," said the captain. "Drink your coffee while I call him."

Bill raised his cup in a salute while the captain dialed the court building and the office of DA Walker. It was as short conversation, "The DA agreed and said he would get the judge to sign it and would personally deliver it to us here at the office."

"Good, I'll go back and brief the team and form an arrest strategy," said Bill as he stood to leave the captain's office.

It was agreed that Bill and Bob would enter through the front office door and speak with the receptionist to determine if North was in the shop. If he was, Ashley and Craig would wait outside the rear entrance of the shop area until Koogan and Barratt entered and confronted North. The strategy was to determine if there were others in the shop and keep the receptionist out of harm's way in case of an altercation in the shop.

The plan was agreed upon and another round of coffee had been consumed by the time Walker arrived with the warrant. He advised the team he wanted to be present on the property as the arrest took place. The team agreed and, with the blessing of the captain, entered two vehicles to drive to the center of town where the auto repair shop was located.

As agreed, John Ashley and Randy Craig drove to the rear of the small shop while Bob Barratt and Bill Koogan parked near the front entrance of the office. Bill and Bob entered the office where Bill stepped up to the desk of the pretty young girl seated there.

"Hello, Miss. I'm with the Alaska State Troopers. We would like to speak with your boss, Mr. Nick North for a moment. Is he in the shop?" asked Bill.

"Yes, he is. If you will wait a minute, I'll ask him to come to the office."

"I would rather you not tell him we're here just yet. We'll go to the shop and see him. I would like for you to stay at your desk until we finish, for your own safety. Do you understand?"

The young girl nodded in understanding.

"Good, we shouldn't be very long. Just stay at your desk." While talking to the receptionist, Bill was attempting to catch sight of the mechanic through the dusty windows of the shop area. There was only one vehicle in the shop that Bill could see. Someone was working under the hood of that vehicle, but the trooper couldn't tell if it was North.

Bill nodded to Bob and the two walked to the door and entered the shop area.

North was working on a Ford pickup truck when they entered. When he heard someone come into the shop, he stood to see who had entered. He recognized Koogan the moment he saw him.

"What are you doing here? I'm working and I don't have time to mess with you. Get out of my shop." North spoke in an angry tone.

Before answering both Bill and Bob moved closer to the mechanic. "Mr. North, we have a warrant for your arrest. Please place your hands behind your back and turn around."

"Who the hell do you think you are?" he shouted.

The man was quick and agile. He stepped back to his small work bench and picked up a twelve-inch crescent wrench and raised it above his head as Bill approached him with Bob at his heels.

"Don't pick a fight with an old guy, North," warned Bill. North took a step forward with the wrench raised above his head.

Bill took a half step forward, toward North and gave him a vicious kick in the groin, sending the man to the floor in great pain while the wrench clattered to the concrete floor.

Bob immediately rolled the man onto his stomach and began to apply handcuffs just as Ashley and Craig came through the back door.

Ashley assisted in lifting North from the floor to set him on a small shop stool to regain his breath.

"I told you not to pick a fight with an old guy. We cheat," commented Bill.

At that point Bill could see Walker standing behind the window of the office, nodding in approval.

"John. You and Randy take him to jail in Kenai and get him booked in. He can call his lawyer once he's booked into jail. Here's the arrest warrant signed by the Superior Court Judge." Bill tucked the warrant into the large breast pocket of Norths' overalls. "Warn the Correctional Officers of the fact he is wanting to put up a fight."

The two officers led the prisoner out the back door to the marked SUV behind the garage. They loaded him into the back seat and secured his seatbelt.

Koogan and Barratt went back out through the office to speak with the receptionist.

"I'm sorry Ma'am but we've arrested Mr. North and he's on his way to jail. I don't know how long he'll remain there, but he won't be back today. If anyone had a vehicle to be picked up today, it won't be ready."

Bill and Bob left the office, the young girl standing behind her desk with her mouth open, wondering what to do.

Walker had witnessed the entire arrest process and followed Koogan and Barratt back to trooper headquarters. They met in the parking lot and proceeded to the captain's office.

"Hello Walker," greeted the captain.

"Hello, Captain," he replied while extending his hand in greeting.

"How did it go Bill?" asked Bradshaw.

"Pretty well. He was surprised to see us in his shop. He attempted to greet me with a crescent wrench, but I stopped him," answered Bill Koogan.

"If he's in custody there is another problem on the horizon. I spoke with Nick North's wife. She was very upset about the whole affair and said she was coming back to take care of the property. She also told me she left the area because her husband was violent and had threatened to do her harm. She also admitted she had had an affair with Lee Woods, our victim."

"How soon before she's expected to arrive back in town?" asked Walker.

"She didn't give me a specific time but did say she'd return as soon as she could make arrangements."

"I would prefer to keep her from entering the property until we have North arraigned. We may have to enter the home again if there's specific evidence we need to look for."

"I think we can arrange that, Walker. But she said he did own a small .38 caliber handgun. She didn't know much about the weapon or where it might be. She said he usually kept it in his reloading room or in his truck." The captain was being candid with the DA.

"Well, I guess I had better get back to my office and start the paperwork for his arraignment," said Walker as he stood to leave the office. He turned toward Bill and again offered his hand in friendship.

"My job today was to verify the correctness of the incident. I want you to know, in my opinion, your team did an outstanding job containing the situation. His attack on you Bill proves he is prone to violence. Good job, Geezer Squad."

"I guess you read the paper," commented Bill, laughing. "I'm going to get Bud Griffin for that one." Everyone in the office was laughing now.

An hour later the last two officers returned to the office and the squad retired to the larger office to complete reports and paperwork dealing with the arrest, and to make the copies their office and the DA would need to present the case in court tomorrow.

CHAPTER FIVE

The previous night had been a very late night, organizing and cataloging photographs, evidence, case notes and a hundred other items that would be turned over to the DA. The four officers worked in the office until after midnight to prepare the case. They came to the office two hours later this morning to begin their day with a new pot of coffee.

Seated at the large, now barren, conference table, Bill Koogan thanked the team for a great effort and timely solution to their first case.

"Just sit tight and I'll check in with the captain to see what our next case might be," said Bill as he stood to leave the office.

He knocked on the captain's office door.

Captain Phil Bradshaw looked up to see who was at his door and smiled.

"Come on in Bill. I was about to call you. How are you doing with the paperwork for the court?"

"We stayed here late last night to finish it up," replied Bill. "I talked to the DA this morning and he was happy to hear our end was completed. North will be arraigned at one o'clock this afternoon."

"Good job! Are you ready for another assignment?"

"Sure thing, Boss." Bill and the entire team were happy to be back in harness. "What have you got for us?"

"There's been a string of armed robberies in recent weeks. They started in Girdwood and worked their way down here. Soldotna had one by this gang of three about a week ago, then they worked their way down to Homer. Homer Police have asked for help with this investigation. I told their chief I'd see what I could do. In the meantime, the robbers have worked their way back up the Peninsula and are somewhere near Soldotna now. They hit in daylight and are armed with what's reported to be 9mm handguns. They seem to target Quick Stop stations and neighborhood grocery stores. I'll send the reports over to your office."

"Thanks, Cap, I'll see what we can learn. From what you say, it looks like the gang is heading back toward Anchorage. We probably won't have them on the Peninsula for very long."

"I agree, Bill. That's why we need to act quickly." The captain picked up his phone and ordered the reports sent to the Geezer Squad office.

Bill Koogan walked back to the office and arrived at the same time the records clerk entered the small office.

"This is all we have on this group," she commented as she set the files on the table.

"Thank you," said Bill as she turned to leave the office.

The Squad immediately began to divide and dissect the files, each officer taking a small section to study for clues as to the identity of the perps. Bob was the first to make any kind of statement about what he had found.

"You know, in the old days these guys would have taken a lot of money, but in today's world most customers use a credit card. In each case I read, the robbers used a different vehicle which, in two cases, turned out to be stolen and later abandoned. Homer police stopped three men in an older green Jeep Grand Cherokee that were questioned and released. The men matched the description of the robbers, but the vehicle didn't match. The license numbers are here, but this report says it wasn't the correct plate for the Jeep.

"These are clever guys," commented John Ashley. "It doesn't make sense to go to this much trouble for the small amount of cash they get from the robberies."

"I think you're right, John," stated Bill. "That would mean they are down here for some other reason. Any ideas what that could be?"

"If they are doing robberies for traveling money it would indicate they haven't done their business yet. Sounds like drug dealers to me." Randy Craig was speaking with authority since he'd been on the statewide drug enforcement team for many years.

"It's possible, but drug dealers usually have a pocket full of cash to spend."

"The captain said he advised his regular patrol officers to keep an eye out for the men, but so far, no results. Bob. You and John go to Homer and interview the clerks on duty at the time of the robbery. Randy and I will do the same at the two stores up this way. In your travels keep an eye open for that green Cherokee. If you see them, call for backup. I think they are more than hoods picking off service stations."

"I guess that means we'll have to start buying our coffee with cash." All four men laughed at that remark. "Take the marked vehicle for the trip. Randy and I will be less conspicuous in the unmarked car."

"Come on Randy. It will take them at least an hour and a half to get to Homer. We can be in Sterling in fifteen minutes if we hurry."

"OK, Boss. Are you driving or am I?" asked Randy.

"You drive, I'll enjoy the scenery," commented Koogan.

It was just twenty minutes to the small Quick Stop grocery-coffee shop-bakery in the center of the small town of Sterling, Alaska. It had been a small, family business for nearly 50 years. The owners and managers of the station were all of the same family. Bill asked to talk with the clerk on duty the day of the robbery.

"She's on break right now but will be back in about ten minutes. Would you like some coffee while you wait?" asked the manager.

"That would be nice," replied the trooper.

The manager brought them each a cup of very good coffee. The investigators stood in a corner of the eating area and sipped the brew while waiting for the clerk they needed to interview. They'd only finished about half the cup of coffee when she returned to the food service area.

"Dolly," called the manager as she arrived, "These gentlemen want to talk with you."

"Oh, sure, come on back to the office where we can talk."

In the office, Bill introduced himself and Randy while displaying official credentials.

"We would like to go over the events of the robbery," said Bill. "There may be some details we didn't see in the report. Is that OK with you?" he asked.

"Yes, of course. I was really frightened that day," she admitted with a smile.

"I would have been frightened too," admitted Bill. "We just want to go over the details to see if there was something we missed. First of all, what can you remember about the men who came inside?"

"Not much more than I told the other officer. They were young, perhaps in their mid to late twenties. They were both very clean but had scraggily beards. They weren't nervous or anything. They just asked me to get the cash from the register. They were polite, but they scared the jeepers out of me with them having their guns pointed at me. I did what they wanted."

"I understand," said Bill. "Do you remember what they were wearing?"

"Oh, yes. They both had camo shirts and Carhartt jeans. They weren't new clothes but were clean. And they didn't smell bad like some of the fishermen who come in here."

Did they have long or short hair?" asked Randy.

"Not really long hair, but not short either. They looked well groomed, actually. They didn't appear to be street bums like some we get in here."

"Did you get a look at the one who stayed in the car?" again it was Randy asking.

"Not really. I saw him as they drove away from the station, and he looked like the other two."

"When they drove away, did they speed like they needed to get away?" he asked.

"No. And that was strange. One got into the front seat of the car and one into the back seat. They just put it in gear and drove away like any other customer." She snickered, "You would expect criminals to be nervous and edgy, looking all around, but these men didn't even seem concerned about who was watching them."

"Were both men armed?" asked Bill.

"Yes, and that was what made me so nervous. They both had semi-automatic weapons and kept them pointed at me all the time. They made no attempt to hide their faces or anything like that. It was late at night, and I was here alone. I was so frightened." She hung her head as if she had done something wrong.

"You did just the right thing, Dolly," stated Bill. "Can you tell me how much they took in the robbery?"

"We were missing two hundred twenty-eight dollars when we balanced the till." She looked at Bill with sad eyes and asked, "Do you think they'll come back?"

Bill reached out to touch her arm with a reassuring pat, "I doubt it, Dolly. They seem to be hit and run types. I don't think you have anything to worry about from these men."

The two troopers stood.

"This is my card, Miss. If you think of anything that might help our investigation, please give me a call. And thank you for being so helpful to us." Bill was trying to be reassuring as he stood to leave.

The investigators walked to their car to drive toward Soldotna and the next interview.

"For someone who was as frightened as Dolly was, she did a great job of remembering the details of the robbers." Randy said to Bill.

"I was thinking the same thing, Randy," stated Bill. "She makes a very credible witness, but we don't seem to have learned much about the perps. I was hoping they might have mentioned something to give us a clue as to what they were up to besides the robberies."

When they neared the other service station-grocery-liquor store that had been robbed there was a dark green Jeep Grand Cherokee at the pumps.

"See that, Randy?" asked Bill.

"You stay with the car and back me up. I'll see who's driving the Jeep," replied Randy.

Bill stopped the car between the pumps and the highway, put the patrol car in park and took his weapon from his hip holster, holding it in his lap. He rolled down the driver's side window as Randy exited, walking to the Jeep at the gas pump. The man pumping gas was young, perhaps nineteen or twenty years old. He was clean shaven and paid no attention to Randy as he approached.

"Hi there," said Randy when he got near the gas pump. "Do you live in this area."

"Yeah, down Jim Dollar Road," was the polite reply.

"Have you lived here long?"

"All my life," replied the young man as he shook the last drops of fuel from the hose.

"I would like to see your driver's license, if you don't mind." Randy displayed his trooper ID as the youngster hung up the hose.

"Sure," he replied as he reached for his wallet. "Have I done something wrong?" he asked.

"I don't think so, but I do need to check your ID. What's your name, son?"

"Roy. Roy Burke," he replied as he handed his license to Randy.

Randy took the Alaska Driver's License to read the name. "I want you to stay here until I check this out. Do you understand?"

"Yeah, I understand, but I have a class at the college in a few minutes and I don't wanna be late."

"This will only take a minute, Roy. I'll be right back."

Randy walked to the patrol car where Bill was sitting and handed the license to Bill.

"The kid looks to be OK, but we should run his numbers anyway."

Bill nodded and picked up the radio mic. Dispatch answered and ran the license through the statewide network. He was who he said he was. Bill gave the license back to Randy who returned to the gas pump where the student was waiting.

"Sorry to bother you, young man, but we're looking for someone in a green Jeep and we needed to check you out. Thank you for your patience."

"It's OK, Trooper. I still have time to make it to class. Hope you catch your guy." With that the young man climbed into the Jeep and drove away.

Bill holstered his handgun and climbed out of the patrol car. The two men walked to the main building and asked to see the manager who came out of his little office to meet the troopers.

Both troopers displayed their ID and asked to talk privately with the manager. He led them back to the small office he had come from.

"What can I do for you men?" asked the manager.

"We would like to interview the clerk on duty the day of the robbery. Is he on duty now?" asked Randy.

"Yes, he is. His name is Luke. Luke Jacobs. I'll go relieve him and

send him to the office. You can use this office to talk."
"That would be great," said Randy.

CHAPTER SIX

Randy and Bill waited in the little office until Luke came to meet with them. He was a tall, skinny young man with a bad case of acne.

"Hi, I'm Luke Jacobs. The boss said you needed to talk to me. Is this about the robbery?"

"Yes, it is, we will need to see your ID if you have it handy," answered Bill Koogan.

The young man dug out his driver's license and handed it to Bill who stepped outside to run the numbers through the system. Randy remained in the office with Luke. When the formalities were finished Bill returned and gave the license back to the youngster.

"Luke, we're here to see if there is anything new you can remember about the evening of the robbery. I've read your statement and I know you told them all you knew, but we need to go over it with you in case you missed something the first time. Is that OK with you?" asked Randy.

"Sure, it's OK, but I think I told them all I knew on the first day."

"For what it's worth, we don't think you did anything wrong. We just thought we might be able to learn something that was missed in the first interview." Randy tried to calm the nerves of the young man and put him at ease.

"That's right, Luke," added Bill. "Were you working alone that evening?"

"Yeah, on the grocery and gas side. There was another clerk in the liquor store. She got robbed too."

"We intend to speak with her as well, but we chose you first because your contact with the robbers was much longer and closer. I understand the robbers made you go to the liquor store clerk and get the money from her cash register. Is that the way it happened?" It was Bill Koogan asking.

"Yeah, that's what happened. I was scared." Luke hung his head as if ashamed.

"Let's go back to the beginning. What time did the men enter the store?" asked Bill.

"It was almost ten o'clock at night."

"Were there any other customers in the store at the time?" asked Randy.

"No, that time of night we usually don't have many customers. Mostly just gas customers and folks wanting to buy cigarettes."

"Did you notice these men before they entered the store?" asked Randy.

"No, I was in one of the aisles stocking shelves when they came into the store. They must have parked out at the side of the building because I couldn't see a car out front. I came back to the counter when I heard the bell on the door. It always tells me when someone comes in at night."

"Did you notice anything unusual about the men when they came into the store?"

"Yeah, they each had a pistol in their hand. Scared the crap out of me."

"Then what happened?" asked Randy.

"The one in front seemed to be the leader, said for me to stay behind the counter and keep my hands on top of it. I was scared and did what he said." Luke looked frightened even now.

"The guy who was doing the talking said I should get the cash from the register and give it to him. He said to put it in one of the store bags. I did what he asked. The other guy kept looking around and he pointed out the entry to the liquor store to his partner. That's when the lead guy told me to go to the liquor store and bring him the cash from that register. He warned me not to make any strange signals or moves if I didn't want to get hurt. He spoke really politely but I knew he meant business." Luke was nearly in tears.

Bill saw the stress in the lad. "It's going to be OK, Luke," Bill spoke in a quiet voice. "We know you couldn't do anything differently than what you did. We don't believe you're to blame for anything. We're just gathering facts that may lead us to them in order to arrest them. Can you describe the robbers?"

"I can do better than that. We have a system of surveillance cameras around the whole store and pumps, as well as in the liquor store. The store manager can probably get them for you."

"That would be wonderful," said Bill. "You can go now, but send the manager back to talk with us, will you Luke?"

"Sure thing officer and thanks for being so nice to me. I thought I was in trouble when you came in."

"No, you're not in any trouble. Just send the manager back to the office."

Luke nearly jumped from the chair he had occupied during the interview. "Yessir, I'll send him back here right now." He nearly ran back to the front counter.

After Luke left the office Bill turned to Randy.

"Is this our lucky day or what. With the video tapes we should be able to print out images of the robbers. At least images of the two inside the store."

"Let's hope the store still has the tapes," commented Randy Craig.

The two troopers stood when the manager entered the office. "Did you learn anything new?" he asked.

"As a matter of fact, we did. Luke told us you had security cameras around the store and outside. Have you kept the tapes?"

"Sure, I thought we could wind up in court over this and I put them in the safe.

"I would like to take them with us as evidence. We can get them copied for you or they'll be returned to you when the case is finished in the criminal trial."

The store manager rubbed his chin, then said, "I'll get them for you if you give me a receipt stating where they are. Our lawyers will need to know."

"We can do that for you," agreed Bill.

"Come with me. The safe is in the storeroom at the back of the liquor store. It was too large to put in this office. There are four tapes. One records two cameras on a split-screen, recording the front door and facing the checkout counter and cash register. The outside cameras record four cameras at a time, all the outside and the pumps. The camera inside the liquor store is a wide-angle type and takes in the entire shop from the counter to the beer coolers. There is one more above the rear door of the stock room that shows the entire back lot." The manager was explaining all this as the three walked to the storeroom behind the liquor store.

Once in the storeroom, the manager opened the safe to remove four plastic cases containing the tapes. After closing the door of the safe, he went to a box on the end of a work bench to get a plastic bag and placed the tapes inside. He handed the bag to Bill.

"Thank you. My partner Randy will write a receipt for you. I appreciate your cooperation today."

"I'm just happy you're looking for these guys. I don't ever want them to come back. No one was hurt this time, but we may not be that lucky a second time."

Randy finished writing the receipt and gave it to the manager. He shook the managers' hand and the troopers returned to their vehicle.

Randy chuckled as Bill started the engine.

"When we started today, I didn't think we'd learn anything new, but I never could have imagined we'd get pictures of the robbery. It's no wonder you were a lieutenant. Magic things just happen when you're around."

It was only a short drive back to the trooper office where Randy took the bag of tapes to a room with video players for this kind of thing. Bill stopped at the captain's office to give him a verbal report.

After being told of this morning's interviews, Captain Bradshaw laughed out loud.

"I don't know if it's skill or dumb luck, but you guys really do get the job done. I don't dare let you get near a computer for fear you will destroy it, but when it comes to police work you do get it done."

"I thought that was what you paid us for," commented Bill. "All these new men you have around here are college graduates and can rule the world with a computer, but most of them never learned to think and reason things out. The times they are a-changin'."

"Have you heard from John and Bob?" asked the captain.

Bill checked the time, "No, but they should be checking in shortly. I'm going back to our office now to help Randy set up the video players to view the security tapes. We might need a computer nerd to print off some pictures for us."

"Just call the young lady handling your paperwork. She's a whiz with the computer," noted the captain.

Bill returned to the little office where Randy had finished setting up the tape players. "I think we can speed through most of the tapes. We only need to see a few minutes when the robbers are visible."

"The captain said the young lady we use as a secretary is a tech whiz and can help us with that."

Randy was leaving the room to go to the secretary's office when Bill's cell phone rang.

"Koogan," he answered.

"Hey, Bill. This is John Ashley. We've finished interviewing the folks down here. Is there anything specific we may have overlooked?"

"No, if you think you covered everything you may as well come on back to the office. Randy and I came up with some security tapes that may have photos of the perps. We'll be in the office when you get back."

Bill found a cup of hot coffee and returned to the little office. Randy was there with the secretary. Her name was Jean; a small, pretty redhead. She instructed Randy on the use of the video players and told him which buttons to push to stop the play at any sights he wanted to print a hard copy of. Randy said he understood and Jean returned to her office.

"I brought you a cup of coffee. Over there on the other desk. We might as well get comfortable and watch movies. Want some popcorn?" Both men laughed.

The troopers knew the time the robbery had been reported and selected the tape within that time frame. Bill and Randy watched the video at a very fast pace on the initial viewing.

Even at this rate they spotted two shoplifters. Bill made notes of times indicated on the video to deal with shoplifting offenses later. Finally, nearly an hour into watching the video, they had the robbers on the screen. The entire incident took only about three minutes.

"These guys are really efficient," commented Bill.

"They certainly are. I'm amazed how calm they are. They don't appear to be at all nervous. Not concerned about who sees them nor if there were security cameras in the store. These men look like professional criminals. They move around a lot from place to place, and except for the robberies, they cause no trouble on the streets. I think you're right about them not being common robbers. They can't get much cash from each robbery. They probably get enough for meals and that's about it. I'll print the best pictures and look for them in the facial recognition database." Randy was pushing buttons to stop the player and make copies of the photos.

"You may as well print the pictures of the shoplifters while you're at it," advised Bill. "I'll tell the captain what we found. When we finish, we can scan the outside camera to see if the driver can be spotted and identified. John and Bob should be back any time now. They can help with that."

Bill carried a fresh cup of coffee back to the captain's office. The captain motioned him inside.

"Well, how'd it go?" he asked.

"Pretty good. We have some pretty good pictures of the two men inside the store. We still need to view tapes from the liquor store camera. John and Bob should be back here any minute. They can help with that. They didn't say what they learned in Homer."

"I just had a call from Darlene North. She said she'll be back by the end of the week. She wanted to know if she could open and stay at her home? I told her she could. I was assuming you found what you could find during the search."

Bill rubbed his left eyebrow in thought, "I guess you're right, Cap. In fact, I think we should check with the crime lab about those reloaded bullets we found. It would be nice to know if they match the ones taken from Lee Woods' body."

"I want you to know I think you and your team are doing a great job. Your methods are a bit dated and you don't use a computer much, but you're effective and efficient. Thank you for that." The captain was sincere in his short praise.

CHAPTER SEVEN

Bill returned to the office where the others were waiting while looking at security tapes taken from the truck stop/liquor store robbery. When he entered, Bob spoke up.

"Hey Lieutenant. John had a good thought a minute ago. What if these robbers aren't robbers at all but looking for someone working nights in one of these Quick Stop stores. That would explain a lot of things about them. For instance, why are they still sticking around the Peninsula? Why do they enter holding weapons? Why do they steal a vehicle to do the robbery? There's a whole list of questions like that could be answered by 'the robberies are a cover for entering these places at a late-night hour.'"

"That is a good possibility, Bob. Good work John. I knew I picked you two for some reason, though it's hard to believe thinking was one of them." Bill was laughing and pointing at the two men. "Really though, I never believed they were just robbing stations for the few dollars they get each time. But I never thought about them searching for someone for a specific reason. I couldn't think of a reason for them to hang around. If they are drug dealers and looking for someone who stole from them or owes them a lot of money this would answer the question."

"We've viewed the exterior cameras and there are photos of the driver sitting at the wheel of a stolen car, but they aren't clear. We can't identify him. We made copies of his photos anyway." Randy reported.

"The good news is Nick North went to arraignment and was remanded back to the jail. He pled not guilty of course. The captain just told me North's wife, Darleen, is coming back to town at the end of the week. We'll contact her and have her give us a statement. Meanwhile we need to catch these robbers. What if we asked the road troopers to make a trip through all the campgrounds to look for the green Jeep? One of these days some young clerk is going to pull out a gun to defend himself and get his head shot off. That makes this a priority search." Bill was genuinely concerned about what he had just described. He felt his job was to protect the public and he took it seriously.

Bob Barratt spoke up again, "I thought we could do that very thing, so I asked Jean to make copies of the photos of the robbers and pass them out to the road troopers. I never thought of having them cruise the campgrounds to look for the Jeep."

"Well, we've had a couple of long days and today is no exception. Give Jean instructions to forward the photos to the local road troopers. I'll buy dinner tonight and we can all turn in early."

The team members were married to understanding wives who were used to all the late nights and odd hours when the guys were working a case.

Bill Koogan liked these men and trusted them fully. They were not easy to work with, but he trusted them implicitly. It was a satisfying feeling which went both ways.

An hour later the Geezer Squad was again seated in a booth at Froso's Family Restaurant drinking iced tea and joking with the waitress. The men never discussed their case while out in public. You never know who's listening from the next booth. All four ordered the special of the day which was a deep-fried shrimp dish. Froso, the owner, came to the table to say hello to the troopers she had known for so many years.

When the owner had gone back to the front desk, Bob asked Bill, "How long do you think they'll keep us on the job?"

"I have no idea," answered Bill. "We were hired because of the fish war in Bristol Bay. The state sent all available troopers out there in hopes of stopping any violence. There's still a fishing season for another six weeks. My guess is that we'll be welcome until the regular troops are back here and on the job again."

"I for one, am glad to have the work," declared Randy. "I've been looking at a new fishing boat I can't afford. This'll give me the cash to buy it. That is, if my wife doesn't have a different idea about it. She may get ideas about remodeling the kitchen or something."

"You'd better not cause me any grief, or I'll call her and tell her what you're making on this call-out." Bill laughed at his own words, along with the others.

After dinner they walked to the parking lot together. Outside and out of earshot of others, Bill motioned the crew to gather around.

"I just wanted to pass the word that Darleen North is on her way home from Oklahoma. Think about it and let me know if you think of anything we need to get from the house with our warrant before she arrives. The judge set Nick North's bail so high I don't think he can afford to get released, but we need to make sure this lady is safe."

With that, the four men shook hands and walked to their own cars. It had been a good day.

It was two in the morning when Bill's phone rang. "Hello?" answered a sleepy Bill Koogan.

It was Soldotna police chief, Bud Griffin, "Good morning, Bill," he said in a friendly voice.

"Oh, hello Bud. What's up?"

"I'm just calling to tell you your Quick Stop robbers just hit again, this time here in Soldotna. My men are there now. I thought you might want to join us in the investigation."

"I'll be there as soon as I can get dressed. Which store was it?"

"The gas station and liquor store on the Spurr Highway at Marydale Avenue."

"I'll be there as quickly as I can. I'll have my guys join us there. We could get lucky and find the vehicle before they dump it."

Bill dressed as fast as he could and drove directly to the small gas station. As he drove into town he called Bob, informed him of the situation and instructed him to call the rest of the team together and meet him at the crime scene. He always drove with his headlights on, even this time of year when there was over nineteen hours of daylight and it was just dusky the rest of the night. To his surprise there was a small crowd gathered at the scene. Soldotna Police had put yellow police tape around the area keeping the onlookers away from the site. Chief Griffin was near the front entry of the store giving instructions to two city officers. Bill stood back and waited for him to finish. As the two officers turned to walk inside Koogan stepped up to speak with him.

"Have you caught 'em yet?" he asked.

The chief turned to see who had spoken to him. "It's about time you got out of bed."

"My team is on the way down here to give a hand if you need it."

"The clerk said they have security cameras around the store and pumps out front. I just told two of my men to secure the tapes as evidence."

Bill reached into an inside pocket of his light summer jacket to retrieve the photos they had copied from the other security tapes.

"Here Bud. See if the clerk can identify these men as her robbers. We just got them this afternoon. In fact, these are the copies I was bringing to your office in the morning."

The chief took the photos and walked into the store. Bill waited outside. A minute later another officer came to take the trooper inside.

"You're sure these are the two men who came inside and robbed the store at gunpoint?" Bud Griffin was saying as Bill approached.

"Oh, yeah, that's them alright. They were polite and nice, but they scared the heck out of me," the clerk was saying. She was an overweight lady in her mid to late forties.

One of the city officers was speaking with an older man who had told them he saw the two leave the store and get into a car parked on the north side of the building. "You know," he was saying, "They were just sauntering along like they'd just bought a pack of cigarettes. If it was me and I'd just robbed a store, I'd be running as fast as I could to get away. It was like they didn't care who saw them."

Bill returned to the checkout counter and took the photos he had given the chief. He returned to where the officer was talking with the witness.

"Sir, I'm a state trooper. Do you recognize any of the faces in these photos?"

The man looked at the several photos and replied, "That's them all right. They're some very cool customers, like I said."

"Can you describe the vehicle they got into?" asked Bill.

"Sure. It was a beat-up old jeep Wrangler. It was red and covered with mud. I couldn't see the driver 'cause it's dark on that side of the store."

"I don't suppose you remember the license number?" asked the trooper.

"Nope, sure don't. But they took off up the Spurr Highway, lickity split headed toward Kenai."

"Thank you, sir. You have been very helpful."

Bill returned to the front counter where Bud Griffin was still talking with the clerk. "The witness says they're in a red Jeep Wrangler, covered with mud and going toward Kenai. If you want to alert KPD, I'll call my team and have them head that way, too."

Bud nodded and reached for his radio while Bill took his cell phone from his pocket and stepped outside the door to make his calls. "Remember, these men are armed and presumed dangerous," were his parting words to each man.

John Ashley and Randy Craig agreed to meet at the trooper office to get the marked car they had been issued. They decided to take the same route to Kenai the robbers had taken instead of the shorter route crossing the bridge in Kenai. Randy was driving while John used his phone to call Bill Koogan.

"Hello Bill. I just thought we may not be looking for the Wrangler. This Jeep may be a stolen vehicle like the other robberies. You might tell the city officers to be on the lookout for the green Grand Cherokee, too."

"Good thinking, John. I'll pass that on to Bud Griffin. Don't try to take them alone. If you find them, call for backup. If you get hurt, it'll cause a whole lot of paperwork and you know how I hate paperwork."

"You got it, Boss," was the reply.

Bill returned to speak with Chief Griffin. "Say, Bud. That Wrangler is probably stolen. The perps likely have a green Grand Cherokee hidden somewhere and will probably leave the Wrangler parked in the trees along the way. You might want to advise your men as well as the KPD officers. That's been their strategy in the past."

"Thanks, Bill, I'll pass that along. I'll have my receptionist type up my report and send a copy to your office. You know, I'm beginning to think you Geezers may have a use after all."

"I'm going to get even with you for that one," said Bill as he spoke over his shoulder, walking quickly to his vehicle.

It was nearly six in the morning and the sun was high in the sky when Bill and his men met back at the office. Each man had a fresh cup of coffee in front of them. Bob Barratt had his feet crossed, resting on the conference table. All four team members were tired and hungry.

Bob was the first to report. "We drove every side road and street we could find. We saw KPD officers patrolling, too. We never found the Wrangler or the Grand Cherokee. These guys are smart and could be parked in a garage or shed somewhere. It's pretty plain to me, they don't move around much in the daylight. But being strangers to the area they sure are invisible."

"Bob's right, Bill. We must have driven a hundred miles tonight and couldn't find any trace of them. I'm wondering if they have a local contact or accomplice hiding them. I still think they're looking for someone who only works at night. I can't see any other reason for them to act as they do." John Ashley was showing his frustration.

Randy Craig was the last to report, "I thought about jumping in with Bob and John but changed my mind by thinking we could cover a greater area with another car on the road. Bob and John covered the area on the north side of the river, and I covered the south side. It was pretty much daylight all night long and I could see into the trees and down driveways. I never caught a glimpse of either of those vehicles."

"I think I'm going to get some breakfast before I come back to report to the captain. Any of you who want to join me is welcome. It's been a long night and you boys need some rest. I would like to have a meeting this afternoon around three o'clock to finish our reports and read the Soldotna Police report. The chief said he'd have a copy for me today. Right now, I'm just tired and hungry."

CHAPTER EIGHT

After he ate breakfast alone, Bill returned to the office to complete his report and await the arrival of his captain. It was nearly eight o'clock when the boss-man came to his office with a fresh cup of coffee in hand. Bill had heard him enter and carried his copy of the robbery report for the captain.

"Busy night was it, Bill?"

"Very. They hit the Quick Stop on the Spurr road. SPD can handle the details of the robbery, but my guys and me looked for them all night without success. I told them to go home until late this afternoon to get some rest. I came in to complete the report and give you a briefing. I don't know where they went,. We couldn't find them. SPD and KPD were looking also. It's still a puzzle as to why they're hanging out on the Peninsula, unless they're looking for someone who may work nights in one of the Quick Stops, but that's only a guess."

"You may as well go home and get some rest yourself, Bill. I know how frustrating these things can get," said the sympathetic captain. "Oh, by the way, Darleen North sent word she will be back on Friday. We better call the DA's office and see if North is trying to make bail. We don't want him coming home and finding his wife has locked him out."

"I'll call Walker before I leave the office this morning. Thanks, Cap."

It was one o'clock in the afternoon when he returned to the office. There was a note on his desk to see the captain. He went to the coffee pot and poured a cup to take with him.

"Howdy Cap," he said as he entered the office.

Captain Bradshaw smiled when he entered, "Did you get some rest?" he asked.

"Slept like a log," Bill replied. "What's up with the note on my desk?"

"I have a little news for you. A kid on a bicycle spotted the red Wrangler stashed in some brush off Beaver Loop Road. I had an officer check it out and look for fingerprints. He said the entire inside of the Jeep was wiped clean. I'm beginning to think as you are, that these are pros. We had better find them before one of our local citizens gets hurt."

Bill was shaking his head in disgust, "I can't help thinking these men have a local accomplice hiding them out during the daylight hours. We never see the green Grand Cherokee they used to travel from town to town. They steal a car off the street during the night, do a robbery, ditch the stolen car and disappear."

"A judge once told me it was like going fishing, 'sometimes you get a fish and sometimes you don't', but you keep on fishing. Don't make it a personal thing, Bill. Just do what you're good at and keep fishing."

The two senior officers stopped talking when they heard voices down the hall in the direction of the officer entry near the offices. It was the other three members of the Squad.

"I guess I should go back and help them find the coffee pot," Bill commented.

"One more thing, Bill. I had a text message from Mrs. North. She will arrive at the Kenai Airport at noon this Friday, day after tomorrow. I think you should pick her up and drive her home. You can explain everything to her and answer all her questions."

"What makes you think she doesn't have a ride?" asked a curious Koogan.

"Mrs. North told me she was not notifying any of her friends she's coming home. She said she was afraid word would get back to Nick at the jail."

"OK, Cap, I'll pick her up on Friday. Right now, I need to see if my guys finished their reports on the robbery."

Back in his office he found the three reports stacked on his desk. "Well, did you boys get all rested up?"

"We are a lot younger than you and don't need as much rest. We're good to go!" reported John with the others nodding agreement.

"The captain just informed me that some kid found the Wrangler stashed in some brush on Beaver Loop. He asked Kenai PD to dust it for prints, but it had been wiped clean. Do any of you have an idea about how to go about catching these perps?"

"Sorry, Bill, we all talked it over and none of us has a good thought about this. I hate to just sit around and wait for them to do something stupid, though." It was Bob Barratt reporting.

Koogan blew out a long breath, "Well, let's brainstorm a little and see if we can come up with something. Since they first arrived on the Peninsula, has there been a time pattern between robberies?"

"We looked at that. They occurred on different days of the week, at different locations, at different times. "We can't find a pattern of any sort." said Bob, shaking his head. "We even looked at their escape routes and there's no single direction of departure from each robbery."

"I've sent copies of the photos to Anchorage Police Department. So far there's no one reporting knowledge of these men. Do any of you have an idea about how to bait them into the open?" asked Bill with frustration in his tone.

"If we knew why they're down here, it would make a difference, but since we don't, we have no idea what they plan to do. I think your idea about them looking for someone in particular is our best yet. I think, until we get something to go on, we're just spinning our wheels."

"I agree with you, Randy, and you know how I hate to waste time. We've alerted all the local police agencies and given them all copies of the photos from the security tapes. I can't think of anything we can do except wait. I'm going to tell the captain to give us something to work on until these men come out of hiding again."

"We all think that's a good idea, Bill. We don't want to sit around the office and drink coffee all day, doing nothing. Get us another assignment." It was Bob making the statement with the others agreeing with him.

"I have a question," spoke Randy Craig.

"What's that, Randy?" asked Bill.

"Have we heard anything from the crime lab about any of the evidence we sent in the Lee Woods shooting? There will be quite a lot of follow-up work when we get that information."

"I'll ask the captain to check on that. Meanwhile, you guys have been putting in a lot of hours. Take a day off tomorrow and spend it with your family. I'll try to regroup and get us back on track."

The following day the entire Squad took the day off. Bill had come to the office to check to see if anything had changed. It hadn't. He spoke with the captain and took the rest of the day off to be with his wife and grandkids. It felt good to relax and act like a retired person.

In the summer in Alaska, there's always lawn to mow, leaves to rake, trim to paint and a long list of other chores dreamed up by the wife during the winter. Bill enjoyed the home chores and especially loved his small grandchildren, here for a few days to visit grandmother and granddad. There were four grandbabies. Two belonged to his son. Two belonged to his daughter. This life was what made retirement worthwhile.

Late in the afternoon he gathered the entire family in the back yard and proposed burgers and ice cream for dinner. Everyone voted in favor of the suggestion. "Should I cook? Or do we go to DQ?' he asked.

"I'll help you cook, Grandpa," shouted Elsie, the youngest grandchild.

"I think that would be a great idea. We can eat and visit out here on the patio." This came from Bill's daughter Myrna, mother of Elsie.

The rest of the day was spent getting things ready for the cookout. Bill loved his family and the time he was able to spend with them. He knew the other three members of the Geezer Squad were doing the same.

They were all family men with close ties to their children and grandchildren. The old stresses were still with him while at work and the office but were nonexistent when he was home with family.

At 10:06pm, Bill was closing the drapes and locking the doors when his telephone rang.

"Lieutenant Koogan, this is trooper dispatch. I was told by Chief Griffin to call you. SPD has a green Jeep Grand Cherokee stopped near the high school in Soldotna. There are four men in the vehicle. The chief asked for you to come to the scene right away. Will you be able to respond?"

"I'll be leaving right now," answered Bill. "Did he request the whole team or just me?"

"SPD has two cars and four officers on scene currently. Chief Griffin asked for you because it was originally your case."

"Tell the chief I'll be in my POV. I don't want him to shoot me. It'll take me about seven minutes to get to the scene."

"I'll inform him, Sir."

Bill called to his wife to tell her he had been called to work. It took eight minutes to reach the scene because he was in his own vehicle with no red and blue lights to warn traffic. When he arrived, he found two city patrol cars had boxed the Jeep between them. One in front and one at the rear. Four officers were behind their respective cars ordering the men out of the vehicle. So far, there had been no movement by the men. As he pulled to the side of the street and got out of his car, there was movement inside the Jeep Grand Cherokee. The driver had started the vehicle and was revving the engine.

Suddenly, the driver revved the engine and put the Jeep in reverse. When the throttle was mashed to the floor, the Jeep lurched backward striking the patrol car and driving it sideways. The two officers standing behind the patrol car were knocked to the ground.

The driver shifted to Drive and again pressed the throttle to the floor, striking the second patrol car in the right front fender, jamming the damaged fender against the wheel. Again, the officers behind it were knocked to the ground.

Bill watched the action and drew his weapon, but the angle of the fleeing vehicle would not allow him a clear shot. The Jeep sped to the first side street and made a U-turn to come back in their direction. Bill stood in the middle of the street near the wrecked patrol cars as the speeding Jeep approached. He fired his Glock .40 at the speeding vehicle, aiming at the driver. The bullet smashed into the windshield, missing the driver by inches.

As the Jeep passed, he managed to get the license number, calling it in to dispatch as he ran to check on the downed officers. It was obvious there were injuries to both officers that were struck first by the Jeep. He ordered dispatch to send medical assistance and turned to check on the second pair of officers at the other wrecked patrol car.

Behind the wrecked patrol car one officer was tending the injuries of his partner.

"Are you OK?" asked Bill.

"I'm alright, but Dean, here, is unconscious."

"I've called for an ambulance. The other two officers are in worse shape. I'm going over to see if I can help them until the EMT's arrive."

As he stepped around the broken patrol car, he could see one of the officers was bleeding profusely. The other officer was regaining consciousness. Bill went directly to the recovering Soldotna officer who was regaining his wits, shaking his head to clear the fog.

"How badly are you hurt?" asked Bill.

"I don't think anything is broken," he replied.

"An ambulance is on the way. Let's check your partner to see if he has anything broken or bent. If you can take care of him, I'll chase after the Jeep. I'll be on the trooper radio."

Bill could see the lights and hear the siren of the approaching ambulance. He ran to his car and climbed inside. There was a portable flashing red light on the rear seat. He placed it on the roof and jumped behind the wheel.

He had seen the Jeep travel the entire length of the street to the traffic light on the Spurr Highway. He didn't dare drive as fast as the fleeing vehicle for fear of striking some citizen driving on the street. At the Spurr intersection, he paused and decided to follow to the right. He cruised down the city street for several blocks trying to learn which way the Jeep had gone.

As he approached the traffic light on the Sterling Highway his radio blared a warning from the dispatch center.

"We have a report of a reckless driver on the Sterling Highway at Binkley Street, Southbound. All units in the area please respond."

Bill slowed and looked for any signs of the fleeing SUV. Crossing the Kenai River bridge in the heart of town, he cruised slowly for another city block to a traffic light where a pedestrian, noticing his flashing red light, pointed to Funny River Road. Bill quickly turned East on the road. He sped up the narrow road, looking into all the driveways and side roads in an effort to spot the green Jeep.

Slightly more than a mile up Funny River Road and approaching the Soldotna Airport, the thought struck him. "What if they decided to steal an airplane to make their getaway?"

Turning off his red overhead light, he passed through the automatic entry gate of the airport. He saw no vehicles driving around the tarmac but decided to patrol the airfield anyway. He turned left toward several large, commercial hangars in that direction. He drove slowly to the end of the paved area, past the last hangar and fuel tanks on that end of the airport. Not seeing the green Cherokee, he turned around to patrol to the other end of the aircraft parking area. It struck him that it would be convenient to hide a vehicle between hangars or in fact, inside one of them. To his left, in one of the open hangars, he saw a Cessna 206 engine start. Not seeing the green Jeep, he continued to the far end of the parking area, with no luck.

He turned around to circle to the south past the open hangars and saw the Cessna taxiing toward the runway. He jotted the registration numbers on the notepad on the passenger seat. He drove to the open hangar he had seen the Cessna come out of and located the green Jeep Cherokee.

While driving toward the large commercial hangar belonging to a church group, he notified dispatch to inform Captain Bradshaw what he had found. At the hangar office he asked who may know the owner of the Cessna. He gave the tail number he had recorded.

"That would be Dwayne Morton. He owns the last hangar in row five. You realize this is an uncontrolled airport and he doesn't need a clearance to take off?" The information came from the young office manager.

"How do I contact the FAA to find out where he's headed and where he lands?"

"Come back here," he motioned, "I have a radio. You can talk directly with them from here." The young man selected a channel and spoke to one of the tower operators in Kenai.

After speaking with the tower supervisor and advising him this was probably a stolen aircraft, Bill waited in the hangar office for other troopers to arrive from a mile down the road.

CHAPTER NINE

Within minutes two trooper cars stopped in front of the hangar where he had waited. When he saw the troopers, he walked outside to talk with them.

"We missed them again, Guys. The green Jeep is in the last hangar in that row," he said, pointing to row five. "I want you to get any prints you can from the inside of it. The last stolen car we found had been wiped clean. They may not have had time to clean this one up. I think they just took off in a stolen airplane."

"The captain asked us to have you come back to the office," instructed one of the officers.

"Have you heard from my squad?" asked Bill.

"Yes, they came into the office to get a marked car and talked with the captain. He sent them uptown to where the injured SPD officers were."

"Have you heard anything of the condition of the injured officers?"

"There were four men hurt. The ambulance took three of them to the hospital. I haven't heard any reports on their conditions. The fourth officer stayed at the scene. It appears he was bruised up pretty good but stayed to help. The captain put your guys in charge of investigating the incident with the SPD officers."

"OK then, I'll head back to the office while you boys check out the Jeep and the hangar where they stole the Cessna. I'll ask the captain to send a wrecker to pick up the Cherokee. I'll change to a patrol car at the office when I finish with the captain and go to help my crew at the crash site in town." Bill blew out a long breath, "I have never seen anything like what those perps did to those two police cars. They disabled both city cars in about ten seconds and did it without severe damage to their own vehicle. I got off one shot at the driver. You'll find a bullet hole in the windshield, but I missed the driver."

Bill went inside the hangar to thank the man behind the counter for his help. He gave the man his business card and returned to the trooper office to speak with the captain, after pouring a fresh cup of hot coffee to carry with him.

"Busy night, eh, Bill?"

"I'll say it was. Has Chief Griffin told you what took place?"

"Yes, and the chief sent his thanks to you for being there for his men. He said you can still move pretty fast for an old geezer," Bradshaw was chuckling now.

"I think I'll cite him for insulting an officer." Now they were both chuckling.

It took over an hour to give the captain a detailed report of the incident and to tell of speaking with the FAA about the suspected Cessna theft.

Confirming federal investigators were involved regarding the stolen aircraft, Captain Bradshaw sent the other three members of the Squad to investigate and report on the wrecking of two SPD patrol cars and the injuries to four officers at the scene. The investigation was completed in just under two hours and the three officers returned to the office. Bill was working at his desk when they returned.

"I've seen a lot of car accidents, but I have never seen one done intentionally, nor as efficiently as this one. They must have practiced that move many times to be able to do it as neatly as they did. I admire their work on this one." Bob had retired after 26 years on the force, spending most of his time as a road trooper, and he'd seen hundreds of car wrecks.

Randy Craig spoke up, "The two troopers they sent to the airport just came back. The green Jeep is on the way to the impound yard. They said to tell you there were only a couple of prints inside the Jeep. Have you heard anything about where the Cessna is going or landed?"

"Not yet, but the FAA will tell us if they show up anywhere. They may not go to a controlled airport to land. With all the private airstrips in this part of Alaska they could be anywhere." Bill Koogan had been entering his own report and reviewing his work. He leaned back in his chair and continued to speak. "I've been thinking. Seeing them in action, they may be ex-military. They worked like special forces men. They acted with precision, were cool and unafraid, they didn't flinch at gunfire but stayed on the maneuver until they made their escape. These guys are good at what they do. One other thing, we've been looking for three perps and there were four in the car. It seems likely they found the person they've been looking for."

"We've always assumed they came from Anchorage, but they could have come from anywhere, and with that airplane they can go anywhere. I think you can forget ever finding them in our jurisdiction any time soon." John Ashley was a grandfather with about a dozen grandchildren to his credit. He also had many hours of training in various aspects of investigation. He always liked his job as a trooper and, from time to time thought he may have retired too early.

"I notified the FAA and had the captain send out a message to all trooper posts to be on the lookout for the Cessna and that these men are dangerous. I think all we can do now is wait to see where they turn up," said a frustrated Bill Koogan.

The rest of the afternoon was spent working on the final reports. It was late when they called it quits for the night. The four officers were having a final cup of coffee in the office when the captain entered.

"I hope you boys don't have plans for the rest of the evening," said the captain. "I just received word they found the Cessna 206 at the Wasilla airport. An airport worker said they landed just over an hour from when they left Soldotna. When they reported their approach, they used a bogus registration number. So no one knew they were there until a few minutes ago. I ordered a trooper King Air to pick you guys up and fly you to Wasilla. Take a crime kit and go to the Soldotna Airport. He said he would pick you up in thirty minutes. Call me if you find anything. The local office will give you a car if you need one."

"Gee, thanks for the kindness, Cap," replied Bill.

"Anything for the Geezer Squad," was the reply.

The turboprop King Air was comfortable and quiet. It was a relaxing flight to Wasilla where one of the local troopers met them when they landed. He took them to the stolen aircraft parked in the transient parking area. The three men worked for almost two hours looking for anything to use for evidence; dust from the floorboards, fingerprints, dropped items, or any other thing to be used as a clue as to who these men were. Though it was still daylight it was very late at night when they finished.

Koogan looked at the local trooper, "Go over to the office and tell our pilot we've finished and need to return to Soldotna."

The local trooper did as directed and returned to the place the King Air was parked within minutes. The entire group followed the pilot inside the large twin engine plane and strapped in for the flight home. They had little conversation on the return flight. It had been a very long and frustrating day, which left the entire group exhausted.

It was just after midnight when they returned to the trooper office to end their day. Bill carried the crime kit into their small office for safe keeping.

The following morning, he was the first into the office, though he was later than usual. There was a note on his desk asking him to report to the captain when he came in.

"You said you wanted to see me, Cap?" he said from the doorway.

"Oh, hi Bill, yes. I had word early this morning they found a body near the Wasilla airport. The local officers think he may be one of the men from the Cessna.

"That may be a possibility. There were four men in the plane when it left Soldotna. There were four men in the green Jeep during the incident with SPD. The guys and I think the robbers may have found the man they had been looking for and took him with them. Perhaps, if we can identify the body, we can make the connection. It must be something like a drug deal gone bad or he didn't come up with the cash to pay for his drugs. Something like that. Let me know when we get an ID on the body."

Bill returned to his office to drink his coffee and write a report on the events of the previous night. An hour later the rest of the team came in with cups of hot coffee in their hands.

Bill looked up when they came into the office. "I had forgotten just how much paperwork there was to this job," he said with a grin on his face.

All four team members were laughing now.

"It looks like they found the fourth member from the plane. Wasilla troopers have a body near the airport. I asked the captain to let me know when they learn the identity of the victim." Bill reported to his men.

He had been working on his own report for another twenty minutes when his phone beeped.

"Koogan," he answered to the unknown number.

"Hello, Lieutenant, this is Sergeant Owens in Wasilla. I just called to let you know we can identify the body we found here. He came from Soldotna. His name is Tino DeLuca. He is from the Soldotna area. At least his driver's license says he lives there."

"Can you determine the cause of death yet?" asked Bill.

"His throat was cut and we assume at this point that was the cause of death. He had a few dollars in his pockets as well as his ID. It looks like whoever killed him didn't do it to rob him. He was wearing a wedding ring, so he may have a widow in your area somewhere. The body has been sent to the crime lab and the medical team for further investigation."

"Thanks Sergeant. Call me back if you learn anything new. We think his killers were the three men we've been tracking for several days. We thought they were looking for someone who worked nights at a Quick Stop because they were robbing them regularly. It looks like they found him. We'll find out who your victim is and what he was up to that got him killed. I'll be getting back to you."

"I take it you think he was one of the men in the stolen Cessna?" commented Owens.

"It sounds like it. I'll let you know when we check him out. If he does have a wife, she may know something."

"Good luck, Lieutenant," said Owens.

Bill scratched his head as he hung up the phone. "We may be in luck men," he said.

"What did you learn?" asked Ashley.

"The Wasilla trooper said the victim was wearing a wedding ring. We need to check all the local Quick Stops and find out where he worked and get a background on him. We also need to find out if he was married and if his wife is here in the area. Split up and go to all the Quick Stops and ask about him. His name is Tino DeLuca. I'll work on his police record. Let's get going on this. See if it leads us back to the men who stole the Cessna and probably killed him. Take my state car, too. Call me if you find out where he worked. I want to be there when you question his employer. Let's get moving, Guys." Bill was hopeful this would lead to information they had never been able to learn during the investigation of the robbers.

A half hour later John Ashley called. "We got it, Boss. He was the night manager at the Soldotna Quick Stop and ran the liquor store at night. I have the day manager here and she says she'll talk to you and give you his home address. He's married and the wife lives here in town."

CHAPTER TEN

When John Ashley called while contacting the day manager of the Quick Stop, Bill Koogan checked his watch. It was nearly time for him to go to the Kenai Airport to pick up Darleen North to drive her to her home. It was one of those chores he did not look forward to. He had always hated dealing with domestic violence disputes and that's what this had turned into.

"John. I'm scheduled to go to Kenai in a few minutes. I'd like you to gather the information and I'll contact you when I return from the airport."

"OK, Bill, we can take care of it. See you when you get back."

"Thanks, John, I shouldn't be more than an hour." Bill finished what he had been working on and walked to the captains' office.

"I'm headed over to pick up Mrs. North, Cap. I should be done with that chore in an hour. Then I'm going to town to meet John and the Squad to interview the wife of the victim killed in Wasilla. I have no idea how long that'll take."

"That's beginning to sound like you're making headway on that case. Keep me posted on your progress. As for Mrs. North, you know our limitations, but give her as much assistance as possible. She looks to be an almost innocent bystander in this case."

"You know me, Cap. I never did like domestic violence cases and that's what this appears to me. They didn't get along, she stepped out, he got angry, Lee Woods was killed. It's not my job to judge motives, only legal issues. I'll drive her home and make sure she's safe, but I can't soothe her conscience."

"Our job is to make her feel safe. Just try to do that with some tact." The captain understood better than Koogan could know.

Bill was parking in front of the terminal as her flight was touching down on the runway. He walked inside to wait for the passengers to come in and claim their baggage. He had never met Mrs. North but was told by people who knew her she was "good looking". One by one the passengers entered the lobby.

She was nearly the last to get off the small passenger plane. She was wearing a dark pantsuit outfit with a white silk scarf around her neck. She was wearing large dangling gold earrings and carrying a small carry-on bag. Bill approached her and asked, "Hello, are you Mrs. North?"

"Yes, I am," she said as she turned quickly to face him. "And who are you?"

"I'm Trooper Koogan. We spoke on the telephone a few days ago."

"Oh yes, Trooper Koogan. Sorry, but I am just a little nervous about coming home, under the circumstances."

"I understand and that's why I came to give you a ride to your home. Perhaps we can have a talk about all that on the way to your place. Do you have more luggage?"

"No, just this. Everything I need is at the house. Can we leave now?" she asked.

Bill carried her bag to the car and placed it on the rear seat of the sedan. Then he opened the front passenger door for her. He climbed in behind the wheel and started the engine. Darleen North hung her head and said nothing for several blocks, but then looked at Bill as he drove.

"Trooper Koogan, I know you're familiar with all the facts as to what happened and you must think I'm a terrible person. I'd like you to know how it was before. Nick and I have been married for over fifteen years. After he decided to open his own shop, he changed. He became distant and abusive. He worked all the time and was mean to me when he came home. Lee Woods lived up the street and was a policeman. He saw me walking on the road one day and stopped to see if I was alright. He knew what kind of man Nick had become and asked if I was safe in the house. After that he would come by from time to time and check on me. One thing led to another, and we had an affair. I don't know how Nick found out, but he became even more abusive. That's when I began to think of divorce and left to stay with my folks in Oklahoma for a while. I don't mean for this to sound like an excuse, but I hope it will give you the reason why I left."

"Mrs. North...."

"Please, call me Darleen," she interrupted.

"Darleen, it's not my job to judge people. It is my job to find out why they did what they did. You're not a criminal and I'm not here to judge your motives. In my career I've seen a great deal of domestic violence. I've seen what abusive men do to wives. Believe me, I'm not judging you. Although, I've often wondered why more women don't do as you did and leave or divorce abusive spouses. I want you to know my department is here to protect you. I'm sorry the situation wasn't reported to us in the past, but I can't change that. I think you're going to be safe while he's locked up. It's unlikely he'll ever get out on bail, but if he does, the court will tell him not to have contact with you, which he'll probably ignore. Don't hesitate to call us if you feel threatened by him or anyone else."

"I hope you're right, Trooper Koogan. He has turned into a very mean person. I don't even recognize him anymore. He used to be kind and thoughtful, but since he started his business he's a mean and spiteful person. It's not just with me, he treats everyone terribly."

"I want you to know I am here to protect you. Not just from your husband, but from anyone who threatens you. Don't hesitate to call any time. Day or night."

"Thank you," she said in a soft voice.

"You know, of course, we searched your home. We were looking for a specific weapon. A small .38 caliber revolver called a Chief Special. We found ammunition in his reloading room, but we never found the gun. Would you have any idea where he may have hidden it?" asked Koogan.

"Perhaps. He hid several guns around the house. He may have stashed it under a table in the reloading room. I'll show you when we get to the house." She paused a moment to think. "Do you have any idea when his next court date will be?"

"No, but I can find out from the District Attorney. I'll call him when we get to your home." Bill was quiet and volunteered nothing further for the rest of the trip.

Darleen North was silent and sullen as she rode to her home.

"I hope we didn't mess your home up too much in our search," commented Bill as they slowly drove down the driveway.

"It'll be just fine. I have nothing else to do but clean the place. Please come inside and I'll show you where he kept the little revolver." As she opened the door to the car, she spied her small sedan parked beside the house. "Oh, good, my car is still here. I didn't know if he had kept it after I left."

Bill didn't comment, but stepped out of his car and opened the back door to retrieve the small carry-on bag from the rear seat. The two walked together up the front steps. She lifted the flowerpot to find the house key which had been returned to its hiding place. She opened the door and offered him entry first. He stepped inside, still carrying the small bag which he placed near the base of the staircase a short distance from the entry door.

"Come with me into the reloading room. I'll show you where he kept the little gun. It may not be there, but this is where he always kept it."

She walked to the bench-like table in the center of the room. She walked to the far side and reached under the table. When she stood upright, she was holding a small leather holster which was filled with a Smith and Wesson Chief Special.

"You had better take this. I don't like guns much." She turned the holster over to show Bill, "He put Velcro on the holster to stick it to the underside of the table."

"I guess we didn't search thoroughly enough. Please put the gun on the table. I need to preserve any fingerprints on the weapon."

Mrs. North complied by placing the package on the table. "Is there anything else I can help you find?" she asked.

"No, and I'm grateful to you for finding this for me. Would you have a paper bag I can place this inside. Again, it's to preserve any possible evidence."

She nodded and walked to the laundry area and opened a cupboard filled with paper shopping bags. "Will this do?" she asked.

"Yes, it will be perfect. Now, is there anything I can do for you while I'm here? If not, I need to get back to the office."

"I don't think so," she said. "Officer Koogan, I want to thank you for being so helpful. I really didn't know what I was going to do about getting home and didn't know what to expect when I got here. I really appreciate your kindness."

"And I appreciate your finding the weapon for us. I also want you to know I'm only a phone call away if you need help of any kind. Which reminds me, I was going to call the DAs office to get you Nick's next court date."

He was on the cell phone for only a few seconds when he said "Thanks" and put the phone back in his pocket. "There will be a hearing in Superior Court next month on the 15th. If there are any changes, I'll call and let you know." He took a card from his pocket and placed it on the large reloading table.

Bill picked up the large brown paper bag with the revolver inside and walked to the entry door. "Don't hesitate to call if you need anything," he said as he opened the door to leave.

She had tears in her eyes when she waved to him as he departed.

Back at the office he stopped by the office of Captain Bradshaw. He held up the shopping bag as he entered. "We have the gun," he reported. "I'll get it ready to send to the crime lab for prints and a ballistics check. I can't believe he didn't just throw the gun in the river, but he had it hidden under a table in his reloading room."

"You see there, Bill? Sometimes it pays to be nice to people." Bradshaw was chuckling at Koogan.

"I'll try not to make it a habit," he said to his boss. "Have you heard from my crew?"

"No, I haven't, they're still interviewing the wife of Owens, the Wasilla victim. They should be getting back before long, though."

"OK, I'll go package this .38 and get it ready to send to the crime lab. I guess I can write another report about locating the weapon." He gave the captain a half salute and went to his own office, stopping for a cup of coffee on the way.

He had just finished his report and had given it to Jean to enter into the system when the Squad returned. "Well, how did it go?"

"The lady was all broken up when we told her about her husband being killed. She wailed like a banshee. I'll bet money she's a meth head. They live in an apartment off Marydale. The lady is in her early thirties and appears to be a heavy drug user. After she calmed down, she gave us a lot of information. First, Tino DeLuca owed a dealer in Anchorage a ton of money. He sent those goons down here to collect. Tino was the night manager and ran the liquor store on the graveyard shift 11pm to 7am, six nights a week. She said he never missed a shift. Tino never used drugs, according to his wife. She said he suspected the robbers were in the area looking for him. She said he had gone to Anchorage and met with the drug dealer to get drugs to sell down here and help pay for his wife's habit. He convinced the dealer he'd be able to pay after he sold some product. The dealer was looking for someone to sell his stuff here on the Peninsula. Tino heard about it and went to see the guy. Tino kept the stuff in his car beside the liquor store and when someone came in and wanted drugs he'd go to his car and get it. He never took it inside the store. She said the problem was Tino had too many broke friends and let them have drugs for which they never paid him. That got him in hot water with the distributer in Anchorage. We have a name and phone number to give the Anchorage drug team. We didn't learn anything about the three goons who drug him out of his apartment and flew him to Wasilla." It was Randy Craig telling the story.

"Was she high when you spoke with her?" asked Bill.

"No, she was out of drugs and having a bad day. We took her to the Emergency Room for treatment, but we had nothing to charge her with at that moment and left her at the hospital."

"Good job, guys. I have some news for you, too. Mrs. North came home. She seems like a nice lady. When we got to her house, she showed me where Nick had hidden the Chief Special under a table in the reloading room." He pointed at the box on his desk. "I packaged it to send to the Crime Lab."

"And we still have half a shift to do our report. Life is good," said John Ashley.

CHAPTER ELEVEN

The next several days were hectic for the Squad. Finding the gun had changed a lot of the information required to file the case with the court. Much of it must be re-heard by the court, meaning new papers to file for the hearing. The defense must be given the opportunity to assess evidence and either allow the evidence to be shown in court or contest the evidence and have it withheld. The old he said/she said argument will not work in a criminal case.

Bill had asked the crime lab to put a rush order on the fingerprints and ballistics found on the weapon. In the meantime, DA Walker had been to the office several times to discuss the progress and accuracy of all forms and writs being prepared. Bill liked Walker for his down to earth attitude and his plain-talking way of discussing the case.

By late in the afternoon the entire squad was totally exhausted and making frequent trips to the coffee pot where the afternoon shift was reporting in for work and the day shift was in the office doing end of shift paperwork. The nickname for the Squad was beginning to catch on with the entire department.

"I heard your call numbers on the radio were 'Geezer One, Geezer Two, Geezer Three and Geezer Four. Is that true?" asked one of the older troopers.

"Do you want to go home tonight and explain to your wife how you got whupped by an old geezer?" It was Randy Craig with the reply.

The good-natured banter went on through shift change, with officers reporting in and others getting off shift. Officers are usually thought to be humorless, but in reality and generally only with another officer, do they become sarcastic jokesters. This is done to protect the image of the uniforms they wear. Police live in a very closed society, forbidden to speak of the job except with other policemen. Bill and his Geezer Squad took teasing well and gave back as good as they got.

Before leaving the office, Bill called Darleen North.

"Hello, Mrs. North. It's Bill Koogan, I'm just calling to check on you, seeing if you're doing OK today."

"Thank you for calling. I talked with the office girl at Nick's shop. She said there were several cars he was supposed to repair. She wondered what to do. I asked if she knew a good mechanic we could hire until everything was settled. She said she did. One Nick had used in the past. She called him and we hired him today. I'm keeping the shop open for the time being. I hope Nicks antics won't drive all the business away. The fact is, I need to make a little money to live on."

"It sounds like a good plan, and I wish you good luck."

"I thank you for being so nice to me during this time. I guess your reassurance is what I needed to get back and restart my life. Nick's lawyer called me today and we discussed a property settlement, but I need to hire my own lawyer to see what I need to do about all this. I could just let the lawyers hash it out if Nick wasn't about to be in jail for the rest of his life. I can't help thinking the lawyer is just worried about his fees for defending Nick. I don't mean to sound greedy, but I guess I own half this property and I don't want to lose the rest to his lawyers. The girl at the shop needs a job and I must make a living for myself somehow."

"Personally, I don't think you're being greedy. I think you're correct in thinking the lawyers just want their cut, and a little more if they can get it. But you're right about one thing. You do need a lawyer to represent your side of the case. Past that point I can't give you any advice about how to proceed. There are several good law firms locally and you've lived here long enough to be familiar with them. I wish you good luck, Ma'am. Feel free to call me if you need anything I can help you with."

"I understand, Mr. Koogan. You've been a big help and I thank you for it. Bye."

Bill scratched his head as he hung up the phone. "This is definitely a domestic problem," he thought. He was nearly to his home when the radio crackled. He picked it up and answered.

"Lieutenant, this is dispatch. The captain asked me to contact you and your squad because there are no other troopers available at this time. There's a large bunch of shoplifters at the Fred Meyer store. Two of them were challenged by the security officer and they hit him in the head, severely injuring him. The store asked for assistance. The shoplifters are fleeing the store now. Can you and your squad respond?"

"I'm returning to the scene now. Contact the other members and have them do the same. I should be on scene in five minutes." Bill braked to a stop and made a U-turn in the middle of the highway as he placed his portable rotating beacon on the roof of the car.

As he approached the parking area in front of the main entry, one of the employees saw the red flashing light and pointed to a tall young man in a long coat. Bill cut off his path with his car. Jumping out of his personal vehicle he displayed his badge and credentials.

"Stop where you are," he shouted. "I'm a trooper. Put your hands on the back of the car behind you. Do it now," he ordered.

"Go to hell, old man," said the fleeing man who continued to walk at a fast pace toward his own vehicle.

Bill took the pepper spray dispenser from his belt. "I said stop and I mean stop NOW!"

The young man continued to stride toward his old van.

"You have no choice! Stop now and place your hands on the car in front of you!"

"I ain't stopping, man. Stay out of my way or get hurt." It was a clear threat by the young criminal.

Bill stepped to the side and edged ahead of the fleeing felon. With a quick touch of the trigger on the pistol shaped dispenser he launched a volley of pepper spray in the direction of the man's face. The reaction was immediate.

The young man tried to wipe the irritant from his face, but only made things worse for himself. At that moment he couldn't see at all, and his entire face burned. He struck out blindly at Bill, but only connected with air and lost his balance, falling to the paved parking lot. In an instant Bill was pulling the man's arms behind him and placing handcuffs on his wrists. Once the man was in cuffs Bill jumped to his feet. The report said there were several shoplifters and he needed to locate the others.

One row of cars over and coming quickly in his direction, Bill saw another young man dressed similarly, wearing a long coat like the man he had just handcuffed. While keeping an eye on the second possible shoplifter he noted John Ashley entering the parking area in his personal vehicle. Bill reached for his radio to speak with his helper.

"I have one on the ground and the guy in the long coat ahead of you is headed in my direction. See if you can cut him off. Watch out, they hurt the security officer and tried to get me."

Ashley swung his car into the lane where the Squad leader and the shoplifter were facing each other. The shoplifter was so intent on watching Bill he paid no attention to the approaching vehicle, expecting it to stop for him as he walked toward Bill.

John braked to a stop near the man and jumped out as Bill came closer. Bill was shouting for the man to stop and to lay on the ground. He paid no attention. Ashley stepped up behind the man and pulled him over backward by the collar of his long coat. Both Bill and John were on top of him instantly. John applied his handcuffs to the shoplifter's wrists.

Now John Ashley turned to Bill, "What you got, Boss?"

"The call said there were about six or seven shoplifters in the store and they had struck and injured the store security officer. These two were out here when I arrived. That one over there didn't stop and I pepper sprayed him. I haven't seen the other shoplifters, but they must be here somewhere."

"Here comes Randy," said John, pointing to an approaching vehicle.

"Good, we may need him. You two take care of these perps and I'll go inside and talk with the manager. Be aware, there are others around somewhere."

Near the apparel department at the front entry door there was a small knot of store employees tending to the security officer. He was bleeding from a head wound and being treated by one of the clerks. The store manager knew Bill by sight and stood to give him a report. He said the security officer asked the man to stop and show his identification. He was discussing the situation with him when another shoplifter struck him from behind with a metal display stand. The other shoplifters, all in long coats, scattered and ran out the door. The two in the altercation stood to watch the injured security officer for a few moments before leaving the store.

"We have two of them cuffed in the parking lot. If they're the ones who attacked your security man, we can charge them with assault and take them to jail. We will need someone to identify them to be sure we have the right assailants," explained Bill.

The store manager turned to two clerks who had administered aid to the stricken security officer. "Nelda, you and Phillis go with Trooper Koogan and see if the two men he has in the parking lot are the ones who attacked Rex."

Rex, the security officer had a deep, bleeding wound on the left side of his head but was conscious. "Have you called an ambulance?" asked Bill.

"Yes, thank you. They should be here in a minute," replied the store manager.

Bill walked back to where John Ashley was standing over the two handcuffed men, still prone on the paved parking lot. The ambulance was arriving as he walked by to meet with Ashley.

"The two clerks will be right out to identify these men. If they are the ones who attacked the security man, we'll haul them to the pretrial facility and charge them with assault. I'm going to call Bob and have him bring the marked vehicle over here to transport these prisoners."

"From the conversation these guys were having, they did take out the security man. They don't seem to be very sorry for it either," commented John as he stood by with Bill awaiting the two clerks for positive identification.

Two minutes after the medics entered the store the two clerks ran to meet the troopers with the prisoners.

Without being asked, both girls, in unison said, "That's the two who hit Rex."

The taller girl, Phillis, asked, "Can I kick him for what he did to Rex?"

"No, Ma'am, that's not a good idea. We'll just take them to jail and let the judge deal with the punishment part of the deal. I am going to need for the two of you to come to the trooper office and write a report for us. When do you get off work?"

"We're off now, Trooper Koogan. We can go to your office now if that's good for you."

"As soon as one of my other officers gets here, I can go to the office and help you give your statements. He should be here any minute."

The prisoners on the ground were silent, apparently contemplating the eminent trip to jail. The first prisoner looked up at them and spoke.

"You can't throw us in jail for shoplifting," he said in an angry voice.

"You're wrong there, pardner," said Bill in a calm voice. "This isn't just shoplifting any longer. I'm going to charge you with a felony assault. You can call a lawyer after you're booked into jail. The DA may decide to add shoplifting to the final list of charges. Enjoy your stay, men."

<h1 style="text-align:center">CHAPTER TWELVE</h1>

The team had been in the office until very late the previous evening preparing paperwork for the shoplifting call and the two assault arrests. Bill had told his men they could come to the office a couple of hours late this morning. Bill himself, came in at the regular time to report to the captain. The head of the Geezer Squad poured a cup of coffee and updated the captain, sitting in the captain's office sipping his coffee while the captain finished a phone call he had received.

"Heard you had some excitement last night, Bill."

"Yeah, Cap, I was on my way home and got called back to a shoplifting at Fred Meyers. I called the crew back to assist and drove to the store. The security officer of the store had been attacked by two of the shoplifters. I met one of them in the parking lot and cuffed him up after he came at me. I had to pepper spray him. The other one came to his aid, and I took him down. John showed up and it got handled. The other shoplifters scattered and we never saw them. Medics took the security man to the ER by ambulance. I haven't heard how he's doing this morning. We all stayed and finished reports last night before going home."

"There was a bad car wreck on Pickle Hill in Soldotna about the same time and both Soldotna PD and our road troopers were busy. That's why we called you back. At the time we thought it was just a shoplifting case. I guess we all get it wrong sometimes. Great job, by the way." The captain was sipping on his own cup.

"Thanks, Cap. My guys know their job. We may be a little rusty, but we can still take care of business. I have a good team."

The captain took another swig of his black coffee, "I agree, Bill. Dispatch reported you handled it perfectly. I can't for the life of me understand why, but the dispatch unit likes you guys." The captain chuckled, "I know you and your team take a lot of teasing, but you're doing a great job keeping the pressure off the rest of the unit. They're still having a bad time over in Bristol Bay and we can't bring the troopers back yet. I'm sure there will be more calls like this before we're done."

Bill stood to leave the office, "That's why you pay us, Cap," he said as he drained the last of the coffee from his cup and returned to his own office. As he stepped into the conference room, he heard uproarious laughter.

All three team members were at the table, laughing. "Here's another fine mess you got us into, Ollie." Quoted Bob as Bill entered.

"Did you get those two tucked into jail OK?" he asked.

John Ashley was laughing, too. "You should have seen all the stuff the jailer took from the pockets of the two long coats we turned over to them. The pockets were full of small items. Wallpaper trim rolls, toothbrushes, condoms by the gross, cans of tuna, just about anything you can imagine. The one you pepper sprayed had two hunting knives and a hatchet in his pockets. Most of his pockets were full of steaks and frozen shrimp. We'd searched the clothes they wore but we removed the long coats and gave them to the jailers without searching them. Bad move. Good lesson."

Now Bill was chuckling with them. "OK guys, write all this up and put it in your reports. The DA will need a copy of the report this morning." He turned back to John, "How is Rex, the security guy doing this morning?"

"I talked with the ER nurse, and she said he was released last night. The docs sewed his up scalp and kept him a few hours for observation before he was released. She said he was lucky they didn't fracture his skull. He was hit pretty hard."

"The cap said there was a nasty accident on Pickle Hill and tied up both Soldotna PD and the Troopers. That's why they called us back. I personally want to thank all of you for responding as quickly as you did. You're a good team and I feel lucky to work with you," adding, "Most of the time." Bill spoke sincerely.

"Do we have a new assignment yet, Boss?" asked Bob.

"Not yet, but we need to get this paperwork done to be ready for one. The captain just said the fish war is still going on in Bristol Bay and the troops can't come home just yet. It looks like we will be on the job for a while. Enjoy the paychecks." After his little speech he went to his own office to finish his reports.

This is the time of year when the days are long and warm. There are thousands of tourists in this small community keeping the local police and fish and wildlife troopers very busy.

Sockeye salmon were beginning to make their run to the spawning grounds upriver. This horde of fish draws tens of thousands of sport fishermen and subsistence fishermen with dipnets to the Kenai River, in addition to the flotilla of commercial fishing boats with drift nets, as well as setnets on the beaches of Cook Inlet leading to the mouth of the Kenai River.

Each evening there is a parade of commercial fishing vessels racing to the canneries, near the mouth of the Kenai River, to unload and sell their catch. All this activity is a spectacular attraction for visitors and locals alike. It also creates a tremendous caseload for the local trooper office. Bill knew it was only a matter of time before something would happen to put his team back in the action.

It was late in the evening when Bill and his wife were watching their favorite TV show when his radio crackled. It was dispatch.

"Lieutenant Koogan, I have a man on the line who wishes to speak with you. He's the manager of the Quick Stop store and gas station east of town. He said he's spoken with you before and this call is related to that case."

"Can you direct the call to my cell phone?"

"Yessir, I can do that. Please hold, I'm switching him now."

Bill's cell phone jingled. "Thank you, dispatch, I'll take the call." Bill set his radio down and picked up his cell phone. "Bill Koogan here."

"Hi, Trooper Koogan. I don't know if you remember me, but I'm the night manager at the Quick Stop east of Soldotna on the Sterling Highway."

"Yes, I remember you. What can I do for you?"

"Three men were just in here and bought some stuff to eat and pay for gas. When they went out it struck me! It was the three who robbed this place. They were in a different vehicle and were all cleaned up without beards. I have them on the security cameras and it's them alright. I thought you would like to know about it."

"That's good work and I thank you. Can I have the tapes?"

"I already took them out of the machines and replaced them with new ones. I have these tapes in the safe. You can pick them up tonight or tomorrow, whichever is best for you."

"I'll have someone come out there and get them tonight. Thanks for being so observant. Good work young man." Bill was excited by the call.

He hung up the phone and called the trooper office to order one of the road troopers to pick up the tapes right away and hold them for his own men in the morning.

Bill came to the office early the following morning to get the tapes and was in the little conference room watching the tapes when the team began to assemble.

"What are you watching, Boss?" asked Bob Barratt.

"We might have gotten lucky last night, Bob," replied Bill. "The manager at the Quick Stop east of town recognized some of his customers last night as the ones who robbed the store. They'd cleaned up and shaved, but I've watched the video and he's right, it's them. Come in and take a look."

By now the whole team was present with fresh coffee in hand, seated at the table. Bill fast forwarded the tapes to where the trio entered the store and shopped for some finger food and drinks. They went to the front counter and paid for the items and the gas they had put in their car. It was a different vehicle. A Toyota Highlander, not the green Jeep they had used when committing the local robberies.

After watching the tapes John Ashley remarked, "That kid has a good eye. I'm not sure I would have recognized them all cleaned up and being customers. Do you think we can hire him?"

The entire group laughed and sipped on their coffee cups.

"I watched the tapes taken of the pumps and when they pulled out of the station they came toward town. They might be in town. I couldn't read the plates, but we have pictures of the car and of them. They could just be here to go fishing, but with such recent robbery and kidnapping episodes I don't think so. I believe they're here for some other purpose. I don't know what, but I'd bet they have a job here. Last time it was to collect a drug debt, it could be the same reason, but different people this time," Bill Koogan was doing the pontificating.

"How do you want to go at this, Boss?" asked Randy Craig.

"I'm open to suggestions. But in my opinion, we should make copies of the faces on the video as well as the photos of the vehicle and pass them out to the road troopers. We're a small team and can't cover enough area on our own," said Bill.

"Dang, you're smart Boss. It's no wonder we work for you," joked Ashley.

"Yeah, yeah, yeah! I'll talk with the captain about it," replied Bill. "Since you're the smart aleck John, you can get the copies made to give the road troopers."

"You're not only smart, but you're also mean and vindictive," complained Ashley.

"Now you sound like my wife," replied Koogan.

All four members of the team were laughing at the exchange when the desk phone rang. Bob Barratt answered it. "Alaska State Troopers, this is Trooper Barratt. How may I help you?" He paused, listening, "That's great, sir. I'm going to let you talk with the team leader, Trooper Koogan." He handed the phone to Bill, "It's the store manager at Fred Meyers. He can identify the rest of the shoplifters."

Bill took the phone, "Hello sir, this is Trooper Koogan. What can we do for you?"

"Oh yes, I remember you. I wanted to let you know we have someone here who knows the other five shoplifters and wants to give you the information. Can you send someone over to take the statement?"

"Is the informant there now?"

"Yes, and he wants to give you the statement."

"I'll be right there. It'll take about ten minutes to get there. Please ask them to wait." Bill hung up the phone and turned to Randy Craig.

"You had better come with me on this one, Randy. John has some copies to make and distribute and Bob can keep an eye on him. Bring a tape recorder to take the statement."

Randy picked up a recorder from the cabinet in the conference room and the two troopers walked to Bill's trooper car. It was a short drive to the Fred Meyer store where they were met at the front entry by the store manager.

"The man with the information is in my office," said the manager.

As they entered the small office, Bill saw an elderly man seated in front of the desk. "Hello, Mr. Daschel. Remember me?" asked Koogan.

The man looked up at Bill. "Sure, I remember you. You pulled me out of my car after I rolled it over two years ago. I don't drive anymore, but I remember you."

Bill shook hands with the man. "The store manager says you know who these shoplifters are. Do you know where we can find them?"

"Sure do, one of them is my grandson. The kid is no good. He runs with a bunch of punks that are always doing something bad. They all came to my house and stole my mechanics toolbox. Rotten kids. The two you have in jail are the worst. Mean, just plain mean. They threatened to beat me up when they stole my toolbox. They did shove me around and knocked me down that day. They all live out by me and have a kind of clubhouse out in the woods behind the houses. An old, abandoned travel trailer. They drink booze and smoke dope out there. I can show you where it is." The old man was nodding assurance.

"Can you give us the names of these men?" asked Bill.

"Sure, Sean Winslow is my grandson. The other four all live in the neighborhood,"

He went on to give the names and addresses of the others. "I hope you don't tell them I'm the one who turned them in. They would come after me for sure."

"Do you still live out there off East Poppy Lane?" asked Koogan.

"Yup, same old place. My daughter lives with me and that worthless grandkid stays there sometimes."

"When do you think it would be the best time to catch them all together in the clubhouse?" asked Randy Craig, holding the recorder.

"They usually go there around five in the afternoon and smoke some dope before going out to get into mischief."

"Would it be safe for you to take us there and show us the clubhouse?" asked Bill.

"Yeah, this time of day, but not after about five. I can show you where it is." The old man was nodding again.

"I have an unmarked trooper car. Would you go with Randy and me to point out the place?"

"Sure, but don't let them see me." The old man was now shaking his head.

"OK then, we'll go find the clubhouse and then go to the trooper office for you to write your report for us. Is that OK with you?" asked Bill.

"Sure, but I gotta ask. Can I get a cup of coffee while I'm there?"

"You bet. Let's go before it gets to be too late in the day." Bill reached to help the man out of his chair.

The three, riding in Bill's official car, drove to the area where the old man pointed out his own home and down the block, pointed to a trail leading into the woods that looked like it had once been a dirt road.

Back at the office they led the old man inside and found him a cup of hot coffee. Bill introduced him to Jean who was to help him write his statement. Meanwhile he and the rest of the Squad geared up to surround and attack the old trailer where the shoplifters were supposed to meet after five.

Dressed in field gear, the Squad walked into the woods to await the gang members. The spruce timber was dense and provided good cover for them to await the gathering. It was a short wait. Four young men walked the trail leading to the clubhouse. They were laughing and joking as they walked. When they reached the club house, they were inserting the key in the door lock when the troopers stepped out of hiding, weapons drawn, ordering them to get on the ground.

"Go to hell," shouted one of the gang members.

Bob Barratt was the closest to them and reached out to grab one of the men by the arm and twisted him to the ground while John Ashley stepped up behind another member and forced him to the dirt.

Immediately the other two put their hands in the air and shouted, "OK, OK," and dropped to their knees. The four were handcuffed and read their rights

Bill called for a road trooper to assist in delivering the men to the pretrial facility.

CHAPTER THIRTEEN

At the pretrial and after they were booked into jail, the Squad took turns interviewing the offenders. All were over the age of eighteen and booked as adults. Each one wanted the troopers to know just how tough they were, until it was explained to them how long they could spend in jail. One by one, they began to talk about their shoplifting careers and how much money they made on each raid into the big box stores. Two of the 'hardened criminals' broke down and cried like babies during the interview.

Every member of the Geezer Squad knew it was unlikely any of the prisoners would be sentenced to jail, but this would be a learning experience for each of the young men. The interviews were done separately, taking more than two hours. Recordings of the interviews were made as references to the mountain of paperwork that would be done when the officers returned to their office.

In the office at trooper headquarters, they were busy writing reports when Bob spoke up. "Hey Lieutenant, we have two assaults and four shoplifters in jail. Leo and Greg for assault. Louie, Burt, Steve and Waldo for shoplifting. By my count we're one short."

"By golly, you're right. I was so busy with the birds in hand I forgot to count. One is still in the bush. That would be Mr. Daschel's grandson. I didn't see him in the line-up. We had better get over to the old man's house and make sure he's safe. The grandson may be back there to harm the family."

"Bob, I want you to come with me to find him. You two stay here and finish the reports. You drive, Bob. We'll take the marked SUV." Bill spoke as he stood to leave.

Ten minutes later the troopers were in front of the old man's house. There was a mud-covered Polaris side-by-side off-road vehicle parked in front of the home.

"I wonder if that belongs to the grandson?" commented Bill.

"Do you know the kid?" asked Bob.

"Not really. I've seen him, but never spoken with him. The old man seemed afraid of him, so we had better be ready for anything. Take the keys out of the bush buggy, Bob."

They exited their vehicle. Bob retrieved the keys from the side-by-side, and the two troopers walked to the open front door.

On the front porch Bill called to Mr. Daschel. "Mr. Daschel are you home?" he said.

No answer.

65

“Mr. Daschel, are you in there?”

Both Bob and Bill heard scuffling inside. The troopers reached for their weapons and entered the open door. There was a short hall with coats and hats on pegs on the walls. Bill led the way to the living room on the other end of the hallway with Bob following close behind. As they approached the next room, they could see Mr. Daschel on the floor, his grandson standing over him.

Bill stepped into the room, his weapon pointed at Eddie, the grandson. “OK, young man. Step away and put your hands behind your head. Do it NOW,” he ordered.

Eddie turned to face Bill and noticed Bob come into the room.

“Hey, man. I was just trying to help my granddad. He fell and I was helping him up,” said the young man.

Bill looked at the old man on the floor, “Is that true, Mr. Daschel?”

There was fear in the old man’s eyes. He said nothing but shook his head.

“Are you injured?” asked Bill.

Again, the old man shook his head.

Now Bob stepped up behind the young man to snap the handcuffs on him. Once he was cuffed, he began to shout that he was an innocent bystander and not guilty of anything. Bob began a pat-search of Eddie while Eddie ranted.

Bill went to the old man and to help him off the floor and assist him to the sofa where he dropped to the seat. The elderly victim seemed to be extremely frightened.

“He drove over here a while ago and came into the house without knocking. He came in and said he had seen his friends taken away by the troopers. He said someone must have snitched them off and I was the only one who knew where the hideout was located.” Daschel took a deep breath with a shaky inhalation. “Then he pulled me off the couch and slapped me. Said he was going to beat the crap out of me. He hit me again and knocked me down. But I was lucky. That’s when you fellas came in and saved me. The kid has gone plumb crazy. Even his mom can’t control him.”

“Are you injured, Mr. Daschel? Do you need medical help?” Bill was genuinely concerned.

“No, I’m alright. I’m just a bit nervous right now.” The old man was still shaking as he spoke.

“Well, Eddie,” said Bill as he turned to the young man, “It looks like you finally made the big time. You can put this one on your resume. I’m arresting you for assault and theft of merchandise from Fred Meyer. Once we get you booked into jail in Kenai you can call a lawyer. I want you to listen very carefully to the rights Officer Barratt is going to read to you."

Bob took the young man by the arm and led him out of the house.

Once again Bill turned to the old man, "Is there someone I can call to come and be with you for a while?" he asked.

The old man shook his head, then reached for Bill's hand. "Thank you for being here, Trooper. He would have hurt me bad." At that he hung his head and sobbed.

"I wish you would let me call someone to come over and be with you for a while," stated Bill.

"No, I don't need anyone. I was really scared after he hit me. I'll be alright now. Thank you again."

Bill reached into his shirt pocket for a business card to give him. "If you need anything at all, you call me at this number." Bill was still concerned for the old man's welfare, but he had refused any help. Short of arresting him, there was nothing else he could do.

Bob searched Eddie, had placed him in the backseat of the police car and was waiting beside the driver door when Bill came out of the house. Reaching into his pocket he took out the key to the bush buggy, "I guess we should leave these keys with the old man," he said, handing them to Bill, who took them into the house and gave them to Mr. Daschel, still sitting on the sofa.

Eddie was quiet on the ride to jail. He sat in the back seat with his head down. Bill thought he may be crying.

"You won't be lonesome in jail, Eddie. Your whole club membership is there. We will need a statement from you when we get you to the jail before we have you booked. The interview will be recorded. Once you're booked into jail you will be allowed to make a phone call to your lawyer. If you don't have a lawyer the judge can appoint one for you, if you want one, when you go to court.

Eddie said nothing.

At the jail, Bob conducted the interview with little result. Eddie said nothing except to identify himself. He denied doing harm to the old man. The interview was short, and Eddie was turned over to the correctional officers.

As they drove back to the office Bill suggested they stop to make sure Mr. Daschel was doing alright. Bob agreed it was a good idea.

As they arrived at the old man's home, they realized the front door was still open. They stepped to the porch and Bill called to the old man. There was no answer. He called again. Still no answer. The troopers entered the home and walked into the living room. Mr. Daschel was lying on the sofa. Bob used the radio to call for an ambulance while Bill stepped over to attempt to give aid to the old man. It was too late. His eyes were open and he had stopped breathing. Bill's shoulders sagged as he stood.

"The ambulance is on the way," said Bob.

"They'll have to pronounce him dead, but they're already too late. He was a nice old man. He's lived in the area for a lot of years. I'm going to miss that old man. I liked him." The sadness in Bill's voice was deep.

The keys to the Polaris were on the floor in front of the sofa.

Bob stood at the front door to await the medics while Bill walked through the house to see if everything was safe and secure. When he finished his walk-through, he went outside to wait while Bob stood at the doorway inside the home.

It was only minutes before an ambulance with five medics arrived. Bill told the captain of the crew what had happened while the others went inside, carrying the equipment necessary for resuscitation, if necessary. It wasn't necessary. Two medics came out of the house to inform the captain of the death and asked what they should do about the body. The captain ordered them to load Mr. Daschel into the ambulance and take him to the hospital. This wasn't the usual procedure, but this death followed a felony assault. The fact was, the captain and Bill were both friends with the victim.

One of the medics had found a ring of keys in the old man's pockets and gave them to Bill who used them to lock the home to prevent further vandalism.

Back in the office, Bill asked Bob to do the report. It would be his unpleasant duty to inform the daughter of her father's passing. She was working at a local insurance company. Bill drove to the office and asked her to step outside with him where he delivered the sad message.

For her, the notification was a double hit. Her father had died and her son, who had assaulted him, was in jail. Hearing the news, she threw her arms around the trooper's neck and sobbed at a near screaming pitch. Bill allowed her to vent her grief for several minutes before pulling her arms from his shoulders and neck.

"Is there someone I can call to come and take you home?" he asked.

"I'm sorry for my behavior, Bill, but this is awful. I don't know what I'll do without my father. My son has been a problem for some time now and I expected something like this for him, but Dad? Dad was always my strength." She was sobbing again. "I'll have Marylou drive me home and over to dad's place. There are some things I'll need to do if no one is living there. I want to thank you for being so kind, Bill. I know you've known Dad for a very long time. It must be hard for you, too."

"Here are the keys to the house, Corrie. I locked it up after the medics left. You call me if there is anything I can do to help you." He squeezed her hand gently.

Bill drove slowly back to the office. Once there he went directly to his small office and closed the door behind him. The sadness was deep within him. He and the old man had not been close friends but had been acquainted for many years. Many times they had sat at the same coffee table with local businessmen for the morning roundtable meetings, solving the world's problems all by themselves.

Daschel had been one of the original citizens in Soldotna, having worked for the Department of Transportation when they moved the thirty miles from Skilak Lake to the new office and shop recently built in Soldotna. All this was prompted by the new highway opened from Cooper Landing to Soldotna and planned to go to Homer on the South end of the Kenai Peninsula.

After a few minutes of personal quiet time with the door closed, he decided it was time to report to the captain.

The captain listened to the account, shaking his head. He, too, had known old man Daschel. "I know how hard this is for you, Bill. It's cases like this that make us wonder why we do this job. Do you realize how this case snowballed?"

"I hadn't given it much thought, Cap."

"Think about it. It started as a simple shoplifting case and look what it became. There are three men in jail for assault, two for theft and a very nice old man dead in his home. We'll have to wait until the coroner gives us a final answer, but there may be further charges for the grandson if the old man died of injuries and not just a bad heart. You and your men have done a bang-up job in the past few days. I want you to continue doing it, but if you think you have had enough, I'll understand."

"No Cap, I'm OK. I just need some time. I'd forgotten that sometimes it gets personal. The guys and I are here for the duration. A cup of coffee and some bad jokes from the guys and I'll be ready to get back at it," said Bill. "I appreciate your sympathy and I promise, I won't tell anyone about it. I respect your reputation. Thanks Phil."

With a short salute he left the office to go to where the rest of the Squad was finishing the reports to be submitted. He and the rest of the crew would be happy to end this day.

CHAPTER FOURTEEN

Once again, the afternoon was a flurry of paperwork to send to the DA's office as information to prepare cases for arraignment tomorrow afternoon. Again, it was late when they finished. Bill told his squad to take tomorrow morning off and come in after noon. They deserved the time off.

Bill was leaning back in his office chair thinking about Mr. Daschel when his desk phone jingled.

"Trooper Koogan," he answered.

"Hello, Trooper Koogan, this is Darlene North. Do you have a minute to talk with me?"

"Sure, what can I do for you?"

"Two men came to the shop today and asked to talk with me. They didn't even mince words. They told me to get out of town. They said I had no right to be in the house, nor any right to keep the business open. I'm sure Nick sent them, but they didn't mention him. They frightened both me and the office girl. They didn't make any specific threats, but the threats were certainly implied."

"Where are you now, Mrs. North?" he asked.

"I'm at the office," was her reply.

"If you can wait there a few minutes I'll come down and take your statement. Given Nick's history, this could be a more serious threat than you may suspect. Do you have time to wait for me?"

"The girl and I are closing the office right now and we'll stay to wait for you."

Bill immediately picked up his recorder and hurried to his unmarked patrol car. The office was dark except for one florescent light over the desk in the office. He tapped on the office door, and it was opened by Darlene North. She motioned for him to come inside, poked her head outside and looked around before closing the door.

"You seem to be very nervous, Mrs. North," commented Bill.

"I've made Nick mad in the past and paid a price for it. Yes, I'm being cautious," was her reply.

She led the way to the reception desk and pointed to a chair in front of the desk. She and the receptionist were seated behind the desk facing him as he took the recorder from an inside pocket and placed it on the desk. After having them state their names for the record he continued, "Mrs. North" ...

"Please, call me Darleen," she interrupted.

"Alright, Darleen, you said on the phone you suspected your husband sent these men to give you a warning, is that true?"

"Yes, it is. I had never seen these men before. They came in and said I had no right to use the house or to run the business. They said it would be best for me if I closed and never came back."

"So, they didn't directly threaten you in any way, is that right?" asked Bill.

"Yes, but I certainly took what they said as a threat," she said in a low voice.

"Can you describe these men?" asked Koogan.

"Yes, I told you there were two men. But our receptionist Susan says she saw one more sitting in the car outside. I only saw the two who came inside. They were kinda young, late twenties or early thirties. Clean and polite but looked like fishermen or tourists. But they had an aura of mean about them. They meant business." Darleen North spoke as if she were still frightened. She went on to give approximate height and weight of the men.

Suddenly Bill had a thought and asked them to wait there while he went to his car and returned with some photos. "Is it possible these are the men you saw?" he asked, showing them the pictures of the recent photos taken from tapes at the Quick Stop.

"Why yes, these could be the men. At least the two I saw. These two," she said, pointing out two of the three photos."

Bill turned to Susan and asked if the third photo could be the other man in the car.

"I couldn't see him clearly, but it certainly could be him," she replied.

"Do you remember anything about the vehicle they were driving?" he asked.

"Only that it was a small station wagon or SUV type. I think it was a Japanese car. Like a Toyota or something similar. It was silver color and fairly new. The driver stayed in the car with the engine running. I was so scared I didn't think to look at many details."

"We know these men and they are very dangerous. I'm going to have Soldotna Police Department do regular checks here until we catch these guys. Don't take any chances and call us if you feel uneasy about anyone hanging around the office. Do you want someone to escort you home this evening?"

"It would be good if someone could follow Susan to her home. She's really nervous and from what you've told me, there's good reason," Darleen North said in a nervous tone of her own.

Bill looked at Susan. "I'm going to call an officer to follow you home and I want you to look your place over and give him a signal that it will be safe for him to leave. Do you understand?"

"Yessir, I do understand. You don't know how much safer you've made me feel."

"I don't have the manpower to keep someone there twenty-four hours a day, but we will be checking on you. Do you live inside the city?"

"Yes, I have an apartment near the middle school on Kobuk," she said quietly.

"I'll have the city officers check on you periodically." Bill then turned to Darleen, "I'll follow you home when you get ready to leave the office. The same advice for you as I gave Susan, check the house, and signal me before I leave. I'll have the local road troopers check the area periodically. Like Susan, if you feel there is a problem, call our office. I'm off duty now, but a trooper will come as soon as possible. Do either of you have any questions?"

Susan and Darleen North looked at each other, then both shook their heads. Bill used his cell phone to order the escort for Susan. It was only a minute before a city police officer drove into the parking area of the shop. Bill asked the ladies to wait inside until he came back from talking with the officer.

Once the short conference with the city officer was finished, he returned to the small office to tell Susan she could drive home now. Bill waited until the two vehicles drove from the office parking area before he turned to Darleen.

"OK, Mrs. North, your turn. I'll follow you home. I live down the main road past your turn. I'm going to have to come back to the office to file my report, but feel free to call the office if you begin to feel uneasy." He looked at her and smiled. "I'll do my best to make sure you're safe here."

Once Mrs. North was locked safely in her home, Bill returned to his office to complete the report. He ordered dispatch to tell the local road trooper in the area of the North home to make regular security checks in the area. He talked with the Soldotna Police evening shift supervisor and advised him of the situation. He added that if there was anything unusual at the address, he was to be notified immediately. After two hours at the computer he was finished and ready to go home for some much-needed rest.

Koogan reentered the office at the regular hour the following morning. As was usual, his first stop was the coffee pot where he poured his first cup of the day. Carrying the cup of fresh brewed coffee, he returned to his office and sat thinking. After reviewing circumstances of the previous evening, he reached for his cell phone and called Darleen North.

"Hello," she answered on the second ring.

"Mrs. North, this is Bill Koogan. I'm calling to see if you intend to open the shop today?"

"Oh, good morning, Bill. Yes, I've called Susan and we agree the shop needs to be open. I think it'll be safe, given the safety precautions you have in place. I want to thank you for being so thorough last evening. Both Susan and I were very nervous and you put us at ease. We both appreciated what you did."

"I don't want you to reveal this to anyone, but we've dealt with these men previously. They are very bad men and if we find them, they will be arrested. You can rest assured we are actively looking for these guys. I have asked the city police to keep an eye on your shop until we catch them. Meanwhile, I want to remind you of the danger and to be very cautious."

"Believe me, Bill, we are very aware of the danger and plan to be extra cautious. Thank you again."

Bill could hear the stress in her voice. "Call me if you think something isn't right. I'll be here for you." He was attempting to be reassuring, but he didn't think it had worked.

The other team members had begun to find their way to the coffee pot. One by one they came into the conference room. One by one they uttered the same word, "Mornin'." Each was carrying a copy of the daily post report which outlined the activities during the night. Bill's report had not yet been entered into the daily sheet.

"OK, Guys, listen up. I have some news for you, pay attention. Last night I was called out to the North Repair Shop. The two ladies running the place had been accosted and threatened while they were closing the shop for the evening. As luck would have it, they identified the men. Two came into the office and a third waited in the car—a Toyota Highlander she thinks, while the two inside made veiled threats against the women. I showed them the pictures of the men from the Quick Stop, and they thought it was the same three men."

"Why in the world would they want to return to this area after killing a druggie the last time?" asked Bob, unable to understand the reasoning.

"Good question, Bob. I think they're being paid a lot of money to be here. A lot of money. Last time they came here we thought they had been paid by a drug supplier in Anchorage. That may still be true, but what would drug enforcers be doing in a divorce case?" asked Bill.

"None of it makes any sense unless the one who hired them was another drug dealer. And if he can afford this kind of help, he must be a BIG drug dealer. Given the targets of the threats, I wonder if North has been dealing drugs and flying under our radar?" It was Bob, once again identifying possibilities.

"I think I should talk with the secretary of North's shop," said Bill. "She may know or suspect something. John, I want you and Randy to come with me as back-up. These goons may be watching the place and I'd rather be safe than sorry."

"What do you want me to do?" asked Bob Barratt.

"In our experience, we've seldom seen these men in the early part of the day. I want you to take copies of the photos around to the eateries in town and see if we can learn where they're eating, what time they come into the restaurant and did they come to the same restaurant more than once. You know, real police work." Bill chuckled as he gave the order. "John, we'd better give the ladies a little more time to open the shop. Have another free cup of coffee."

"Gee, Bill, you're such a good boss. I think Randy and I should order you some flowers," was the sarcastic reply.

Bill just shook his head and smiled. "Randy, I want you to interview the mechanic in the shop while we speak with the women in the office. We really don't know anything about him at this point. I don't think he's involved in the case, but we had better check him out anyway. Try not to be threatening but find out who he is and if he could be involved with North in any under the table business, like drugs."

John finished his coffee and the team left the office to pursue the tasks they had been assigned. Each man has years of experience in this sort of investigation and they were very good at what they did. They agreed to meet back in the office at lunch time.

CHAPTER FIFTEEN

Bill was an hour late getting to the office the following morning. On his way into the trooper complex he stopped at the captain's office to learn of any new developments overnight. There had been no new calls that affected Bill or his crew. The one item that did interest him though, was a note from the receptionist that the funeral for Mr. Daschel was scheduled for Monday at 1:00 p.m. He took the note to his office where he sat, drinking his first cup of coffee of the day. His quiet time was interrupted by John Ashley.

"Hey, Boss, there's a call for you on Line 1. It's Mrs. North."

Bill turned in his chair to face his desk and picked up the telephone. "Hello, Darleen, is everything OK this morning?"

"That's why I called you. Good morning to you, by the way. We had a break-in last night. The back door was jimmied, and someone came in and left a note on my desk. I didn't pick it up but read it. I'll read it to you. 'You are not safe in this office nor at your home on Smith Way'. Nothing else was disturbed, as near as I can tell. Do you want the note?"

"Yes, I'll be right there to pick it up."

He turned to John, still standing at the doorway, "Grab a fingerprint kit and come with me to the auto repair shop. Someone broke into the shop but only left a note on the desk for Mrs. North. If it was done by our suspects there probably won't be any prints, but we can try."

"I'll be right out and meet you at the car," replied Ashley.

The two men were silent during the one-mile trip to the auto repair shop. Ashley knew his job and did it without any further instruction. Bill walked Darleen outside to talk while John did his print gathering.

"You said you didn't find any other items disturbed in the office, is that correct?"

"Yes," replied Mrs. North.

"It's hard to tell for certain, but this appears to be another threat directed at you."

"Well!" she said sternly, "I'm not closing the shop and I'm not leaving town."

"I don't mean to alarm you or frighten you. But these are very bad men. They killed a man on the last encounter we had with them. This was done for a drug debt and had nothing to do with you or your husband. I only mention this because they are the same bunch, and they're ruthless. Be very careful and don't take any chances."

"I understand and I realize this is my choice. I don't hold you responsible. You've given me warning about how dangerous these men are. This decision is mine, and I'll have to live with the outcome." Darleen North was speaking with a determined tone.

"I hope you know what you're doing, Darleen. I don't have the manpower to protect you full time."

"I understand, Bill, and I don't want to hold you to blame for what happens. I want you to also know I don't want to lose everything I have because of fear. I intend to fight for what is rightfully mine." Again, there was determination in her voice.

At this point John Ashley came out of the office to tell his boss he was finished with his fingerprinting chores.

"OK, John. Wait for me in the car. I'll be right with you."

Ashley nodded and walked to the patrol car. Bill turned his attention back to Darleen North.

"Please be careful and don't take any chances. Call me if there is anything you need or feel any further threats. I'll have the Soldotna PD keep a constant eye on you and the office."

"I thank you for caring. I'll do my best to protect myself and Susan."

John Ashley was behind the steering wheel and Bill took the passenger seat.

"Did you find any prints?" asked Koogan.

"None, they had wiped the entire door and frame clean. And the same went for the paper the note was written on. They must have worn gloves. These guys are real pros. I'm beginning to think your theory about North being involved in the drug business may not be so far-fetched. If he was a dealer, I think we would have heard a rumor at some time. He may be a money man or distributor behind the scenes. I've been out of the loop for quite a while, so I don't have any snitches I can ask about it." John had made several good points in his summary.

"Let's run this by the captain when we get back to the office. He may have heard a rumor that we're not aware of yet." Bill blew out a nervous breath, "I'm concerned for the safety of Darleen North. I would hate to see anything happen to her."

"You're right about asking the Cap. Every piece of information in the post goes across his desk. Would you let me sit in on the meeting?" John was nodding agreement as he turned the vehicle into the parking lot at trooper headquarters.

Bill and John stopped at the door of the captain's office. Captain Bradshaw motioned for the men to enter and have a seat in the office.

"What have you two been up to this morning?" he asked while writing on a pad on his desk.

"We've just come from the auto repair shop in Soldotna. When she and Susan went to open the shop this morning, Mrs. North found the rear door of the shop had been damaged and someone entered. The only thing they found inside was a note left on the desk that seemed to be an implied threat. We have the note. Mrs. North refuses to close the shop. I've asked Soldotna PD to keep an eye on the place. Mrs. North identified the men who came to the shop as the three we identified from the Quick Stop robberies. We think that all had to do with a drug deal where the dealer didn't get paid. To make a long story short we were wondering if you've ever seen any indication Nick North was involved in the drug business?"

Captain Phil Bradshaw leaned back in his chair a moment, thinking. "No, I haven't. But there were rumors of a local financier backing drug buys for wholesalers in the local market. We were never able to confirm the rumors, though. Not to say we were able to rule them out either. We get information about street sales and who the dealers are in this neck of the woods, but seldom do we get information about the big money guys. North could be one of the big money men, but I can't say for sure."

"We're still trying to locate the three men we identified as the robbers and as suspects in the murder of the local dealer they abducted to Wasilla. So far, they've been invisible, but Mrs. North and the receptionist both agree they are the same ones threatening them. I have men looking for them, but no luck so far."

"It's pretty tough to make a legal case when all you have to go on is guesswork. 'Suppose' and 'Perhaps' are not specific legal terms. We need to have evidence. You and your team are doing a great job, Bill. Keep digging and let me know what you learn."

"We will, Cap, but something in this scenario doesn't add up. We'll try to figure out what that is and who's responsible. I'm having a meeting with the team to discuss it this afternoon."

Bradshaw went back to making notes on his pad as Bill and John left his office.

It was just after lunch when the team gathered in the conference room to discuss the case. Bill gave a short summary of the morning meeting with Darleen North. At the end of his statement, he asked for each man's thoughts on the case, "I think we need to pool our thoughts and discuss any possible alternatives to the path we've been following. John and I agree we are missing something. These three enforcers aren't here simply to terrorize Mrs. North and stop her from operating the auto shop. That simply doesn't add up. I'll start with you, Randy."

" I'm sort of relieved to hear how you feel. Bob and I have been talking about it and we agree, these men are professional enforcers. We never believed they came back here to be involved in a domestic dispute. I can't imagine them coming back just to threaten the wife of a drug dealer or even a money man. Nick North is going to go away for a lot of years for killing a police officer. He would never be able to go back into business in this town again. I agree with you. There has to be some other reason they came back. We've seen how ruthless the men can be and we know they're talented killers."

"John and I feel as you do, Randy. We're missing something. That's the reason for this meeting." He turned to Bob Barratt, "What do you think, Bob?"

Bob was a softspoken man who always seemed to think past the obvious. "I don't know why you ask me," he said. "I'm usually wrong about everything, but in this case we all seem to agree. Somewhere in this case we've made a wrong assumption about an obvious outcome. Somewhere we misread the evidence. I think we should make a story board listing all the deeds, places and characters in the case. Maybe we can determine where we got off track."

"That's a very good suggestion, Bob. I'll have the office girl find us a large white-board and markers. We can get started on that chore after we finish our meeting." Bill turned to John Ashley, "Your turn, John. I know you and I spoke of this earlier today, but lay out your thoughts for the group,"

"You always make me walk at the back of the pack and pick up the broken pieces," Ashley joked. The others laughed, including Bill. "Bill and I discussed this earlier. I think we've all reached the same conclusion: we seem to be going down a wrong path. Somewhere we missed something, and we need to go back and correct our conclusion. My thought is Nick North killed Lee Wood because he was making it with North's wife. What if that's where we went off-track? What if North killed him because Woods found out he was involved in the local drug trade. Mind you, I have no evidence to prove that's true, but it seems to me it's a possibility."

"Dang, John," commented Bob, "I didn't know you owned a crystal ball. You've become a real Swami."

Again, everyone at the table laughed. Using this small distraction as a break, Bill called Shirley on the in-house phone and asked her to bring a large whiteboard and some markers to the conference room. The meeting adjourned for a few minutes while they waited for the board and used the time to go to the coffee pot for refills. By the time they returned to the conference room Shirley delivered the three by five-foot board and stand to the room, adding an eraser to the tray at the bottom of the board.

Randy Craig was assigned the task of writing the list of items on the board. Each item and known fact in the case was written on it. Since there were so few characters in the case the format was changed to boxes with a character name over each box. The connection to the case was listed in each box. The last box on the board was labeled WRECKING CREW, since there was no positive identification of the three robbers/enforcers. It seemed imperative the team find these men who were wanted for the murder of the Quick Stop manager.

Mrs. Darleen North's name identified box number two. Box number one was Nick North. And so the outline began. Any item of evidence attributed to the name was listed in the small box. It took the rest of the afternoon to finish listing each item. Late in the day the team members sat at the far end of the long table and gazed at the board. Some items had been moved from one box to another and some were listed in multiple squares.

Bill checked his watch to see it was long past quitting time. "Let's call it a day, guys. We can take it up again tomorrow. I'm going to lock the conference room door tonight. I don't want anyone messing with or seeing what's on the board. Good job men," he added.

As he drove from the parking lot in the front of trooper headquarters his cell phone jingled. "Bill Koogan," he answered on speaker phone.

"Hi, Honey, are you coming home soon?" It was Bill's wife asking.

"I just pulled out of the parking lot."

"Would you make a stop at the grocery store for me on your way home?"

"Sure, what do you need?"

"There is a good movie on TV tonight, and I thought we would have some popcorn with the movie. Just pick up a box of microwave double butter popcorn."

"Will do, Babe. Do you want any sodas or anything?" he asked.

"No, just the popcorn. I'll start dinner while I'm waiting for you. Hurry home. Bye."

The clerk behind the counter recognized the frequent customer as he entered. Bill walked directly to the snacking shelves and found the double butter microwave variety. The clerk smiled as he stepped up to the counter. "You are sure becoming famous in these parts, Bill," she commented.

"How so?" he asked while reaching into his trouser pocket for some cash.

"Don't you read the newspapers?" she asked.

"Not much, why?" he asked as he placed a ten-dollar bill on the counter.

She reached under the counter to retrieve a copy of the local newspaper. "Have you seen the article in today's paper about you and your team? They keep calling you and your team the Geezer Squad. Everyone I see thinks it's just great and I've heard you were doing a great job.

Bill just shook his head, "Your police chief, Bud Griffin started that name. I'll have to figure out a way to get even with him one day."

The clerk was chuckling as she counted out his change.

As he walked to the front door she called after him, "See you later, Mister Geezer." She was chuckling once again.

<h1 align="center">CHAPTER SIXTEEN</h1>

Bill Koogan had eaten dinner and was nodding off in his recliner, a bowl of popcorn in his lap. His wife was on the couch eating popcorn and watching the TV movie she thought was going to be so wonderful. The movie didn't offer enough action to keep Bill interested. He finally said he was going to go to bed.

"I'll be up soon," she answered with her mouth full of fresh popcorn.

Bill just smiled and walked to the staircase, looking back to see her engrossed in the gushy love story on the television. It had been a very long and tiring day for him, and he wasn't as young as he once was. He was very tired and decided to forgo his normal nightly ritual of reading for a half hour before turning out the light. An hour later his wife joined him in bed without turning on the bedroom light and disturbing his rest.

It was just after three in the morning when Bill sat bolt upright in bed. In his restless sleep a thought had come to him that awakened him with a start. Not wanting to lose the thought he got out of bed and went to his office desk down the short hallway where he found a sheet of paper and a pen to write down the thought that had struck him and woke him from a sound sleep.

Satisfied he would remember his thoughts he returned to bed. Now relaxed, he fell into a deep and restful sleep. He slept until shortly after six that morning. When he came downstairs after his shower, his wife had breakfast cooking and a cup of hot coffee next to his plate on the table.

"Good morning, Honey," she said as she turned the eggs in the skillet. Did you have a bad night?"

"It started out that way, but I had a thought that made it better. I think I may have solved a problem my team and I had worked on all day yesterday."

An hour later, with the notes he had made during the night, he drove to the office for his morning meeting with the captain and to go to work on the problem the team had left open the night before. When he had finished with the captain, he went to the coffee pot for a cup of hot, fresh coffee and then to the conference room to unlock the door. Inside, he sat at the table looking at the white board. "Yes," he thought, "This is where we went wrong in our thinking."

Minutes later the team began to assemble in the small room. John Ashley had brought a box of Safeway donuts to go with the morning coffee. One by one the team found a seat at the table and exchanged bits of sarcasm to go with the coffee and donuts.

When things settled down Bill asked, "Have you come up with any new thoughts on the problem we discussed at quitting time yesterday?"

He looked around the table and saw only blank faces staring back at him. "OK then. I came up with one possibility and I want to run it by you guys before I try it out on the captain."

The team looked at each other, curiosity on each face. "Would you let us in on it, then?" asked Bob Barratt.

Bill was smiling, "It's so simple I don't know why we didn't think of it yesterday. Think about it, Guys. We agreed we must have missed something and we couldn't figure out what it was. A thought came to me after I went to bed last night. What if Nick North is a financier in the local drug trade. What if the Quick Stop robbers were working for him? What if he was so distracted by his wife fooling around on him, he sent for the enforcers and told them to solve the problem. He lives a good lifestyle, but his business is small and probably doesn't generate nearly enough money to keep him in that level of living. He doesn't seem to be a drug dealer, or we would have heard about it. I think he may have had a complaint from one of the local dealers asking for help collecting from the Quick Stop manager. He would have connections with the enforcers through his contacts in Anchorage and sent for them as a favor to the local drug supplier, perhaps, since the Quick Stop manager was in so deep, he'd become a problem."

Bill looked around the table at the bewildered faces. "I know this scenario has a lot of what-ifs and maybes, but let's see if any of this really does apply to our case."

Randy Craig was shaking his head. "That leaves a lot of dots to be connected, Bill. If the trooper office doesn't have any information to suggest any of this, and we've only been at it a few days, where do we start?"

"You guys stay here and think about it while I take a trip to the SPD office and have a word with Bud Griffin. I have a couple of other items to speak with him about. I'll be back in about a half hour."

As he rose from his chair, he received a couple of halfhearted waves and a low murmuring of non-believing voices. "Meanwhile you can try to come up with another, more plausible scenario to follow."

Bill was smiling as he left the office, knowing the team would do their best and be as objective as possible with their discussion.

Five minutes later Bill was at the reception desk of the Soldotna Police Department to see the chief.

"Just a minute, Trooper Koogan. I'll see if the chief has time to see you," said the receptionist.

She spoke to the chief on the in-house phone. When she finished, she came back to the window, "The chief will be right with you, Sir."

A moment later Chief Griffin opened the door to the secure area. "Come on in, Bill. What can I do for you today?" he asked.

"First of all, I want you to know I owe you a big one for all the nice publicity you created for me and my team." Bill spoke with a sneer on his lips.

"Aw, c'mon, Bill. You know I wouldn't do or say anything bad about you or your team. I thought you'd like the notoriety." Griffin was chuckling.

"We can discuss that later. Right now I have a bigger problem to deal with. I'm still dealing with the Nick North case. There are some new elements that lead us to believe we missed something in the initial investigation. Have you heard anything more regarding the death of your officer?"

"Nothing since we last spoke about it. Why do you ask, Bill?"

"This is between you and me, Bud. I'd rather not have any of this conversation leaked."

"You know me, Bill. I'll share what I know with you, but I don't tell stories out of school. What's going on?"

"Some things have come up making us rethink our first conclusion."

"What kind of things?"

"Do you remember the Quick Stop robbers?"

"Of course, they stole an airplane from the Soldotna Airport in the get-away."

"They're back in town. They came to North's Auto Shop and threatened Nick North's wife. This set us to thinking about why they would risk returning to Soldotna. My favorite theory is these men are enforcers for the drug wholesalers in Anchorage. You said you hadn't heard of any connection between North and the drug business locally. What if he's not in the drug business but financing some local dealers. Last time they were in town was to collect from a local distributor, the Quick Stop manager. We've tried to think of a reason for them to return unless someone with power and connections sent for them. I showed Mrs. North and the receptionist photos of the robbers, and both were certain they are the same three men."

"Wow, Bill, I would never have thought of that. The way you explain it, it makes perfect sense. Do you have any evidence to back up your theory?" Bud Griffin was now leaning forward in his chair and listening intently.

"That's the reason for this meeting, Bud. We don't have anything except educated guesses. I was hoping you may have heard something we could add to our guesswork." There was frustration in Bill Koogan's tone.

"Lee Woods was our lead drug investigator and when he was killed, we lost a lot of information about local drug dealers. In the old days the local dealers bought from a single supplier. That's changed in these new times. Local dealers can still buy from local suppliers but can also call Anchorage to have drugs delivered, eliminating one of the middlemen and cutting the cost by quite a lot. Most of those abandoned cars you see when you drive to Anchorage were left there, stripped by drug runners. Most of those cars were stolen in Anchorage. If Nick North was financing some of the drug distributors on the Kenai Peninsula, I never heard about it." Chief Griffin held up a finger and a light came on in his eyes. "Hey, Bill, I just thought. What if Lee Woods came across something implicating North in the drug trade? That would be a better motive for murdering my officer than to find out my officer was making it with North's wife, wouldn't it?"

"I guess it's possible, but there are so many possibilities and none of them are backed up with proof. I thought about going to the jail to talk with North, but he wasn't too interested in talking the last time I had a conversation with him."

"What about Mrs. North, do you think she may know something?"

"I've spoken with her several times, and she doesn't seem to know anything about Nick's drug dealings." Bill was shaking his head, "Remember when catching drug dealers was simple? Now-a-days, there are too many layers. Today, it seems anyone can get into the drug business and there are so many new drugs on the market, it's just crazy. I remember when one of the North roaders was a big drug dealer. He sold marijuana and cocaine. He made a lot of money doing it. In today's world, what with fentanyl, heroin, methamphetamines and who knows what else, dealers are more specialized. Some are even manufacturing their own stuff. I'm beginning to realize I'm not qualified to investigate it any longer."

"I guess that's why we have special drug teams." Griffin was shaking his head. "Have you seen the statistics on drug related deaths here on the Peninsula?" he asked.

Bill shrugged his shoulders in disgust, "I've seen the stats and they're horrendous. It looks like I have my job cut out for me, Bud."

"Sorry I couldn't be of more help, Bill. I'll do whatever I can to help you, but, as you know, that layer of the business is pretty difficult to penetrate. I'll let you know if I hear anything useful." Bud Griffin stood to shake hands with the trooper investigator.

Koogan smiled, "This still won't get you off the hook for the Geezer Squad label you invented."

As he drove back to the office, Bill attempted to find another scenario that would fit. He couldn't. At the office he walked directly to the conference room where the rest of the team was working on the charts.

"It looks like we're on our own on this one, Guys," said Bill as he entered the room.

"If it makes you feel any better, Boss, we didn't come up with another story that justified all the facts as well as yours. We're all believers, now," voiced Bob Barratt as Bill entered. "Where do we go from here?"

"Those three robbers are the only real evidence we have. We have pictures of the car they're using, and we have pictures of them. I think it's time we did some real police work.

Bob. You and John take the marked car and search for them. You take Kenai, the North Road and Nikiski. Randy and I will take Soldotna, Kasilof and Sterling. Remember, the last time they were in town they used some well-hidden hideouts."

The team left the office to patrol their assigned areas, each with great hopes of finding the three men who threatened Mrs. North and the receptionist, Susan.

Patrol is boring and monotonous work, but it makes an officer feel useful and important when working a case. Bob and John headed North while Bill and Randy began by patrolling the less populated areas of the City of Soldotna.

CHAPTER SEVENTEEN

It was a little past eight in the evening when the four teammates met again at the office. The team was tired and disappointed with the results of the day's search.

"Well, I hope you two had better luck than Randy and me," Koogan uttered in a tired voice.

"I think we covered every sideroad and driveway from Kenai to Captain Cook Park. We never found anything close to the car or the men we were looking for. We drove a lot of miles without finding any clues as to where they went. We even asked a couple of folks we knew out north but didn't find anything. Even worse, I had to sit in the car with Bob all day."

John Ashley and Bob Barratt had been friends and hunting partners for years, never missing a chance to goad each other.

"OK, Guys, let's call it a day and do our reports in the morning. We don't need to beat ourselves up any more today. I'll write a short report for the captain before I leave the office."

When the team left Koogan sat at the table, thinking. It had been a long, frustrating day with no positive results. The team leader could not think of what to do next. He wrote his summary of the day's activity and placed it on the captain's desk as he left the office for the day.

Early the next morning Bill stopped at the Safeway Store for a Starbucks coffee. Waiting in line for his order, a voice behind him said his name.

"Good morning, Officer Koogan," said the lady next in line behind him. It was Susan the receptionist at North's Auto Repair Shop. She spoke in a soft tone.

Bill turned to see who was speaking to him and recognize the lady immediately. "Oh, hello Susan. You're out early."

"I stop here every morning for coffee on the way to the office. How is everything going in your investigation?" she asked.

Bill smiled, "We haven't found those men yet, but we're working on it."

"I just wish I could be more help," she said, looking at the floor.

Bill reached to pat Susan on the shoulder. "You've been a big help already, young lady. Because of you we now know who these men are. It's our job to find and arrest them. Not just for what they did to you and Mrs. North, but also for kidnapping and murder in a recent case. These men are dangerous. You should be glad if you never see them again. Chief Griffin has his patrolmen checking on you at the office frequently. Meanwhile my men and I are doing everything we can think of to find these men."

"There is something I would like to speak with you about, but not in the office. I just want this to be private. Between you and me. Can we do that?" asked Susan.

"Of course. Call me at my office number and we'll set a time and place to meet," answered Bill.

It was then the barista called for Bill; his cup of Cappuccino was ready.

Bill entered the trooper building and stopped at the office of Captain Bradshaw, still carrying his Starbucks cup. As he entered the office Phil Bradshaw looked up to greet him.

"Another late-night last night, eh, Bill?"

"Yup, the others are holding up better than me. We covered the whole north end of this borough and never saw any sign of the vehicle or the men."

The captain rubbed his chin, "I'll have the patrol troopers keep looking for any trace of them. Do you think they could have left town?"

"They appear to be in town to make threats, so leaving town doesn't seem likely. It's frustrating working without evidence of any sort. There's no way to know if we're headed in the right direction or not. It wouldn't be so urgent if it didn't put Mrs. North in such a dangerous situation."

"I understand your position Bill. I sympathize with you, but we have to keep looking." The captain had been in this position himself on occasion.

"I saw Susan, the receptionist at the auto shop, this morning. She wants to have a private meeting with me and is supposed to call with a time and place. She didn't say what it was about, but she may have something we can follow up on. I just don't know at this point."

"Just keep me informed of the progress or lack thereof, Bill."

Bill nodded as he stepped into the hallway to go to the conference room. When he entered, the other team members were already at the conference table. "Good morning boys. Anxious to get to work, I see."

"You know us, Boss. Always ready to serve," quipped Ashley.

"I knew I could count on you," answered Bill with a chuckle.

It was Bob Barratt's turn. "Say Boss, do you remember that last time we dealt with these guys they kept their vehicle hidden at an old homestead house in the woods on Beaver Loop Road. It doesn't seem likely they would use the same place again, but I think John and I should cruise over there and look around. We don't have much else going for us, as I see it."

"OK Bob, but be careful and if you spot the vehicle call us in. Don't try to take them alone. I think I'm going to take Randy and go over to the jail to see if Nick North will talk with us. It just baffles me to know there's something we're missing. We'll see you two later." Again, frustration had creeped into Bill Koogan's tone.

It was shortly after noon when the team met again in the conference room. "Well, what did you find?" asked Bill.

"A whole lot of nothing!" answered John Ashley. "How did your interview with North turn out?"

"About the same as your search. He refused to talk with us and said we could request answers from written questions directed through his lawyer. He's a very angry man." The team was running out of things to investigate and Koogan felt their frustration. "What say we all go to lunch at Froso's and clear our minds a little." It was a statement and not a question.

"I think it's a great idea as long as you're buying," answered John.

Froso, the wonderful Greek lady and owner of the restaurant, came to the table to visit with Bill and his men. She always teased Bill about running away together. Bill was always embarrassed.

Bill was reaching for a credit card to pay for lunch when his cell phone jingled. "Trooper Koogan," he answered.

"Hello, Trooper Koogan, this is Susan from the Auto Repair Shop. You said to call and let you know when we could meet privately."

"Yes, have you decided on a time and place?"

"I hope so. I have a hair appointment in an hour at Crissy's Salon. Do you know where that is?"

"Yes, I know it. What time do you want me there?"

"Can you meet me there in an hour? We can talk in your car in the parking lot." She asked Bill as he checked his watch.

"I'll be there in an hour. I have an unmarked vehicle. I'll see you then." Bill turned off his phone and finished paying the tab.

When he finished Randy asked, "Hot date?"

"Perhaps, Randy. That was Susan, North's receptionist. She says she has something she wants to see me about privately. She's never been anxious to talk before, but Mrs. North was always around. I'm hoping she may know something we've overlooked. Let's go back to the office and study the whiteboard for a while. I'll meet her in an hour." Bill seemed deep in thought as he and Randy drove back to the office.

The four men spent the time revisiting the little squares of information on the board. There were a lot of 'what ifs' but nothing new came from the short meeting. A half hour later Bill instructed the men to keep at it and that he'd return shortly. "Hopefully with something new."

Susan was seated in her car waiting for the trooper when he arrived. He parked next to her in the parking lot. She stepped out of her car and into the passenger seat of his patrol car. "I hope no one saw me get into your car," she said as she scanned the parking area to see who was looking.

Bill reached for his recorder, turned it on and placed it on the dashboard. "I'm going to record this conversation, if it's alright with you, Susan. If it is, just say your first and last name and date of birth for the record."

While still scanning the area she did as instructed.

"OK, Susan. You said you may have something I need to know. Can you tell me what that is?"

She seemed to relax a little. "Yes, I just want you to know that I think you seem to be off track in your investigation."

"How so Susan?" asked Bill.

She took a deep breath. "You seem to think Nick North is some sort of ogre and Darleen is a sweet, innocent victim. That's not the way it is at all. Nick is a very intense person, and his business has been losing money in recent days. He's under a great deal of stress and works very long hours. He told me he thought the cash flow was finally turning around and things were getting better."

Susan took a long, deep breath before continuing. "Darleen, on the other hand, never worked. She never came to the shop, and she only worried about herself. She spent a lot of money on clothes and whatever else she wanted. I know she seems like the mistreated wife, but that's not the case. She never worked and yet always had cash in her purse. Nick never had two nickels to rub together and worked endless hours to make this business a success while she was always going to Anchorage on shopping trips and always had a purse full of cash. It never seemed right to me. When those men came to the shop I was terrified, but she didn't seem to be very upset. It was almost as if she knew who they were."

"Do you think she was spending all Nick's profits? Or do you think she had something going on the side?" asked Koogan.

"I can't say. I would only be guessing, but I think she was the reason Nick was so stressed out. I heard she was having an affair with someone here in Soldotna, but I don't know that for certain. All I know is she treated Nick like crap and spent money like water. I've seen her having lunch and associating with some really weird types of people. I really don't want to speculate on her private life, but I don't think it was very respectable."

"Can you give me any names of these people she was seen with? I'd like to check them out and learn what they had in common."

"You know that Quick Stop manager who was murdered recently?" again she scanned the parking lot. "I saw her talking with him outside the liquor store a while back. She was shaking her fist at him when I drove by on the highway. And I've seen her with people I've heard were drug dealers around town. There were at least three of them I've seen her talking with. I know this isn't evidence, but to me it's a good indication of her basic character. As soon as I can find another job, I'm going to quit this one." Tears were forming in Susan's eyes.

"I know this has been tough for you Susan, but what you're saying makes a lot of sense and changes the way I think about some of our evidence. You may have put us back on the right track and I thank you for helping. Now go get your hair curled and take comfort you did the right thing." Bill gave her a big smile. "Call me if you need to talk again."

"Thank you for listening, Trooper Koogan. Thank you for being so kind." She gave a short smile and opened the car door to go into the salon.

Once she was inside the building, Bill started his patrol car and tucked the recorder into his shirt pocket. This information was needed back in the conference room. Information on the white board needed to be adjusted using this new statement. Five minutes later he was walking into the conference room with a smile on his face. "I think we have something, guys."

CHAPTER EIGHTEEN

"Gather around guys. We may have something here," Koogan announced as he entered the conference room. He took the recorder from his shirt pocket and placed it on the table as he pulled a chair out to sit. "This is the meeting I just had with Nick North's receptionist. If what she says is true, we have a lot of adjustments to make on the whiteboard. You may want to make notes for questions it'll generate."

The team sat quietly, listening to the recording. Each made notes in their notebooks as the tape played to the end.

"Wow Boss, if any of this is true and we can prove any of it, we have a lot of work to do with our whiteboard. Do we have any evidence to back any of this story?" asked Randy.

"No, but it does make me think she could be right about Mrs. North. Susan's version of events leading up to the murder of Lee Woods is certainly a good one. North is probably the one who shot Woods, but not for the reason we've been following," opined Bill.

"That still makes North the killer and our assessment of the evidence at the scene will still be the same," concluded Bob Barratt.

"That's true Bob. We should contact the DA to advise him there may be a different motive for the murder. I'll ask the captain to send us a couple guys from his drug team and we can compare notes. We've been away from the drug scene far too long and we need to talk with an officer who has current information. Randy, I want you to drive to the courthouse and let the DA know what we've learned. I'll try to have the drug team in here by the time you get back."

"I guess Bob and I will be mopping floors and washing windows while we're waiting," uttered a sarcastic John Ashley.

"I was thinking the two of you could work on the whiteboard, but if you'd rather wash windows and mop floors, I'll have them send you a couple buckets," said Bill, returning John's sarcasm.

Bill was smiling as he walked to the captain's office.

"What's so funny, Bill?" asked the captain.

"Just sparring with the guys. We think we have a new twist to follow and wondered if there are any of the drug team around the office? We need a little background on the local drug trade. Our team has been away from it much too long. Are any of the team in the office today?"

"None of the undercover officers are in the building, but two investigators are here catching up on some reports."

"Do you think we could interrupt their day for a few minutes and have them give us the lay of the land with the local drug scene?" asked Bill.

Captain Bradshaw punched a speed dial button to talk with the drug team. "Burt do you and Glen have time to meet with Bill Koogan and his team?" the captain listened, then looked up to speak to Bill.

"When do you want to meet with them?" he asked.

Bill checked his watch, "A half hour would be about right. I'm waiting for Randy to get back from a meeting with the DA."

The captain nodded and spoke again into the telephone, "Half an hour, in the conference room."

"Thanks Cap," said Bill as he turned to leave the office.

Bill stopped to pour another cup of coffee before returning to the conference room. When he returned, he was pleased to see Bob and John working with the facts written on the white board. "How's it looking, Guys?" he asked.

John turned to answer, "You may have something here Bill. Bob and I agree the story line works much smoother with this outline than it did before. Lee Woods was the lead drug investigator for Soldotna Police Department. What if North heard Woods was asking questions about Darleen North? He may have killed Woods to protect his wife. Everyone who knows them says Nick was madly in love with his wife and would have done anything to protect her."

"Mrs. North has told me she had an affair with Lee Woods. She may have lied to me to cover her real reason for being sought out by Woods. If Lee Woods called Nick and said he wanted to talk to him with reference to Darleen's possible connection to the drug trade, Nick being the volatile person he is, waited for him and shot him when he stopped to talk." Bill paused and rubbed his chin, "You know that makes a lot more sense than Woods stopping to talk about an affair he was having with Darleen."

"Well, where do we go from here?" asked Bob.

"The drug team investigators will be here to brief us on the local drug trade and perhaps we'll learn the reasons at that meeting. Randy should be back by then and we'll have a chance to learn whether Darleen North is a possible financier in the local drug trade or not. They'll be here in a few minutes. Grab some coffee and wait for Randy to get here." Bill realized his men hadn't been wasting time while he was away from the office but worked with great diligence on organizing facts on the whiteboard.

Glen Simms and Burt Taylor had finished introducing themselves when Randy returned. There were handshakes all around. Bill gave a short introduction to the investigators about the case before asking if they could be on the right track.

Simms, a corporal, stood to give the answer. "I understand you and your squad have been away from the drug scene for a while. The methods of sales have changed in recent times as well as the product being sold on the streets. Burt and I will try to give you as much information as possible, but the whole scene has changed, not just the local drug business."

"You say the entire drug scene has changed. How so?" asked Bill.

"The greatest change is the drug import business. We no longer have a southern border. Drugs are coming into the country by truckloads every day. The drug trade is based on a much different product than we had in the past. Cartels are sending TONS of heroin and fentanyl into the country. The heroin is a much more concentrated form than the old days. It's much more potent, and when mixed with fentanyl has become even more deadly. Many states legalized marijuana which, as you know, is the gateway to other drug use. Politicians seem to think the way to stop crime is to make everything legal. I disagree with that policy. I think it only opens the door for heavier drug use, and in the end, more deaths and dangerous side effects. The changes I've mentioned have had a gigantic effect on the Alaska drug trade. I'm sure you can remember when marijuana and cocaine were the big drugs used on the street. Then came methamphetamines which the locals cooked right here in town. The business was operated by local addicts wanting to make enough money to pay for their own habit. Cooking meth is dangerous and caused many deaths from fires and fumes generated by the process. Marijuana has become legal and cocaine too expensive. The drug trade in Alaska has changed in the past few years." Simms ended his overview of the drug trade changes. "Any questions so far?" he asked.

Each member of the squad had been taking notes, deeply interested in what had been presented. There were no questions now, but there would be many questions later.

"OK then, I'm turning the meeting over to my partner, Burt Taylor, a CPA and a good man with a pencil. He knows about business organization and profit and loss stuff. Your turn to amaze the Geezer Squad."

Burt stood, "Thanks, Glen," greeted the new speaker, smiling at the crew. "I became a trooper to get out of an office and onto the street, but now here I am back in an office doing accounting. Can I come to work with you guys and get away from a desk?"

There were chuckles from around the room.

Burt continued, "Like most businesses the drug trade has changed because of the costs involved. You remember when an addict would steal some propane tanks and go into the business of cooking meth. Well, like Glen said, the price of goods has gone down and the volume has increased. The quality of meth was unpredictable, and folks were dying from the product. Users gradually changed to heroin, mostly for that reason. Then, along came fentanyl to enhance heroin. Fentanyl began as a tranquilizer for elephants in Africa. I don't know how or why anyone would want to pump it into their own veins, much less mix it with heroin, but here we are, and that's the lion's share of the drug trade today. Fentanyl is the most dangerous drug on the streets. To shorten the story, the volume of these two drugs is so great that dealers need backing to finance their buying power. Without a southern border we have no way to stop the flow. Virtually every hospital in Alaska sees at least one overdose patient every day. In the major cities the rate is much higher, but too many people are dying."

"Let me get this straight. You're saying there are financiers on the street backing buyers in order for them to acquire enough product to satisfy local markets?" asked Bill.

"Basically, yes. Private bankers, so to speak. Financing large drug buys," answered Burt.

"What about locally?" asked John Ashley, "Do we have any of those financiers in the local area?"

"The short answer is yes. The more complicated answer is, we really can't identify most of them. As a rule, they never handle any drugs, only cash. And as a rule, they only deal with wholesale dealers, the large suppliers. The financiers back large shipments. They finance the shipment and are paid a large fee for the services."

Bill Koogan had the next question, "Without jeopardizing any of your cases, can you identify any of these financiers?"

Burt smiled, "Do you have anyone in mind?" he asked.

Bill blew out a long breath, thinking, "I can only say we may have a suspect, but at this point, it's only speculation. Can we keep this off the record?"

"If that's the way you want it," noted Taylor.

"Our investigation has information, connected with a murder investigation, that the wife of the man charged with the killing may be one of those financiers. Her name is Darleen North."

Burt Taylor looked at Glen Simms who stood to close the door of the conference room. "How did you come by that name?" asked Simms.

"I take it the name strikes a chord?" asked Bill.

"I don't know where you got your information, but I wish I could talk to them. We've heard the name many times, but no one will give us any proof. She's a big, and I mean BIG, financier in the local area. We thought her husband Nick was in it with her, but the rumors I hear are that she is becoming too big for the mechanic. We also heard she was about to divorce him. You guys have stumbled onto something very important." Again, it was Simms making the statement.

"Well, Glen, we may be on the same page with this one." Bill opened his notebook, "she told me she was visiting her parents in Oklahoma when I called to tell her Nick had been arrested for murder. She admitted later she was considering divorcing him, but after she returned, she reopened the auto repair shop and is running it with a hired mechanic. It makes me wonder. Does she intend to use the shop as a front for her other business?"

"Bill, I'd like to work with you and your squad on this, if you're willing to work with us." Glen Simms was opening a door that is usually locked to other the law enforcement agencies. Because of the need for secrecy and the number of snitches on both sides of the law, the team was now considered one of the drug team's assets.

"You have to know we're only temporary here. We really are cops and do a cops work every day, but we're only a short-term detachment, tasked with investigating special crimes. I know my team and they're all good at policework. That's why I picked them, but I would be willing to help you in any way we can. The other side of this is that you can trust every man in this room with anything you have. We have no axes to grind. If the captain says it's OK, we'll be happy to help you out."

Two hours later, with the blessing of the captain, the Geezer Squad had access to information not open to the rest of the police unit for security reasons.

CHAPTER NINETEEN

Minutes later the group was back in the conference room with fresh cups of coffee. Taylor and Simms returned with a stack of files. When they were all settled in their seats Bill Koogan turned to Bob Barratt.

"Bob, would you be good enough to spin the whiteboard around so we can all follow it? Let's give these men our view of the case as it stands now."

Bob stood and walked to the other end of the table to turn the board so the entire group could see the little squares and notes written there. Bob reviewed the board, using both the original and new versions as it had been revised in the past few hours. When he finished, he asked for questions, but there were none.

Glen Simms finally spoke, "I'm curious," he said. "What about the three men you've been looking for? Have you identified them yet?"

"No, but we suspect they're still in the area. We spent the entire day searching for them yesterday with no luck. We showed Darlene and her receptionist photos of the three from Quick Stop security video, and they seemed to agree these were the same men who came to the office and threatened them. These are the men who kidnapped and killed the Quick Stop manager recently. I saw them in action and it's my opinion they're ex-military and well trained. So far, we've had no response from the Feds about help in identifying them."

"We have a few contacts with the Feds. Let me see if we can get something from them," Burt responded as he made notes.

"At this point, I think finding these three Bozo's should be our top priority," uttered Ashley.

Bill was nodding his head, "I agree, John. These are very dangerous men. They've killed one man already and are making threats we can't ignore toward Mrs. North and Susan. I believe they're in danger as long as these men are running the streets."

"Burt and I will get busy on an attempt to identify these guys. I'll put in a call as soon as I get to my office, but it may be a couple of days before we hear back from the DEA. They have access to FBI files, facial recognition, and profiling programs we can't access. Hopefully we'll get an answer quickly." There was a note of confidence missing from Glen Simms's voice.

"I want to thank you fellas for helping us to get some insights we didn't have before. But at this point, we don't have much to go on and need a good break." Bill stood to shake hands with Simms and Taylor. It looked like this new association was going to work well. "I hope you guys bring us a little luck." His parting remark was sincere.

"We'll get busy on this right away and get back to you as soon as we hear anything," said Burt.

The rest of the team remained in the conference room to assess the information they'd just learned. In the end nothing had changed, and the frustration levels were climbing.

"OK, Guys, I think it's time for us to take a day off. Since there's nothing pending and no new info about the case we're dealing with, let's take today and tomorrow off, or at least until we get a call from the drug unit identifying the three men we've been searching for." Bill knew this dead-end feeling. He'd felt it before and taking time off always seemed to be the best answer.

"Good," said John, "now I can go home and wash windows and mop floors, just like I do here."

The men laughed, stowed their notes and locked the conference room for much-needed time off.

Bill checked in with the captain on his way out of the office to give him a rundown on what had happened during the meeting, and the decision to give his men some time off. The captain agreed it was the best course to take.

Two days later, after much-needed rest, Bill was the first to return to the office. He was sipping his coffee and reading the weekly reports on his desk when the in-house phone disturbed him.

"Koogan," he answered.

"Bill, this is Glen Simms. I'm just checking to see if you were in this morning. I have some news for you about the men you're looking for. Do you have time to meet with me?"

"Sure, Glen, come on down to the conference room. I'll be waiting for you."

Five minutes later both drug unit officers appeared. They had a large file folder with them. Glen tossed the folder onto the table in front of Bill Koogan.

"Take a look at this, Bill," he said. Bill took the folder and opened it to the second page, the first being the request for information. He read the page and flipped to the second and third pages. He read all the information, which took several minutes, before returning it to the table and looking at the two uniformed officers.

"Wow!" Bill commented. "No wonder we've had so much trouble finding these men. I would have never guessed they were ex-Navy Seals. This file only says they were court martialed and discharged, but it doesn't describe the charges. Do you know why they were kicked out of the military?"

"Nothing official, but one of my contacts in Washington knew of the case and said they went off the reservation and began to deal large quantities of heroin and steal state treasures from the Iraqi government. The Navy seized the treasures, mostly gold artifacts, paintings, and some ancient religious treasures. He didn't specify what these treasures actually were. He also said the Navy confiscated most of the heroin shipment which was sent to the U.S. on military aircraft. He said the reason they weren't sent to prison was because of their military records. All three were decorated heroes in Iraq."

"Can I keep this file?" asked Koogan.

"Yes," answered Burt Taylor, "We made another copy for our files."

"I have a question for you, Bill," interrupted Glen.

"What's that?" asked Bill.

"Do you think Burt and I could join forces with you on this investigation? If we can find and arrest these men, we may be able to get inside information about the heroin and fentanyl trade in Alaska. I know you and your team are looking for them with respect to the murder of the Quick Stop manager and we don't want to interfere with that case. It just seems we could be useful as extra officers on the case."

Bill thought for a moment. "We could use the help, but you must realize you will be branded with the name 'GEEZERS'?"

The three men laughed and were still chuckling when the rest of the team arrived.

"What's so funny?" asked Randy as he set his coffee cup on the conference table.

"Good morning, guys," announced Bill. "I want you to meet the newest members of the Geezer Squad. When you get settled you should read the report on the three men we're looking for. We have names and mug shots of all three."

After the initial hubbub settled down, Koogan turned to the two new men. "I have something to discuss with you two. The Squad and I were looking into a new angle with this case and came up with something you should know about if you're going to work on the case with us."

"Sounds interesting, what is it?" asked Burt.

"A couple of days ago I had a private meeting with Susan, the receptionist at the auto shop. Originally, we thought Nick North killed Lee Woods because he was having an affair with Nick's wife, Darleen. Now we aren't so sure. Susan claims Nick was a hard-working guy with a lot on his mind for financial reasons. Darleen, on the other hand, spent money like there was no tomorrow. She always had money for shopping and trips to Anchorage. In the beginning we thought Nick was the one who contacted the three enforcers and brought them to town. Susan's statement makes us want to change all that. We assumed Nick was the local drug financier. What if Darleen is the financier? What if she didn't have an affair with Lee Woods, but Woods was asking questions of Nick about the drug business. He told Darleen and she concocted the story about having an affair with Lee, knowing Nick would do something drastic."

The new members of the squad sat quietly for a moment, thinking. Burt was the first to reply, "Somehow that makes perfect sense. You must have had a reason to discount the original story about the affair?"

"A weak reason, at best. Susan claims Darleen acted as if she knew the enforcers when they came to the office and supposedly, threatened the ladies. She also said she saw Darleen having some sort of heated conversation with the Quick Stop manager some time prior to his kidnapping and death. I'll admit this is all pretty thin, but our next move is to try to verify some of the facts," admitted Bill.

Glen was the next to contribute, "We always suspected there was someone with money behind the amount of buying being done for local dealers. Neither Nick nor his wife were ever on our list. We know Nick. He's a man working hard hours to make a living. We never heard a word about Lee Woods having an affair with anyone, even though he'd do a lot of bragging when he drank a couple of beers."

"Do you have any leads as to who's supplying the local dealers?" asked Bill.

"No, but there are a few dealers we might be able to put pressure on. You know how they are; nobody wants to rat their suppliers. Leave that to Burt and me for now. We'll see if we can come up with something."

"OK, Glen. In the meantime, we'll get back to finding the enforcers as soon as we figure out where to look."

Bill followed the two troopers out of the conference room to make a report to Captain Bradshaw. A few minutes later he returned to discuss the search with the rest of the squad.

"I have an idea, Bill," announced Bob.

"Good, because I'm out of ideas," replied the squad leader.

"How about John and I go to the Soldotna airport and ask around about any strangers hanging around or airplanes recently parked there. You and Randy go to Kenai and do the same there. We might get lucky."

"That actually sounds like a good idea," admitted Bill. "It beats just sitting here doing nothing. Bob is a pilot and knows several of the operators at the Soldotna airport.”

“We’ll call you if we come up with anything,” said Bob as the entire team stood to leave the office.

John and Bob drove to the Soldotna Municipal Airport in their marked patrol vehicle. This is a very nice local airport with 5000 feet of paved runway and another 1500 feet of dirt overrun. The length limits larger commercial flights but is ample for business jets and some local operators. The airport is well maintained but has no tower. About 120 aircraft call this airport home. The number varies with the seasons.

“How about you hike around and go through all the open hangars over there and I’ll check with the commercial operators on this side of the airport. I’ll meet you back here at the car in a half hour or so.”

“Good idea Bob. If they aren’t here, they may have left their car parked in one of the hangars and we have a picture of it. I think it was a Toyota Highlander.”

Both men stepped out of the patrol car onto the hot expanse of the parking area beside one of the commercial hangars used by several aircraft mechanics as well as the headquarters for a Missionary Air group. Bob walked into the big hangar while John began his walk toward the large array of open hangars on the other side of the taxiway.

Bob spoke with everyone he could find in each hangar with no success. There were four of these large, commercially operated hangars in a row on the north side of the airport. One of the hangars was unlocked, but no one was inside. His tour of the hangars took a little less than an hour and when he finished met John at the patrol car.

They climbed inside and closed the doors. Bob started the engine and engaged the air conditioner with the blower fan on high.

“Did you find anything?” asked Bob.

“Nothing,” said John. “I found a guy working on his airplane and asked him about the men and the Toyota, but he didn’t know of one parked around the hangars.”

“OK then, lets drive up to the other end of parking area and check out those large hangars up that way.”

Another hour was spent checking out these parking areas and offices with no information to be found.

“I hope Bill and Randy have more success than we did.”

CHAPTER TWENTY

While Bob and John had spent the afternoon canvassing the Soldotna airport with no positive results, Bill Koogan and Randy Craig had been at the Kenai airport doing the same. Kenai has more commercial operators and many more hangars at the airport than the Soldotna airport.

Interestingly, the total number of aircraft on the Soldotna airport is usually ten to twenty percent more than at Kenai. The big difference is the types of aircraft. There are a few commercial and business aircraft at Soldotna while a large percentage of airplanes at Kenai are commercially used.

The Kenai Municipal Airport has several daily commercial passenger flights from and to the terminal. There are several air taxi operators and freight hauling companies operating from the Kenai Airport as well.

Bill and Randy spent the entire afternoon stopping to talk with the operators in each office on the airport property. Bill was friends with many of the operators and was at ease talking with them. The result, however, was the same as achieved at the Soldotna airdrome. No one had seen the men in the pictures they'd shown the operators. At the end of the day Bill and Randy were totally frustrated.

Bill was behind the wheel of his unmarked patrol car, the engine running to supply air conditioning. He turned to Randy, "Well, Partner, where do we go now?"

"I know it's getting late in the day, but let's drive out to Nikiski and check with the air taxi operator out there. He sort of manages the local airport."

"Good thinking, Randy. I'd forgotten about that airport. We should be able to do that in about an hour. Are you sure you have the time today?"

"Yeah, Bill, I don't have any plans for this evening."

"OK then, I'll buy you a soda pop for the ride back to the office."

The Nikiski airstrip is on the south edge of the industrial village of Nikiski. The oil industry makes up much of the business on the airport: drill pipe inspections, exploration companies, oil field supply companies, helicopter operators and many other related businesses, including many local businesses that supply residents with food and other supplies.

When they arrived at the Nikiski Airport, they found the air taxi office open and the owner behind the counter. Bill and Randy entered the office to speak with him. "Hello there, Gene," greeted Bill.

"Well, I'll be darned! Haven't seen you in a while, Bill. How have you been?" asked the operator as he stuck out a large hand to shake with Koogan.

"I've been great, Gene. I've been retired for a while now, but I came back to investigate a crime for the troopers. They had to send a bunch of troopers to Bristol Bay to help with the fish war going on out there and were shorthanded, so me and three other retired troopers took the jobs. That's why I'm here. We're investigating a situation in Soldotna where some threats were made and we're looking for three men. They may have come from Anchorage in an airplane and parked it somewhere. These are the men," said Bill, showing Gene the pictures of the three ex- Navy Seals. "They're real bad guys, Gene. Have you seen them?"

"I don't think—Wait! Maybe I have. Let me see the pictures again." Gene took the pictures and studied them for a full minute. "Yeah, Bill, they parked a Cessna 206 here. It's over by the AN-2 at the end of the airstrip. I remember they called and rented a car from some private guy who advertised on the internet. Haven't seen them for a while, but the 206 is still here."

"Are you sure they are the same men?" asked Bill.

"Yeah, I'm sure. They were fit looking guys. You know, muscles everywhere. They were very polite and paid for a month in advance. They didn't give me an address to contact them, though. I thought that was strange. You'd think someone with an airplane worth about $350,000 bucks would want to be contacted if something happened it. I asked about that, and they said they'd contact me from time to time. I haven't heard from them, though. That was strange, too. I asked for a contact number. They said they didn't have one, but I saw a cell phone in one of the men's shirt pockets. They did say they were going to be fishing with a guide who was flying them out to some lakes on the other side of the Inlet. They paid in cash and parked the plane over there," Gene pointed again to the spot on the other side of the airstrip. "That's about all I can remember about them," Gene concluded.

"Finally, some good news. If these men show up again Gene, call me immediately. Don't confront them. They're dangerous men. I'll alert the trooper patrolling this area and have him stop by from time to time. Now, if you don't object, we'd like to go out and make a walk-around. We should record the tail numbers and see if there's any evidence visible from outside the plane." Bill was excited, but at the same time worried for the safety of his old friend, Gene.

"You go ahead and look all you want, Bill. It's the gold and white job beside the old Russian biplane. The owner of that old plane uses it to haul clams from the other side of the Inlet. The clam processing plant is closed for the rest of the season, so it's not in service right now."

Bill reached inside his suitcoat to find a business card to give his old friend. Handing the card to Gene he said, "Call me if you hear from them. I'll get here as fast as possible. Again, Gene, don't confront these men. They're very dangerous."

"I don't know what they did, but if you're that set on it, I'll leave them be." Gene was smiling as the two troopers walked from the office.

Bill told Randy to bring the patrol car as he walked across the unpaved airstrip to where the Cessna was parked. He took several pictures from different angles to include the registration numbers. When he returned to the patrol car, he reached for the radio mic to ask for an ownership check on the "N" numbers he was reporting. It took several minutes for the FAA to return an answer to his request. The Cessna was registered to a corporation in Houston, Texas. Bill wrote down the name of the corporation and a contact telephone number. Since it was after business hours in Houston he decided to wait until morning to follow up on the ownership information.

Bill walked around the car to get behind the wheel, then drove out of the Nikiski area. As they drove toward Kenai, he stopped at the Quick Stop to buy himself and Randy each a soda pop for the ride back to the office.

When he opened his office the following morning there was a file on his desk. It was the FAA report with details about the airplane and the names of corporate officers in Texas Westward Corp.

Four of the eight names on the corporate officers listed home addresses as countries in South America. Nicaragua and Costa Rica. Bill scanned the folder and reached for the in-house phone.

When a voice came on the line, Bill announced, "I have some new information I think will interest you. You and Burt come to my office as soon as you can."

Ten minutes later the two new members of the Geezer Squad arrived with coffee cups in hand. "What ya got, Bill?" asked Glen.

"Randy and I found the plane. We asked for an FAA registration check, and this is what was on my desk this morning." Bill handed the file to Glen and waited for the uniformed troopers to finish digesting the information.

By the time they finished, both Glen and Burt were excited. "This is all new information. I don't believe the central office for our drug team has ever seen this. If you'll allow me, I'll copy this and ask for a federal search of the names on this list. It looks as if the cartel owns the Corporation. You may have uncovered something here. Something with international consequences." Glen looked at Bill, "Damn, it makes me proud to be a Geezer".

All three men laughed as Bill gave permission to copy the folder.

"Get back to me when you learn the identities and occupations of the men on this corporate board. We need to check all the names and not just the ones from South America."

"We'll do that, Bill." Glen turned to Burt, "I guess we'd better go to the office and get busy."

When the two men left, Bill walked to the captain's office to give him a short report on what had taken place. He reminded the captain of the importance of him being called immediately if the men were reported back at the airplane. The captain agreed and picked up the phone to notify dispatch.

A few minutes later the rest of the team arrived in the office. "Mornin' Boss," greeted Ashley. "Did you find anything in Kenai?"

"No, but Randy and I went to Nikiski, and we did find something there," replied Bill.

"You did?" replied John with surprise.

"Yes, we found the airplane. The air taxi operator there and I are old friends. He recognized the photos of the three men. They have a Cessna 206 tied down out there. They didn't leave a contact number. I ran the registration number and the folder on the desk gives us some interesting information. The plane is registered to a corporation. Half the officers in the corporation are from South America. You can read the details for yourselves." Bill finished the statement by taking a long drink of his now tepid coffee.

Several minutes later, when the team finished reading the new report, Bob Barratt was the first to reply, "Wow, Boss, this is great. But I have a question about how we're going to pursue surveillance of the plane?"

"Right now, we don't have a good answer for that. I asked Gene, the air taxi operator, to call me if they show up or contact him. I warned him about how dangerous these men are, and I think he understands. The problem is we don't know when they'll be back for the airplane. We can't just station one of you out there until they return, but we can't leave it all to chance either. Anyone have a suggestion?"

"Hey, Randy. You have experience with aviation activities, why don't you get a job in the office for the air taxi operator. You can book clients, sweep floors, and even load and unload the airplanes while you wait." Bob was laughing as he spoke.

"You know, Bob, that may not be a bad idea. We're sort of at a dead end until we can locate these men and you're right, I do know what to do in the office. At least I can fill in there until I'm needed somewhere else," was Randy Craig's reply.

Bill was listening to all the banter and held up his hand. "Hold on guys. I think it's a good idea too, but we need to do a little planning if we intend to get away with the charade. The trooper office still has that old State DOT pickup out back. If it still runs, Randy could use it to go to work. He has a cell phone and we can arrange a portable radio for him. I'll call Gene and see if he would make room in the office for Randy. He'll probably be glad to have the extra help around the office. He usually closes the office when he has to fly. Now, he'll be able to keep it open all day."

The idea took root and Bill went to the captain with the plan. Captain Bradshaw agreed to the plan and authorized the use of the old pickup for Randy. Bill returned to his office to call Gene and arrange for Randy to become the new office help and ground crew for his air taxi service. Bill noted that he did, indeed, seem pleased to have the extra help with no payroll involved. By lunch time Randy was driving the old pickup to the North road and the Nikiski Airport.

When he arrived, Gene gave him a short course on his duties: tend the office, answer the telephone, help with cargo loading and unloading, fuel aircraft and 'other duties as assigned'. Randy took all the instructions well and seemed to enjoy working in the office with Gene. He had no idea how long this assignment would continue but was looking forward to a successful end. After all, now he knew what he was to be doing while the others in the trooper office were still attempting to figure it all out.

CHAPTER TWENTY-ONE

Bob and John spent the rest of the afternoon doing internet searches, investigating exactly what sort of business the Texas corporation was into. It was noted as a legitimate corporation in the State of Texas, but the exact nature of their dealings was a mystery.

The State reported the business paid $105,000 in corporate State taxes the previous year. However, they couldn't determine what business the corporation earned the money through. The only address listed for the company was a postal mailing box in Houston, Texas.

Company assets included three aircraft: the Cessna 206, a Cessna Citation business jet and an old C-123 Caribou twin engine cargo plane.

Bob turned to John and asked, "Have you ever seen anything like this?"

"No, but I can say this is the weirdest corporate filing I've ever investigated. The whole thing smells of drugs to me," commented Ashley. "I wonder why the State licensing office didn't question this application. Off-hand I'd guess someone was paid NOT to ask questions."

"I think you're right."

John looked at his watch. "Oh, well, it's quitting time anyway. Do you want to go to the river and catch a couple of Sockeye for dinner?" he asked.

"I can't tonight, John. We have the grandkids tonight and the wife suggested we take them to Dairy Queen for dinner. I'll see you in the morning."

The men stopped at the small office occupied by Bill Koogan. "We're leaving for the day, Bill. We didn't find out anything about the owners of the Cessna 206 except that they seem to be a shadow company with no footprint. They pay a lot of taxes, but for what business we were unable to learn. Something's fishy, but whatever it is they hid it well."

Bill was nodding his head, "OK Guys, I'll see you in the morning. No more than I'm accomplishing, I may as well leave, too,"

The following morning Bill was in his small office early. He checked his mailbox for messages but found none. He was sitting at his desk sipping his morning cup of coffee when his telephone rang. It was Burt Taylor.

"Good morning, Bill. Do you have time to see me and Glen for a couple of minutes?"

"Sure but bring your own coffee."

"Good, we have some information about the members of the

corporation that owns the Cessna you found."

Bill moved from his small office to the larger conference room to wait for them. The new team members were smiling when they entered the room.

"Glen and I are amazed at what you stumbled into."

"How so?"

"We went to the national database to check the names on the list of board members, and it's really strange. Two of the board members are deceased, one is in prison, one has disappeared and two don't seem to exist. There are two South Americans. The remaining two are very wealthy men. The one from Costa Rica is a billionaire. The one from Puerto Rico is only a multimillionaire. He lives in a villa in San Juan and technically is a U.S. citizen because it's a U.S. territory. The one from Costa Rica has homes in several countries as well as a 230-foot yacht. Sails the entire world. Being a billionaire, I guess he can afford it." Burt had been reading from a thick file folder in his hands.

"Do you think these men are the cartel responsible for the heroin and fentanyl being shipped to this country?" asked Bill.

"It appears that way," said Glen. "The folks we know on the national level say yes, but they have no evidence to support that. They were surprised to learn of a connection with the corporation and someone, an individual, here in Alaska. If you're thinking about Mrs. North is correct, and she's backing local drug distributors, she must be very high up the ladder in the cartel. If we can obtain any evidence whatsoever that this is true, the Feds will give us all medals."

"It would also explain how she was able to summon this quality of muscle. These three men are professional grade killers. Military trained and with endless financial backing." Bill was massaging his chin, "This is uncharted territory for me and my team. What do you suggest as we move ahead with this case?"

"I asked that very question of the folks at DEA headquarters. They're putting together a plan for us to use, but I don't think they understand Alaska and our limited resources. For now, I guess we should just wait and see what they have to say on how to proceed." It was Burt making the prediction.

Bill exhaled a long breath, "I have a man working at the air taxi office where the Cessna is parked. If he reports seeing the three enforcers, I'm going to need help. I hope I can count on you and your team to back us up."

"You can, Bill. The captain gave us a free hand in dealing with these mercenaries. I'm not looking forward to a firefight with these men, but I think it'll come down to that if we see them." Burt was being honest with the Geezer Squad leader.

There were voices in the hallway. It was Ashley and Barratt.

"Howdy Guys. Are you here on official business or just for the coffee?"

"Just bringing Officer Koogan his report card, which he can share with the rest of you," replied Glen.

"I hope I got an A in deportment," commented John. The entire team was laughing.

Burt turned to Koogan, "We need to get back to our office to do some police work. Call us if you need anything at all."

When they had gone, John Ashley asked, "So, what did they really want?"

"It's a bit complicated, but you can read the file sent from the feds. It appears Mrs. North and the folks she's associated with are probably members of a large drug cartel supplying heroin and fentanyl to Alaska. There is no physical evidence yet, but the possibility looks very good. I want you two to read it and give me your opinion of this report. I'm going to see the captain for my morning briefing. I'll be back in a few minutes.

The captain was given the details of progress on the case including Randy being sent to Nikiski to keep an eye on the Cessna. He was also briefed on the facts included in the report from the Feds.

"This is turning out to be a far-reaching case. It's been a long time since we had word of someone being involved in the international drug trade," commented Captain Bradshaw.

"I agree. Not since that guy, I don't remember his name, who owned a trucking company in the southern states was building a lodge at Lake Illiamna. That was a lot of years ago."

"I want you to stay on top of this and keep me informed every step of the way. If the Feds get involved, I'll need to contact the colonel."

"Sure thing, Cap. I don't know what we can do at this point. All of this is supposition with no hard evidence. The Squad and I are going to have a meeting about all that in a few minutes." Bill stood to leave, then turned back to the captain, "I don't remember life being this complicated in the olden days."

As he returned to the conference room he asked the two team members a question, "OK Guys, what's your opinion on what the Feds have concluded?"

Bob was the first to answer, "It looks as if they have come to the same conclusions as we have. Mrs. North is most likely the big money behind the local dealers. But like us, they don't have any real evidence, only guesswork."

Koogan turned to John, "What about you, John?"

"The same as Bob, speculation with no evidence."

"Any suggestions as to how to proceed?" asked Koogan.

"No, but we might want to ask that question of the two new members of the squad. They'd know more about the local drug trade than all of us." Bob made the statement without emotion. "Can we get them to come down here and give us an overview of the pecking order in the local drug business?"

Bill was nodding agreement as he picked up the inhouse phone. When his call was answered he said, "Burt, can you and Glen come down to the conference room and give us some information?"

When he hung up the phone he turned to John and Bob, "They're on the way over. He said they'd been expecting our call."

The offices used by the drug team were on the other end of the building. It took only a couple of minutes for the two newest members of the team to arrive. The rest of the Squad was seated in the conference room when they arrived.

"Well Fellas, what do you think?" asked Glen.

"We think we need to learn more about the drug business as it is today," answered Bill.

"Where do you want us to start?" asked Burt.

"I guess we should start by learning the way the business is structured. In our day, dealers bought drugs from the importer, paid cash and went to work on the street selling them. It was simple in those days. There were no big money backers. The dealers were mostly independent businessmen. It seems like the structure of it has all changed. We need to know how it works today." Bill had laid out the basis for needing their explanation.

Burt stood to answer, "In days gone by, the framework for all the drug importation was random and chancy. Today the volume being introduced into this country is huge. Heroin has been replaced for the most part by cocaine and methamphetamine use. Most marijuana is now grown in the U.S. and isn't being sent here in such quantities as you were used to seeing. There's still some coming across the southern border, but not like it was in the old days. Not that we can ignore importing weed, but heroin and fentanyl are a thousand times more dangerous and are killing thousands more users. In Alaska, heroin and fentanyl are an epidemic. Marijuana is now legal to use and sell. We still arrest people for illegal use and sale of it, but our resources are taken up with the lethal drugs on the street. The expense and volume have increased the cost of these hard drugs to where local distributors need financing to operate. The cartels have gone into the business of backing local distributors. Now, they're essentially drug bankers. The three killers roaming the streets are like bank guards keeping an eye on money being deposited."

Bob raised his hand with a question, "Are you saying this whole thing is set up like a large corporation?"

"Yes," replied Burt, "That is exactly how it works, only more lethal. The drugs are deadly. Fentanyl is one of the deadliest drugs on the market today. Some pills are too pure and will kill almost instantly. Some are poisonous and will kill almost instantly. The mix of heroin and fentanyl are another deadly combination. We're told fentanyl is more addictive than heroin. I can't imagine why anyone would want to put that stuff in their bodies."

"It sounds to me like we need to start with what we do know. Like local drug dealers. Squeeze as much information out of them as possible. I'd like to remind everyone that at this point, we still have no evidence Mrs. North is the actual financier. We're still speculating. We need to find some real, factual, identifiable information. Unless you're doing it differently these days, we should go out and shake some trees and see what falls out."

Bill was doing his best to make sense of the way things are done today. He understood the old system and helped develop it, but this was all new to him and his team.

"Don't lose faith, Bill," stated Glen. "We've already learned a great deal that even the Feds hadn't uncovered. Today's crime syndicates are more organized and better financed than they once were. The criminals are also better educated. We're not just dealing with street bums making a living. We're dealing with corporate executives in big offices getting rich. Because they never get out of the office and onto the street, we seldom get to see them. The dealers on the street are still the same dirt bags we've always had. You and your men have learned more about this problem than our drug team and the DEA have learned in all the time they've been chasing them. You and your team should be very proud of what you've done thus far."

"Where do we go from here?" asked Bill.

"Burt and I talked about that. How about we split the team into two units, going to different areas and questioning some of the dealers we know?" Glen asked Bill and his team.

"That's probably a good idea. We know how to be cops and you know how to locate the local offenders. How soon do you want to start?" It was Bill speaking with John and Bob agreeing by nodding approval. "When do you want to start?"

"Burt and I thought first thing in the morning, if it's OK with you."

"We'll meet you here first thing in the morning to get started," replied Koogan.

CHAPTER TWENTY-TWO

The following morning the team met in the conference room to discuss how to proceed with this investigation. Glen and Burt looked somber as they entered.

"Change of plans, Guys. We got overruled by the big guys. They want us to hold off making inquiries until they send undercover troops out to test the waters. They think poking around is OK, but if done by uniformed officers it won't work well. We have several undercover officers inside the organization and the bosses think they can do a better job of looking than us. Sorry boys. They're in charge of all of us in the area of drugs." It was Glen speaking while a glum looking Burt stood by his side.

Bill scratched his head, thinking. "How long did they say they needed?" he asked.

"They didn't say. Nothing ever happens on schedule when it comes to drug investigations," replied Burt. "I'm thinking we should give them a week before we step back in and do it ourselves. I understand the reasoning behind the decision but, as you've said before, we're looking for some very dangerous men. We can't stop you from doing it on your own, but we work for them and will have to do it their way. Sorry, Guys."

Again, Bill was scratching his head before speaking. "OK, we'll do it your way for now. We don't have any specific information to work with, so we'll let them do what they do unless we come up with some new leads to follow. You've been great to work with and I hope when we take the case up again in a few days, you'll be back with us."

"Thanks, Bill. We were hoping you'd feel that way. Burt and I will let you know of any progress or good information the undercover boys find and report back to us. I hope you'll do the same if you hear anything on your end."

Bill only nodded as the drug team members stood to return to their offices. When they were gone, he turned to the remaining two team members. "Anybody got any good ideas?" he asked.

Neither John Ashley nor Bob Barratt had any.

"Then, I'll go speak with the captain and we can all go fishing this afternoon."

Bob was the first to reply, "Do you suppose Susan at the auto repair shop has heard anything new since you last spoke with her?"

"I haven't heard, but I wouldn't mind going by to ask, if Darleen isn't in the office."

"Don't you think it might be productive to speak with her before you report to the captain?" asked Bob, with a grin.

"It might not be a bad idea to just stop by for a minute," agreed Koogan.

By now John had a feel for this conversation, "And it's about time to check on Randy out in Nikiski. Sometimes that area isn't very friendly. I'd hate to see Randy get captured by North Roaders."

"OK Guys, you're right. There are some things we can do while we wait for the professionals do their thing." Bill was happy to note the team wasn't disheartened by the news from the two drug team troopers. In fact, it made him a little prouder of his Geezer Squad.

Bill returned to his little office where he dialed the auto repair shop. Susan answered on the first ring.

"Soldotna Auto Repair Shop," she said.

"Hello, Susan, are you free to talk a moment?"

"Yes, but I'd prefer you come by to speak face to face."

"Would it be convenient for me to stop in a few minutes?"

"Yes, my boss has gone to Anchorage today."

"Good, I'll be there in ten minutes." Bill was happy to learn the two of them could talk without interruption from Darleen.

As he drove into the lot beside the office, he noted there were several cars parked alongside. Business was good. Inside he surveyed the small office area. There was no one else in the office.

"Hello, Susan, how is it going for you?" he asked.

"Everything in the shop is fine. We're very busy and the mechanic seems to know his business. Darleen comes and goes, but she spends an awful lot of time on her cell phone. She's careful to make sure I can't hear the conversations. She either goes into the shop or outside when she gets one of her important calls. As a person I like her, but I don't trust her."

"If what I suspect is true there's good reason for the feeling. Have you seen or heard from the three goons since we last talked?"

"Not a peep. I have noticed one thing, though. Darleen has had a lot of appointments with the man who owns the used car dealership between here and Kenai. I know the man who manages the place, but he doesn't own it. He's a good guy. The owner is never here. Doesn't even live here. He lives in the MatSu Valley. Darleen is forever making another appointment with him and going to lunch with him. They may be dating, but I don't think so. Once I asked if she was dating the guy and she said I must be crazy, that he's a creep."

"Why do you think she's meeting with him?" asked Bill.

"I don't know for sure. She may be trying to sell the shop to him. I asked and she said no, she's keeping the shop."

"What makes you so suspicious of her, Susan?" asked Bill.

"She keeps a large, expensive briefcase in her car. If she gets a phone call she goes to her car and opens the case. I've never been able to see what she has in it, but I think it's just files and papers. I don't know what else could be in it."

"Can you think of anything else you'd like to tell me right now?"

"No, I guess not. But now you see why I don't trust her. All her actions are very suspicious in my mind." Susan was becoming edgy and nervous.

"OK, Susan. I'll check out what you've told me and get back to you as soon as I can. If you think of anything else, just call me. You have my card." Bill waved as he reached the door and exited the office.

He stopped at Dairy Queen for a chocolate malt to take back to the office with him. In the time he was away from the office his two Squad members had used the marked patrol car to drive to Nikiski to check on Randy Craig. When they arrived, Randy was helping to load a group of fishermen into a Cessna 207, an extended version of the Cessna 206.

Bob and John waited in the patrol car until the plane was loaded and taxied to the runway for takeoff. Randy watched it go and sauntered back toward the office building where the patrol car was parked.

John powered the window down as Randy approached. "How does it feel to have a real job, Randy?" he asked.

"Exhilarating," he replied. "What are you two government employees doing out here in Nikiski?"

Bob opened the driver side door and stepped out onto the gravel parking area. "We 'government employees' are just checking on the working-class folks," said Bob.

Randy stepped closer to keep the conversation at a low volume. "Glad someone is interested in my welfare," he said with a grin. "How are things at the office?"

"We're doing what we do, but there may be a turf war brewing with the drug unit and the undercover men. The uniformed guys in the office are good to work with, but the people they work for like secrets. Bill's trying to work something out, but you know how those things usually work out."

"Dang, Bob, I'm glad I'm not in the office these days. It's peaceful out here and the gas hose and baggage never give me an argument. For what it's worth, I haven't seen or heard anything from the owners of the Cessna over there," he said, pointing at the airplane.

"Do you have everything you need, Randy?" asked John.

"Yeah, I don't need much to keep watch on a parked airplane. I've been hanging out late at night to see if those men sneak after dark, but so far, nothing. Of course, dark is around midnight these days. But I do appreciate the two of you coming out to check on me, though."

"If you need a day off or have something to do, call me and I'll come out and give you a break," said John. "Otherwise, I guess we'll leave you to your tasks. Just let us know if you do need something." Ashley slid into the passenger seat as he was speaking.

"What he says is true, Randy. Call if you need or want anything. Don't take any chances," Said Bob as he climbed into the driver side of the patrol car.

"See you later, guys," shouted Randy as the car eased away from the parking area. He walked slowly back to the office.

An hour later at trooper headquarters, they found Bill in his office reading a report delivered by the newest members of the Squad. It was a DEA report on the owner of the car lot. His name is Gordon Tullis.

Bill looked up as the two came in, "Well, how is Randy making out?" he asked.

"He's doing fine, according to him. He said he didn't need anything and that he had been staying late to keep an eye on the Cessna. I think he likes it out there," Bob reported. "How about you? Did you learn anything?"

Actually, I did. I was sitting here reading the report I just received from DEA. Susan gave me the name of someone who owns Big State Motors. Darleen meets with him quite often and has numerous phone calls to and from him. I asked Burt and Glen to see what they could learn about him. They just brought me this report. He has a home in Wasilla, where he lives when he is in the State. He has a primary residence in Florida north of Miami, and another family home in Oklahoma. I checked it out and it's the same area where Darleen had been visiting her family. It may just be coincidence, but it may be the link that connects her with Gordon Tullis, the car lot owner. Go on over to the conference room and I'll bring the report over there where we have more room to think."

Once they changed offices, they began to study the DEA report in depth. In Miami, he was associated with a company owned by the drug cartel. DEA investigated and could not find any business connection tying him to the drug trade, but they were suspicious and put him on a watch list. The reason for a report being returned to Alaska so immediately was due to the watch list. They were requesting any information about him from Alaska State Troopers.

"Hmmm," mumbled Bob, "I wonder what connection Darleen has with Old Gordy?"

"Good question, Bob," commented Bill. "I wonder if she's the agent for Gordon Tullis and the one bankrolling cash to local dealers?"

"Why don't we call Glen and Burt to see if they have any insight about this?" asked Bob.

Within minutes the two troopers came to the conference room. They were both excited about a connection between Darleen, Gordon Tullis, and the local drug scene.

Burt read the file sent by the DEA with a great deal of excitement. When he finished reading, he looked at Bill. "I don't know if you guys are very good, or just plain lucky. We've been trying to find the local connection to the cartels and crime syndicates for years. You four breeze in here and hand it to us." Burt handed the pages to Glen to read. How did you do it?"

"Just good old fashioned police work, Burt. Nothing special." The Geezer Squad members were laughing now.

"Let me take this to my bosses and we'll try to make a plan about how we should proceed," it was Glen bringing back the seriousness of the moment.

"OK, I think we'll leave it with you tonight and start again in the morning. Let's plan to meet here first thing in the morning." Bill knew some things had to be authorized by bosses of his bosses; inconvenient, but necessary.

CHAPTER TWENTY-THREE

The next morning Koogan came in, retrieved a fresh cup of coffee, and walked to Captain Bradshaw's office. He was on the telephone when Bill arrived, so he waited outside the door for the Captain to finish. A minute later he heard the voice of Captain Phil Bradshaw, "Come in, Bill."

"I just wanted to come by and fill you in on what the Squad is doing these days. We may be making some headway, at last."

"That was Burt Taylor on the phone. He briefed me on your finding a link to Darleen North and the local drug business. Congratulations! It seems that your connecting Gordon Tullis with the Alaska drug trade is a giant step forward. One the drug team was never able to identify. He also said he was to have a meeting with you this morning to discuss where to go and what to do next. Bill, I can't tell you what an asset you and your squad have been in recent days. It looks like you'll be here a while longer and personally, I like the thought."

"I appreciate the kind words, Cap. I picked these men because they're good cops. They've proven I made the right choices. I guess if Glen and Burt are headed my way, I should get back to my office." He walked back to the conference room with a measure of pride in his step.

John and Bob were drinking coffee at the big conference table when he arrived. "OK, Guys, what did I miss?" asked Bill.

"Nothing," answered Bob. "But we were wondering if you had heard from the drug team this morning?"

"They should be here in a few minutes." Koogan hesitated a moment, "I want to pass on to you that the captain is very happy with the Geezer Squad and results we've attained. I want to add my own personal seal of approval with how you men have performed since we started. You're a great crew and I appreciate your skills and diligence."

"If you're going to get all mushy, I'm quitting right now," commented John Ashley.

"I'll second that," said Bob.

Bill was about to add another snide comment when Glen and Burt entered the room.

"Is this a private party or can we join?" asked Glen Simms.

"Come on in," offered Bill, "We were just having a friendly discussion. What have you decided about a plan of attack?"

Burt had a file folder in his hand and stepped up to give the answer. "Since we have no way to prove any of the accusations we're putting forth, there is no way we can do a raid on Gordon Tullis' home or office. What we can do is put surveillance techniques into play. We'll follow and record him wherever he goes. It'll be up to you and your men to keep tabs on Darleen North. I know she's been out of town for a couple days, but when she returns, we want you to keep a close eye on her. We still have no word on where to find the three enforcers we've been looking for, but one of our mechanics is headed out to make sure the Cessna in Nikiski won't start when they return. We'll have additional manpower available when we need it. Our team has been contacted by DEA to assure us they'll be available if, and when, we can come up with something tangible to base an arrest warrant on."

"Are your undercover guys going to be able to work that side of the street?" asked Bob.

"Yes, they are, but you know how that goes. They can ask questions, but getting answers is never guaranteed," Glen replied.

"I'll let our man in Nikiski know your mechanic is headed his way. Do you have an ETA?" asked Bill.

"No, but he's local and it should be soon."

The drug unit troopers left the office to the other end of the building. When they'd gone Bill turned to John and Bob.

"You know?" he said, "I think I should make another try at speaking with Nick North. He's been sitting in jail for a short time and may be ready to talk with someone."

"Well, good luck with that, Boss," answered John.

"I know, but perhaps he's had a change of heart," replied Bill as he rose from his seat.

Fifteen minutes later the Geezer Squad leader rang the bell at the front gate of the pretrial facility in Kenai. A lady corrections officer answered the bell and admitted the trooper.

"Hey there Trooper Koogan, how's it going?" she asked.

"Fine, Crissy, just fine. I'd like to talk with Nick North if he'll see me." Bill was speaking as he signed the guest book.

"His attitude has changed in the past few days. He might just be in the mood to talk. Where do you want to see him? In visiting or the attorney visiting room?"

"The attorney visiting room may be better and a little more private," answered Bill.

"Come on into the shift office and wait while I go and ask him if he wants to see you."

He followed her into the secure part of the jail and was admitted to the shift supervisor's office where he was handed a cup of coffee by the jail boss-man.

"We haven't seen you in a while, Bill. I thought you retired and was fishing all the time." quipped the sergeant.

"I was, but they called me and three others back to do some investigations for the troopers. We'll be going back to retired life as soon as the Bristol Bay fishery ends. I guess those poor guys up there are having a time keeping the peace."

Just then a buzzer sounded a warning of the door of the inmate area of the jail being unlocked. Crissy was leading a large man in handcuffs to the attorney visiting room, located just outside the door she was bringing him through. She led him into the small room and shackled his ankle to a set of ankle cuffs attached to a ring on the wall. This was done for security reasons. In the past, on rare occasions, an inmate had attempted to attack an interviewer. The ankle cuff allowed the visitor to make it out the door of the small office, but the inmate was restricted from moving that far without being unlocked from the wall. When North was secured, Crissy came out of the office and motioned for Bill to come.

Bill had locked up his weapon in a small safe outside the secure area but unfastened his duty belt before leaving the supervisors office to go into the small interview room with the prisoner. Once inside he took a seat across the desk from North.

"Mr. North, I don't know if you remember me. I'm Bill Koogan, with the troopers."

"Yeah, I remember you. You're one of the cops that arrested me," stated a gruff North.

"Normally I would've sent someone else to speak with you, but this doesn't pertain to your case. It has to do with some things that, frankly, we did think you had a hand in doing. We no longer believe that's the case. My questions have to do with the drug trade in the local area. Initially, we thought you were involved in the sale and distribution of drugs around here. We now suspect someone else is. Do you know anything about what I'm saying?"

"No, and if I did, I wouldn't tell you!" he said.

"Listen, Nick. I'm willing to put in a word to the DA if you cooperate. You'll still do a lot of time, but it could shorten your stay by several years."

"I ain't sayin' nothin'", he repeated.

"OK, Nick. But it looks like your wife is making a lot of money these days, as well as running the repair shop. I was hoping you could give me some insight on who she's working for and who she's backing in the drug business. But if you'd rather spend extra time in prison while your wife becomes a rich lady, then I guess we're through here," Bill said as he stood to leave.

"No. No. Sit down. I guess I'm just mad at the world. For what it's worth I shot Lee for having a good time with my wife. Since I've been in here, I've learned he was doing an investigation into the same thing you're talking about. I didn't know anything about her doing any of that business. I worked so much, and I felt guilty about it. I wanted to blame everyone but me for my mistakes. I really didn't want to shoot Lee, but I was so hurt about what I thought was true, that I just couldn't stop myself." Nick was staring at the chain on his right leg, very close to tears.

Bill waited a few seconds before continuing. "Look, Nick, I can sympathize with you. Your wife is a very beautiful lady. I can see why you'd be angry thinking she would be unfaithful. I must say I don't know if she was or not, but at this point it looks like if she was having an affair, it wasn't with Lee Woods. She is, however, implicated on some other things, probably the same things Lee was investigating. I'd like to know if you can tell me about those dealings. The reason we need to know is these people she's working with are very dangerous and wouldn't hesitate to do away with her when they think they don't need her any longer. We think she's an agent for the man financing local dealers. She's in a very dangerous position and may not know it."

There was great sadness in the big man's sagging shoulders and watery eyes. "Trooper Koogan, I never knew about any of the drug stuff she was doing. I wouldn't even believe she was doing them, but since I've been in here, I've heard a lot of things from the other prisoners that prove to me it's true. She's in cahoots with some money man from maybe Florida or somewhere. I really don't know what she does, except she loans cash to local drug distributors. Not to street dealers, just suppliers. I only learned that since I came in here." Once again, he was staring at the floor.

"Can you tell me the names of any of the local distributors she's loaning money to?" asked Bill.

"Like I said, I didn't know any of this until I came in here. I don't know anything else." He went quiet and stared at the floor.

"OK, Nick. I thank you for what you've told me. If you hear anything else, have the jailers call me." Bill stood to leave, then turned back, "Is there anything I can do for you?" he asked.

Nick only shook his head.

Back out front, he buckled his duty belt into place and signed out. In the lobby he picked up his weapon and said goodbye to Crissy.

On his way back to the office he considered how his opinion of Nick North had changed since their first meeting. He felt sorry for the man. Life had played some dirty tricks on this guy. He was a hard-working man with a goal, was working hard to attain it, but was blindsided by the beautiful woman he loved dearly. Now he lived with a heavy heart, his dreams shattered. The woman he loved had gone on with her own life and left him with prison life as his future. It was sad.

He radioed ahead to ask Burt and Greg to meet him in the conference room when he returned.

John Ashley and Bob Barratt, as well as Greg and Burt, were waiting when he arrived. He spent the next several minutes telling them what Nick North had revealed.

"Again, this is not evidence, but it does confirm we're on the right track. What I need to know now is, what do we do next?"

Glen Simms was the first to answer, "You guys are amazing. You've come up with information our investigation has never been able to obtain. I agree this isn't evidence, but now we know what we're going to investigate. The best chance of finding real evidence will be with the undercover officers. We'll have to investigate any crimes or possible physical evidence the undercover men report to us. For me, the most productive thing we have is your man in Nikiski. We still need to find those three men from the Cessna. They're dangerous and they're here for a purpose. We should find them before they find what they're looking for."

"It sounds like we're back to square one," said Bill. "OK, thanks boys. You get the undercover team to work, and we'll work something out from here."

CHAPTER TWENTY-FOUR

It had been two frustrating days of fruitless searching and research attempting to learn the whereabouts of the three enforcers. It seemed they had vanished from the face of the earth. In the conference room the Squad members searched files, re-read reports, re-thought all their suppositions, and came up with nothing new. It was beginning to look as if they needed to go back on patrol and attempt to find the men and the Highlander.

Bill was about to ask John and Bob if they had any new ideas when the intercom phone rang. It was Glen Simms.

"Got a minute to talk with us?" he asked.

"At this point, time is the only thing we have," responded Bill Koogan.

"Good, we'll be right down to see you."

Minutes later, the two uniformed drug unit members entered the conference room with a fille folder. After saying hello to the Squad, they took a seat and opened the folder.

"OK, Guys. We finally got something from the undercover troopers. The three men you're looking for have been making the bar circuit all up and down the North Road. They've been asking a lot of questions about one of the local drug dealers out there. This one distributes everything. He handles meth, heroin, coke, marijuana, and fentanyl tablets. He's said to be the largest distributor on the North Road. No one seems to know why they're looking for this dealer, but it's our guess he owes someone, probably Mrs. North, a lot of money. It looks like he got word someone was looking for him and has made himself scarce. The enforcers haven't begun to break legs yet, but they did offer a nice reward for anyone who can tell them where this dealer is hiding." Glen Simms gave the rundown.

"Do we have a name for this distributor?" asked Bill.

"Yes, we do. His name is Billy Forsythe. He's local, born and raised. His family, all his uncles and cousins, were big in the management of the refineries and other facilities on the North Road. Most of them have moved away or retired from the oil business. Billy has a house just north of Nikiski, but he hasn't been home for several days." Simms was giving the information.

Burt Taylor now took over the file and continued. "Billy has a record for drug sales, DWI and extortion. This last charge was filed by a bar owner who claimed Billy wanted exclusive rights to sell drugs in his bar. The owner refused and Billy threatened to burn the place down. The owner had a video camera and microphone set up to keep tabs on his bartenders, but this time he caught Billy threatening him and did it on video. The DA threatened to prosecute him. Somehow, Billy was found guilty and paid a fine, but never went to jail." Burt paused to check his file.

"Our informant is familiar with the local druggies and claims the resident banker, a good-looking lady, met with Billy Forsythe several times to arrange for the cash to back large purchases he wanted to make. A deal that would make him the largest heroin and meth dealer in the area. A deal was made for him to buy from several different suppliers. The word on the street is he couldn't renege without serious repercussions. Sounds like he managed to fail in his obligation."

"Will we have a witness to identify Mrs. North is the lady making the deal?" asked Bob Barratt.

"We're working on that as we speak," said Glen. "We are also attempting to learn where Billy's hiding right now. By the way, do you have a current picture of Mrs. North?"

"The best I can do is a driver license photo," said Bill.

"OK, but we can bring that up ourselves." Simms thought a moment before adding, "You might advise your man in Nikiski to keep his head down. Both sides of this, the three assailants and the potential victim, are dangerous."

"I'll give him a call and let him know what you've told us. You're right, these men are very dangerous. I wish we could find them and arrest them before they hurt someone else, even if the someone is Billy Forsythe." Bill had been taking notes during the meeting and thought it was time to update the captain.

After finishing his report to Captain Bradshaw, Bill decided to drive to Nikiski and speak with Randy Craig face to face. When he arrived at the airstrip, he spotted Randy loading an airplane with fishing gear and passengers. He waited at the office until the airplane took off and Randy came back to the small office building. Bill had parked his own car behind some fuel tanks at the side of the office to stay out of sight. As Randy approached, he stepped into view.

"How's it going, Randy?" he asked.

"You know how it is, I like to complain that I can't get a day off during fishing season." Randy and Bill both laughed. "What are you doing out here, Boss?"

"We have had some developments in the case." Bill took the time to give Randy the latest update about the three enforcers and the possible identification of Darleen North as the financier for the drug dealers. He also passed on information about Billy Forsythe and his connection with Darleen. "It's time to be extra careful, Randy. Would you like for me to send someone out here to stay out of sight and able to back you up if you needed it?"

Randy thought a few seconds, "Not yet, but if I call, I'd like you guys to make it a priority. It could get ugly in a short period of time. We've seen these men in action before and they play dirty. If I hear they're coming, you know they may call ahead or something. It's not likely, but if they do, you need to head this way pronto."

"You can count on us doing that, Randy. But you should take all precautions to protect yourself until we arrive."

"The only one who knows what I'm doing here is my boss and he knows what's going on. He's my other set of eyes at this point."

"OK, if that's the way you want to play it, but don't take any chances. Call us if you suspect they may show up." Bill was uncertain about this decision, but knew Randy was a very capable officer with a world of experience. Bill turned to return to his patrol car, giving a small wave of his hand as he walked.

"Thanks for caring." Randy said as Bill walked away.

Bill had just turned onto the Kenai Spurr Highway when his call numbers came across the police radio, "Koogan here, what is it?"

"We just received a report from a bar owner in Nikiski that Billy Forsythe was back at his bar."

"Is he still there?" asked Bill as he slowed to return to Nikiski.

"Not inside, but he is sitting in his car in front of the bar talking on the phone," reported dispatch.

"I'm headed back that way now, ETA five minutes. Please advise the bar owner." Bill didn't use the siren or red lights so he could approach without being noticed by Forsythe. As he turned into the small parking area he could see a man in the front seat of a vehicle, speaking on the telephone. Parking behind the car, he stepped out to approach the driver. He stopped and waited near his own front fender to call dispatch and give the license number of the vehicle he was looking at. Seconds later he heard back that this was, indeed, Billy Forsythe's vehicle.

Billy was so intent with his phone he didn't see Bill staring in the side window. Bill smiled and tapped on the glass. Billy jumped with surprise.

Laying his phone on the front seat, he rolled down the window, "What do you want," he demanded.

"Hello, Billy, I'm Trooper Koogan. Please step out of the car. I need to speak with you for a moment."

"I ain't gettin' out. What do you want with me?"

"Now Billy, is that any way to talk. I just want to ask you a few questions. Unless you've been threatening people, I don't have a reason to arrest you. Now get out of the car."

Billy was shaking his head as he opened the door to get out. "I ain't done nothin' wrong, so just leave me alone."

"Hey Billy, I just wanted to talk. I didn't want to arrest you. Why are you so jumpy. You should respect an officer of the law," chided Bill.

"You guys don't respect me, why should I respect you?" argued Forsythe.

"You seem awfully touchy, Billy. Have you been doing bad things again?"

"That bartender called you, didn't he? I never said anything he could take as a threat. He just doesn't like me."

"Billy, Billy, calm down. I just got here. Have you already been in the bar?" asked Bill.

"Yeah, I was inside a few minutes ago. That crumb told me to get out, so I came out and got in my car to call a friend. I was about to leave when you showed up."

Bill Koogan thought he should take a chance on spooking the drug dealer, "Who were you calling? Was it your banker?"

"What in the world are you talking about?" asked Billy.

"You know; that pretty banker you've been dealing with. The one keeping you supplied with the cash to buy drugs."

Billy was turning beet red, "If you can prove I'm dealing drugs, then arrest me and let me call my lawyer. Otherwise get outta my face!"

"I've already told you, Billy, I didn't stop to arrest you, only have a little talk. I don't know why you're so angry."

"I don't like being jerked around by a cop, or anyone else for that matter. Just go away and leave me alone."

"OK, if that's what you want. I just thought you might introduce me to your pretty banker."

Again, Billy became irate, "Darleen would never speak to you. You piece of crap."

"Now there you go, Billy. I never mentioned her name and you just blurted it out. Not smart, Billy. Another thing that isn't smart is you trying to outwit those three goons looking for you. They won't be as nice as I am. Have you seen them?"

Billy now had a shocked look on his face. "How did you know about those men? I never said anything about them."

"You should know by now your private life isn't private any longer. You might want to ask me for some help. These men are bad men who do bad things and I need to find them before they find you." Bill's attempt to make Billy nervous was working.

Billy reached for the door handle on the driver door. "I can't stay out here all day talking with you. I have important things to do. Now get out of my way."

Bill stepped back to allow Billy to enter his vehicle but reached inside his coat to find a business card to give the drug dealer. "Here's my card, Billy. You may find a need for my help soon, just call if you want me to help you."

Billy snatched the card from the trooper and dropped into the seat behind the wheel. He was shaking his head as he hooked up his seat belt. "Fat chance, Koogan," he said as he slammed the car door.

Bill watched as Billy drove away to the north toward his home. When he was gone, Bill walked to the bar to speak with the bartender. "Howdy, Dave," greeted Koogan as he entered.

"Oh, hi there, Bill. You just missed Billy Forsythe. He was here wanting me to reconsider his offer. I turned him down again. He can't seem to remember I sell liquor here, not drugs."

"Yes, I know, we met in the parking lot. He's not a happy person today. I hope I had something to do with that."

"Thanks for coming out to check on me, Bill. I don't want anything to do with that Forsythe character."

"No problem, you can call us anytime. Good to see you again. I'm going back to the office now but call if he comes back." With that Bill waved and left the bar to drive back to the office, anxious to report the confirmation of Darleen North as the agent for the drug banker.

CHAPTER TWENTY-FIVE

By the time Koogan returned to the office he'd calmed somewhat, from the excitement of learning Darleen North was the financier they were looking for. He also suspected the three men they were looking for were somewhere in the North Kenai area. That bit of news would narrow the search area dramatically.

He walked to the coffee pot on his way to the office to meet with John and Bob. With a fresh cup of hot coffee in hand he returned to the conference room where the Squad members were studying files. Both men looked up when Bill entered.

"How was the trip out north?" asked Bob.

"It was worthwhile. I came across Billy Forsythe and had a short conversation with him. He managed to spill the fact that Mrs. Darleen North is the banker for the drug dealers locally. He was at the local bar attempting to coerce the owner into distributing drugs from the bar.
Dave, the bartender-bar owner threw him out."

"Well, at least we now know who the drug team should be looking at. How's Randy making out?" asked John.

"I offered to have one of you come out as a backup in case the enforcers returned unexpectedly, but he refused the help. One thing, though. I'm convinced these enforcers are staying somewhere in the North Kenai area. When we have nothing else to do, we can go out there and patrol all the side roads and backwoods driveways. There's a lot of area out there to cover. We can split up and cover a lot more country. I think I can get the captain to have the patrols in the area help with that search." Bill had not yet talked with the captain but was sure he would agree.

"We haven't seen or heard from Darleen for a couple of days. Do you think she's been out of town?" asked Bob.

"Yes, I do. I'm guessing she is in Wasilla to see Gordon Tullis." He looked down and shook his head, "We need to get some tangible evidence on these two. Sooner or later, they'll claim harassment and file a complaint on us. They've played it smart this far and not allowed anything that would connect the two of them. I sort of tricked Billy Forsythe into saying Darleen was the banker. He got very angry about the slip-up. I think we should have the drug guys come over here and meet with us to plan our next move," Bill was rubbing his forehead from the tension.

Minutes later the two uniformed officers joined the Squad in the conference room and seemed excited to be joining in the investigation. Bill briefed the men on what he had learned on his trip to North Kenai.

"Finally," said Burt, "We finally have information confirming our suspicions about Darleen North. Now all we need is evidence."

"Darleen has been missing for a few days. I think she's in Wasilla conferring with the big money man, Gordon Tullis. It would be nice if your drug agents in that area could verify that she's there. I also think we should begin to document her movements. Until now we've been operating on suspicion, but now suspicions have been unofficially confirmed. Sooner or later, she'll make a mistake and we'll connect her with a crime," Bill stated.

"If we can confirm she really is in Wasilla, can we call her in and ask her to explain what she is doing with Gordon Tullis?" asked Bob Barratt.

"That may be a little premature, but we're getting closer to that very thing," answered Burt Taylor.

Again, Bill's frustration was getting the best of him, "OK, Guys. Enough speculation. We need to concentrate on the facts we have. We need to find the enforcers. We need to shake the drug sales tree and see if anything else falls from it. We need to quit guessing and do some real police work."

Everyone was silent for a few seconds, then Bob spoke up. "You're right, Boss. We need to get back to doing what we do. Randy is out there without backup while we sit here in the office discussing possibilities. Would it be permissible for John and me to find Billy Forsythe and make him a little nervous?"

Bill snickered, "You know, Bob, that might just be a good idea. He was pretty shaken up after his admission that Darleen was the local banker. He owes her pile a of money, and we think the enforcers are after him to collect. Someone in that circle should know where he's hiding, since he hasn't been home for several days.'

"It sure beats sitting in the office mopping floors and washing windows," commented John.

"Burt and I agree, Bill. We'll have the undercover team step up their efforts. I think Burt and I will be able to get out of the office to lend a hand in locating the three goons." Simms said with a smile. "You sure know how to light a fire under a crew," he said with a chuckle.

"Come on, John, let's go to Nikiski and earn our wages," said Bob as he stood to leave.

The rest of the team also stood to leave, "Thanks for being a team," Bill said to the Squad as they filed out of the conference room. It was time for him to report to the captain on the progress being made.

The briefing was lengthy, and the captain listened intently. When Bill had finished, the captain sat quietly, thinking before speaking.

Finally, he said "Good job, Bill. It sounds as if you and your team are making progress. I think I'll assign Glen and Burt to work with you on this. Since you've made the connection between the drug business out there to your case, the use of the drug unit officers will be legitimate. Is there anything else I can do to help you out?"

"We're finally getting a lot of loose ends to tie up and can use the help, but we're still a long way from making a legal case against anyone. Right now, I think the weakest link is Billy Forsythe. Glen and Burt were on their way out to find him. My greatest concern is Randy. He's out there alone with no backup. He said he's OK and didn't need it, but it's a rough neighborhood and I'm not comfortable with him being there alone.'

"I guess you still haven't learned anything about the enforcers?"

"No, but that's our next priority. John and Bob are headed out there now. It seems probable that these enforcers are staying somewhere near Nikiski. We're intensifying our search efforts out there. Randy is very busy in his new sideline and I'm afraid he'll be distracted and not see a threat coming his way."

"Sorry I can't spare any more manpower, Bill, but you know how it is right now. If you get into a bind, call it in and we'll send all on-duty officers to back you up. That is about all the promise I can make you at this point. Sorry, Pal."

"I understand and for what it's worth, I'm grateful for the promise. So far all we have is guesswork, but some of that has paid off when we learned Darleen was the 'lady banker' we've been hearing about. At least we know who the evidence is pointing at. We keep looking, Cap, and sooner or later we'll come up with some answers." It was time for Bill to join his men in North Kenai.

Bill was putting the finishing touches on his list of chores before leaving the headquarters building when his cell phone rang. It was Susan from the auto repair shop.

"Hello Trooper Koogan. This is Susan. I was wondering if you could come by the office for a couple of minutes," she said.

"I was just about to leave the office and I can stop if now is a good time."

"It would be perfect," she said.

Minutes later he drove into the small parking area beside the shop. As he walked inside, he looked around the area to see if there were any signs of a threat. There didn't seem to be any and he saw no signs of the Toyota Highlander near the business.

As he entered the shop, he noticed Susan was busy adding up the costs from a billing sheet she'd been working on. She looked up when she heard the door.

"Ah, hello, Trooper Koogan. Come in and have a seat."

She closed the file she was working on and looked out the windows to see who was in the area. She saw nothing that worried her in any way. "I just had a call from Darleen. She's on her way back from Anchorage. You said to let you know if I heard from her."

"Did she say she'd stop by the shop on her way through town?" he asked.

"Yes, she did. She said it was just to check on how business was going and to see if I needed anything. I told her things were just fine and I didn't need anything, but she said she was going to stop on her way through before going home."

"When do you expect her?" asked Bill.

"Said she was in Cooper Landing, and it would take her about an hour to drive here. That was almost a half hour ago. She should be here in about thirty minutes."

"I was about to go to North Kenai, but I'll hang out in town in case you need me. In fact, perhaps I'll just drop in while she's here; just to chat with her. I'd like to know where she's been the past couple of days."

"All this is very uncomfortable for me," said Susan.

"I understand, but without any evidence we can't arrest her. I will tell you that there are some things coming together in the matter. Just hang in there a little longer."

"OK, I have plenty to keep me busy until it does. Thank you for being so kind to me."

"It's what we do," replied Bill. "Just be extra careful about slipping up and telling her I've been here asking questions."

With that little warning he walked to his car and drove out of sight of the auto shop. From a block behind the shop, he could see the parking area and was watching when Darleen drove in. He waited another few minutes before driving to the shop, parking near her car.

Darleen noticed Bill as he walked to the office door.

Bill opened the door and stepped inside. He acted surprised when he saw her beside Susan's desk.

"Hello, Darleen, I saw your car out front and thought I should stop and see if everything was good here. I hadn't seen you around in a few days and was curious."

"Oh, hello, Bill. How have you been?"

"I've been just fine, thank you. Have you been out of town? I haven't seen your car around lately."

"Yes, I've been to Anchorage and Wasilla on personal business for a couple of days. Nothing important, mostly shopping," she lied. "Was there something specific you wanted to talk to me about?"

"No, mostly just curiosity. I'll get out of here, so long as you're safe and don't need anything." Bill was attempting to appear friendly.

"No, we're just fine," she explained.

"Well, just call if you need anything." With that short note he turned to leave the office. He could feel her eyes on him as he walked back to his car. Inside the patrol car he reached for the mic and reported he was on his way to Nikiski to meet with the rest of the Squad.

As he approached the Nikiski airport, he called Bob and John on his radio, "Where are you," he asked.

Bob answered, "Halibouty Road. We had a tip. Meet us out here. We'll wait for you to get here."

Bill drove to North with excitement building inside him. Was it possible they had found the enforcers? He also wondered if they had contacted Glen and Burt to also meet them. Then minutes he saw the marked SUV parked alongside the road and stopped behind it, got out and walked to the driver side window of the trooper vehicle.

"What's up?" he asked.

"Glen and Burt had a tip from an informant that some strangers had been staying in an old cabin out here. He said they were driving a new Toyota Highlander."

"That's good news. You men go ahead, and I'll follow you. How far?" asked Bill.

"Two miles," said Bob.

CHAPTER TWENTY-SIX

Bill followed the marked SUV down Halibouty Road to an old homestead road on the left side of the paved thoroughfare. It was badly grown up with tall grass and willows, indicating no one was living on the property on a regular basis. Burt and Glen were parked about a hundred yards into the drive and waiting beside their car. The three Squad members stopped and walked to where the two uniformed troopers were waiting.

"Are there any other residents in the area?" asked Bill.

"No, the man who owned this property died a couple of years ago and it's been abandoned since then. One of the locals from down the road likes to come out here to fish the lake, but he saw that someone was staying in the old homestead cabin and called us to report it. He and the old man who owned the place were good friends and the caller didn't think anyone should be using the cabin," reported Burt.

"I know this place," said Bob. "The old guy who lived here was a pilot and had a short runway just this side of the main house. He sold off all his old airplanes a long time ago. He was in poor health for a long time before he died. There's no other exit to the property, but if we continue walking on this driveway, they'll see us coming. I think we should split up into three units and hike through the trees until we get within sight of the cabin."

"That sounds like a good plan, Bob. You and John take the right side. Glen, take Burt. Swing over to the left and I'll go straight in but stay in the trees beside the road. Turn down the volume on your radios and we'll stay in touch by voice. Try to stay concealed until we're all in place with a view of the cabin. I don't expect them to comply when we ask for them to come out. Knowing their background, I think they'll put up a fight and we don't know what kind of weapons they have with them," Bill Koogan was directing the plan of attack.

"We should have them boxed in since there's a small lake behind the cabin and a swamp on the other side of the lake. The old man used to have a small boat behind the house, but it was gone the last time I was out here," said Bob.

"Good," said Bill, "We'll all work our way into position and when we're all set, I'll order them out of the house. Don't take any chances and stay out of sight if you can."

It was agreed, and the men went into the woods on opposite sides of the road. Bill stepped into the trees and walked directly toward the cabin. He stopped when he came to the edge of the trees near the front of the house.

He could see the Highlander parked alongside a woodshed near the house. He stepped behind a small spruce tree to conceal himself and wait for the others to reach their vantage points.

When the two teams reported they were in place, Bill shouted to the men inside the cabin. "You inside the cabin," he ordered. "Come outside and identify yourself." There was no response. Again, he called to the men in the cabin, "You men in the cabin, come outside where we can see you. This is the Alaska State Troopers. Come outside and identify yourself."

Still no response.

Glen Simms was the only one carrying a shotgun. Bill addressed him on the radio. "OK, Glen, pepper the front porch with buckshot." Bill drew his .40 Glock semi-automatic handgun.

"Five seconds," Glen replied.

The entire team counted down, "5-4-3-2-1" One second later a shotgun blast echoed across the lake. Still no response.

"OK, guys, cover me. I'm going to move closer. When I get close enough, I'll throw something at the front door." Mic clicks were his answer.

Bill moved through the trees until the view of the front door was obscured by the Highlander. He moved closer to the house using the Toyota as cover. Once in place he found a large stone he could pitch at the front door. He made a mental judgement on speed and arc of the throw and hurled it toward the door. It made a loud clunking sound as it bounced off the door, then fell onto the porch.

"Come out of the house with your hands raised," he shouted.

Seconds later the door opened a crack and the barrel of an automatic rifle, probably an AK-47, showed at the door. "Gun!" shouted Bill into his radio.

His voice seemed to be the signal for the rifleman to fire of a burst of gunfire. Then all went quiet. Bill waited about another minute before shouting another message to the men inside.

"We have food, water, and heat out here. We can wait longer than you men will be able to stand. Come out one at a time after throwing the weapon out the door."

Still no response from inside.

Five minutes went by until Bill called out again. "OK, men, have it your way. We can wait. This time of year, you don't even have the dark of night to use by waiting. We'll wait for you to throw out the weapon."

On his radio he warned the other team members, "There's probably more than one AK-47 in there. Be careful. We'll wait until they get nervous and decide to make a run for it."

In the woods to his left, Glen was changing the channel on his radio to ask for backup from more uniformed troopers. These are well-trained mercenaries and extremely dangerous. The extra help should ease the danger somewhat. However, it also presented the enforcers with more targets.

It seemed that no matter how many times you're involved in an armed stand-off, the tension was almost unbearable. And so, the waiting began. It was almost an hour before the back-up troopers arrived, staying out of sight, maneuvering through the spruce trees to meet the on-scene troopers.

Glen gave the new team instructions to be quiet and use the assigned voice channel on the radio to communicate with the other team members. Now they were all waiting. Their arrival boosted the number of troopers to ten.

An hour passed with no response from inside the cabin.

Bill selected another large rock to pitch at the front door. It too, clattered to the porch. Again, the door opened a crack and a gun barrel appeared and again another short burst of automatic gunfire erupted. This time Bill was ready and leveled his own weapon to fire into the cabin striking the door only an inch from where the gun barrel had been belching bullets. The door closed and again things went silent.

"I said throw out the weapons and come out with your hands raised. That hasn't changed," he shouted.

Again, there was silence.

Bill suddenly heard something behind him and turned to see what it was. It was one of the backup team belly-crawling toward him. When he was hidden behind the Highlander he sat next to Bill.

Bill knew the man well. "Hi, Bill, can I play with you guys?" he asked.

"Sure," replied Koogan. "Did you bring any toys?"

"Yup," replied the trooper corporal, "Right here," he said holding up a flash-bang canaster.

"Oh, wow," commented Bill. "Do you think you can put that close to the door?"

"Yeah, I brought a burlap bag to put it in so's it won't roll around when I toss it."

"Get ready and let me know when you are, and I'll pop a couple of rounds at the door."

Tony Faraday dropped the canaster inside the bag and felt around it to find the ring on the pin he'd pull to activate the explosive inside. "Are you ready," he asked Bill.

"Just say when," replied Bill.

"Now," said Faraday as he raised up to throw the bag at the front door, pulling the ring as he stood.

Koogan fired three shots at the door at the same moment Faraday threw.

Bill dropped back behind the Highlander as Faraday ducked behind the SUV. Seconds later there was an explosion and a flash of blinding light at the cabin's front door, blowing the door off its hinges and scattering debris into the cabin.

Two officers ran to the cabin from the left side. They approached the broken door and carefully peered inside. Acrid smoke and dust blurred the scene. Burt Taylor was the man doing the peeking.

"I don't see anyone inside," he said over his shoulder to Glen.

Just then there was movement in the rear of the room. Burt could see the movement behind a mattress at the back of the room. Suddenly there was automatic gunfire from inside the cabin. Bill stood behind the Toyota to fire into the cabin giving Glen and Burt time to run from the porch to the side of the cabin.

Bill turned to Faraday, "We need a rifle or another shotgun to shoot through the door. That mattress will protect them from pistol fire, but a heavy slug should penetrate and do some damage."

Faraday nodded and spoke into the mic clipped to his lapel, "Eddie, bring me a twelve gauge and some slugs."

About a minute later another trooper was crawling toward Bill and Tony. He handed the Remington shotgun to Tony, reached inside his shirt to retrieve a full box of slugs. "Do you want me to wait here, Tony?" he asked.

Faraday quickly surveyed the entire area, "The other side of that shed, see the big stump and stand of willow?"

"Yeah, I see it," said the trooper.

"Get one of the rifles and try to get to that position. With a rifle you should be able to take anyone shooting from or in line with, the front door. Be careful and keep low," warned Tony.

Inside the cabin the troopers could see movement behind the old mattress. They had pushed it up straight and propped it up with two kitchen chairs, giving them a small measure of protection and blocking the view from the outside. These men were adept at 'adapt and overcome' tactics.

"You know," said Bill, turning toward Tony, "With that mattress propped up like that and not much support behind it, the shotgun may not penetrate."

"I know, but that's why I sent Eddie to that other spot over there." He pointed with his thumb to the spot he had pointed out to the other trooper. The rifle has a higher speed and smaller diameter bullet and should penetrate the mattress. Me shooting at the mattress may let Eddie know where he is behind the padding.”

The two waited behind the SUV for a signal from Eddie that he was in place and ready. It took more than five minutes for him to get into place and signal Tony.

“OK, Bill, let your men know what we’re about to do. I’m going to disturb those guys with the shotgun slugs.”

Bill spoke into his radio to inform the rest of the team about the plan. Mic clicks gave the answer of understanding. Bill then made eye contact with Tony and nodded.

Tony rolled to his knees, then stood behind the SUV and fired two blasts into the mattress. The men inside moved around behind the barricade to avoid another round. Tony stood up and fired two more rounds into the mattress and again dropped below eye level to avoid giving the men behind the mattress a target.

A rifle barrel became visible over the top of the mattress. Faraday looked to where his man Eddie was positioned and signaled.

Eddie peered through the rifle scope and saw the gun barrel atop the mattress. It was moving as if someone were holding it to shoot but could see no human target. He adjusted his aim to where he guessed the rifleman should be located and fired two shots.

There was a loud scream from inside the cabin. There was also a loud burst of profanity heard from behind the mattress. Suddenly another rifle barrel appeared over the top of the mattress and fired blindly through the open doorway. It was a short burst and then went silent, disappearing once again.

Eddie had seen the movement and adjusted his sighting crosshairs to a lower point and slightly to the right, firing two more rounds into the mattress.

There was another loud scream, then silence. Bill waited for almost a full minute before calling out to the men inside.

“Hey you, inside. It sounds like we hit two of you. Throw out the rifles and stand up with your hands over your head.”

It seemed like an eternity before he heard an answer from inside.

“OK, OK. My partners are hit and need medical attention.” A rifle flew over the mattress as he was speaking, followed by two others. Now a head appeared as someone stood from behind the mattress. He placed his hands behind his head as he stood. “Get my friends some medical help, now!” He shouted, obviously disturbed by the injuries done to his partners.

Bill turned to Tony, “Order an ambulance,” he said.

Turning back to the person inside, Bill shouted, "OK, walk out onto the porch, keep your hands where they are."

The man stumbled over something and moved from behind the mattress shield. He moved slowly to the porch area and stopped. Bob and John were at the corner of the cabin and waited for him to step out. Once he was outside the two troopers leaped to the porch. With one trooper on each arm, they placed handcuffs on his wrists.

"My partners are wounded, get them an ambulance," he demanded.

Bill was walking toward the cabin, the Glock still in his hand. "It's on its way," he said as he walked past the prisoner and stepped inside the cabin. Faraday followed closely behind. They inched toward the back of the kitchen where the mattress hid the bloody forms of two men.

Bill kept the Glock pointed at them as Tony checked their condition. "This one's dead," he reported as he moved to the other wounded man. "This one is alive, but he needs medical help very soon. He grabbed a towel from the sink and pressed it to the man's chest to stem the bleeding.

Stepping back to the porch he looked at Bob, "Read them their rights and the two of you take him to the pretrial facility at Wildwood."

The rest of the troopers began to filter into the open area in front of the cabin. "We need to secure the area and search the other buildings. You men can clear the weapons and secure them for evidence." Bill directed the other troopers.

It was more than ten minutes before the Nikiski ambulance arrived and the skilled medics examined the two men on the floor of the kitchen. One was pronounced dead while three medics administered aid to the third. He was in extremely serious condition.

When the immediate flurry of medical attention had been taken care of, Bill contacted Tony Faraday. "Thanks for the help, Tony. Your men did an outstanding job of supplying what we needed when we needed it. You guys did a great job. We can handle it now, if you want to go back to the office and make your reports."

"I guess we'll do that, Bill. For what it's worth, I think your Geezer Squad handled the situation better than any of the new troopers could have done. It just proves, experience and wisdom are important commodities. I'm putting it in my report along with the other details. Good job, Bill. Tell your men we were impressed."

With one man in jail, two men shot, one dead and one sent to the hospital in critical condition, the crime scene photographed, evidence bagged and marked. This had been a very long day. Bill led his Squad back to trooper headquarters.

CHAPTER TWENTY-SEVEN

Randy Craig was still at the Nikiski airport. Bob and John were delivering the prisoner to the jail facility. Glen and Burt had gone to the hospital to guard the injured prisoner. Bill was left to report to the captain and complete reports about the arrest and shooting.

Bill went directly to the captain's office when he returned to the headquarters building.

"Were any of our men injured?" asked Captain Bradshaw.

"No sir, we were lucky. We were able to capture all three of the enforcers and I can tell you they are the same ones that kidnapped and killed the store manager the last time they came to town. One is dead, one is wounded and one is being booked into jail as we speak. It's going to take me a while to complete the report." Bill was speaking in a weak and tired voice.

"Have you interviewed the survivor you took to jail?" asked the captain.

"Not yet, but John and Bob are at the jail now and when the booking is completed, they'll try to interview the man. Our report from DEA gave us names, but we don't know which one is who yet. I still gotta call Randy and tell him he can come home now." Bill leaned back in his chair and stretched.

"OK, Bill, get some coffee and do your report. Call Randy and tell him to come back to the office. Then take the rest of the day off. I'll read the report in the morning. At this point I have to congratulate you and your team on a job well done." Captain Bradshaw reached over his desk to offer a handshake.

Bill stumbled to the coffee pot to pour a fresh cup of brew. Carrying it back to his desk he thought of someone else he should notify. He dropped into his desk chair and dialed Susan at the auto repair shop.

"Soldotna Auto Repair," she answered.

"Susan, this is Bill Koogan. I'm calling to let you know we just caught up with those men that were threatening you and Darleen. You can't say a word about this just yet, but one is dead, one is shot and laying in the hospital and one is in jail."

"Oh, that's such a relief. I can sleep tonight. Where did you find them?" she asked.

"In North Kenai. I can't say any more than that" advised Bill, "Have you heard from Darleen?"

"Not really. She left a message on my machine sometime last

night."

"I'd prefer you not tell her about the arrests but have her call me about the details."

"Whatever you say, Trooper Koogan."

"I've got to go now. I have a long report to write. I just thought you should know we took them off the streets. I think you can relax now."

Bill hung up the phone and took a sip of coffee. He picked up the phone again, this time to call Randy. It was answered on the second ring.

"This had better be good news, Bill."

"It is. You can come home now. We caught the three enforcers this afternoon." Bill went on to give a brief account of the arrests. "Get your stuff and come on back. We need you around here. We don't usually want you to gas the cars or handle our baggage, but if you would like to do some of that I can arrange it for you," Bill was chuckling.

"I'll be there as soon as I say goodbye to my new boss."

"Thank him for us, Randy. We'll have to impound the Cessna, but we can worry about that tomorrow. I'll need to speak with the DA about it in the morning. See you in a while."

He returned to his computer to begin translating all his notes into details of the raid and putting them into his official report. He'd been working on the report for more than an hour when someone entered his office. He turned around to see Randy standing in the doorway.

"Good to see you, Randy. Get a cup of coffee and come on back. I need a break anyway."

Bill stood, picked up his coffee cup and followed Randy to the coffee room. Back in the office he pointed to the other chair for Randy to be seated.

"OK, Boss. Give me the details."

Bill gave Randy a careful description of the events of the afternoon and complimented the uniformed officers sent to back him up at the old homestead. "Those boys did an outstanding job of aiding in the attack on the cabin. Faraday, the leader of the team, threw a flash bang at the door took it off its hinges. The men inside made a protective barricade with a couple of chairs and a mattress. When the smoke cleared, I pumped a couple of rounds into it. When they fired back the sharpshooter behind us used a rifle to shoot through the mattress. He killed one and wounded another. The third didn't want to play and was busy helping his wounded buddy when we came in. He's been taken to the jail facility in Kenai. All things considered, it went well and none of our men were injured."

"Has the one in jail talked at all?" asked Randy.

"John and Bob are still over there to try to interview him. These men are military trained, and I doubt he'll even give us his name. Who knows? Maybe he's had enough and wants out." Bill was shaking his head and shrugging his shoulders.

"Well, unless you need for me to do something, I'm going home."

"Yeah, go ahead, Randy. I'm going to finish my report, then I'm going home, too."

Randy left the office and Bill turned his chair back to face the desk and computer to finish the report. He was just wrapping up the final details when Bob and John returned.

"How did it go?" asked Bill.

"The only thing we got out of him was his name. He wanted a phone to call his lawyer. The corrections folks are keeping him in a single cell until he goes to court," said Bob.

"Did he give you the names of the other two?" asked Bill.

"Yes, he did. They must have been a close team for a long time. He was very emotional about his two friends. The one we booked into jail was Steve Town. The one wounded was Greg Swift and the one killed was Douglas Ritter. He wouldn't tell us where they came from or who he worked for." It was John Ashley giving the details.

"Did you advise the jail about their connection to Nick North?" asked Bill.

"No, we didn't. I guess we just never thought of it," answered John.

"OK, I'll call over there and let them know it could be a conflict. Go and do your report and go home. We'll cover the rest of the details in the morning. I'll call the jail and advise them about North."

Bill turned in his chair to put these new details in his report. When he was finished, he turned out the light and called it a day. He was totally exhausted.

At home that evening, needing to relax, he fell asleep in his reclining chair. About an hour later his wife awakened him. She was concerned for his welfare because it was rare for him to sleep while sitting in his chair.

"Bill," she said as she shook his shoulder. "Are you alright?" she asked.

He opened his sleepy eyes and said, "Oh, was I snoring?"

"No, but you were sleeping so sound, and I was worried about you."

"I'm OK, honey, I've just had a very stressful day. I think I'll go up to bed."

"Are you sure this job isn't too much for you? I know you like it, but I think it's getting to you. I don't want to see you getting sick because of your work."

"No, I'm fine. I didn't want to say anything to worry you, but we were in a shootout today. I wasn't in any danger, but it was stressful. It won't last much longer." Bill sugar coated the truth a little to pacify his loving wife.

"Well, don't you go and do something that will make you sick. I have enough to do around here as it is." She, too, was adjusting the truth so as not to worry him.

Bill climbed the stairs and fell into bed where he slept soundly until the alarm awakened him the following morning. When he came from the shower his wife asked, "Are you doing alright this morning?"

"Yes, I'm fine," he said as he went down the stairs to eat breakfast.

An hour later he was in the office reading reports Bob and John had written and left on his desk. They seemed complete and he forwarded them to Shirley for typing. He began to wonder when Darleen was going to call. He also was beginning to wonder if his wife was right in her assessment that the job was too much for him at this stage of his life. His thoughts were interrupted when his telephone rang.

"Trooper Koogan," he answered.

"Hello Bill, this is Darleen North. I had word you wanted to speak with me."

"Oh, hello Darleen. Yes, I want to speak with you, but I think my office is the place for us to meet. There have been some developments you should be aware of. Can you come to my office this morning?" he asked.

"Certainly Bill, can I come there now?"

"Actually yes, right now is a very good time. Everyone around me is busy and I am forced to wait until they get caught up. The girl at the front desk will bring you to my office."

"I'll be right over," she said.

Ten minutes later the receptionist brought her to his office. He greeted her and dismissed the receptionist. "Have a seat, Darleen. This may take a while to explain."

She sat in the other chair next to him. "Is something wrong, Bill?" she asked.

"No, but yesterday we had an incident you should know about," he began. "We had a tip about someone using an old homestead cabin on Halibouty Road. When we went to investigate, we found a vehicle, very similar to the one the men who threatened you had been using. When we arrived at the homestead, we tried to get them to come outside, but they wouldn't respond. We identified ourselves as troopers and they took a shot at us. We called for backup and more troopers came. Since they had automatic weapons, we decided to wait them out. We tried to talk them out but were met with no response. The short version of the story is that there was a gunfight. Two of the three men were wounded, one died, the other is in the hospital. The third man was taken into custody and was booked into the jail facility in Kenai.

"These men are ex-military and well trained. We've tried to interview the man we booked into jail, but he refuses to give us any information. I was wondering if you had ever talked with these men except for the time they came to your office and made threats to you and Susan?"

"Oh my, no. I have no idea who these men are," she explained.

"Hmmm, strange. Tell me, Darleen, do you know a man by the name of Gordon Tullis?" asked Koogan.

Her face flashed an instant of curiosity. "Why, no, should I?" she asked.

"I don't know, but his name has come up in recent days. He owns a used car lot here in Soldotna, and I thought you might know him. By the way, I was told you were out of town for a few days. Can you tell me where you went?"

"I just went to the city to do some shopping. Why do you ask?"

"Just curious, I thought you may have gone to Wasilla for some reason," said Bill in an off-hand manner.

"Why would you think that?" she asked.

"That's where Gordon Tullis is living, and I thought you may have gone to visit him."

Instantly anger flashed across her face. "Are you inferring I'm lying to you?"

"Oh no, Darleen. I'm just trying to make all the facts fit into some sort of sense," said Bill in a calm voice.

"Well, I don't like what you're inferring. Now if that's all, I think I should leave." She stood to leave the office. "I think the next time I speak with you I should have my lawyer with me." When she finished the short statement, she marched out of the office.

CHAPTER TWENTY-EIGHT

Darleen was angry and frightened as she left the trooper headquarters building. She opened her car door and sat in the seat without starting the engine, thinking of what to do next. She didn't like the tone Bill Koogan had taken in his conversation with her this morning. Did he know of her side business or was he just on a fishing expedition? She had been cautious and discreet in her dealings with local drug dealers.

Someone may have talked and given the troopers her name, but who would do such a thing? She had been careful to only deal with major suppliers and never with street dealers. It seemed likely Koogan was attempting to get her to admit to something but had no real evidence of her involvement in this business.

She started her car and drove away toward the auto shop. On her way she had a thought. She pulled into the parking lot of the local Dairy Queen, sitting, trying to sort through what she thought the troopers knew and what they were guessing. It was obvious to her that they suspected Gordon Tullis of something, but probably didn't know his full involvement with the drug trade.

Darleen also knew she was more vulnerable than Gordon, the man financing her involvement in the drug trade. The same question arose, "does he know what I do or is he just guessing?" If he knew, where did he get the information? If he's guessing, it means the troopers know about Gordon and are attempting to connect her to him. She was becoming more frightened and decided to call Gordon. She dialed his Wasilla number.

When he answered she wasted no time in explaining, "Hello Gordon. I just came from a meeting with a trooper who asked me if I knew you. He asked if I was with you this week. I don't know if he really knows about you or is just guessing, but he does suspect something."

"What did you tell him?"

"Nothing, I just left his office and called you." Her voice was weak and shaking.

"Calm down, Darleen. They don't know anything, or they would have arrested you. Go back to your office and wait. I'm going to be down there this afternoon and we can meet to discuss this. Have you heard from my men?" asked Tullis.

"The trooper said they had found them and were in a gun battle where two of the men were wounded and one of them died. One is in the hospital and one is in jail. Things are falling apart around me. We need to figure out what to do next." Darleen was speaking with desperation in her tone.

"Go to your office and wait. I'm going to drive to the Peninsula right now. I'll call you when I get to my home there. Try to stay clear of the troopers and don't talk to anyone. I'll call you when I get into town," said Gordon Tullis.

"I'm scared, Gordy," she said.

"We'll figure something out. Go back to the office and wait," he repeated.

Gordon, too, needed answers and decided to contact his local lawyer to investigate.

"Hello, Ben, this is Gordon. I have a job for you."

"What kind of job?" asked the attorney.

"I need for you to go to the jail and speak with Steve Town. He was arrested after a shootout out in North Kenai. Three of my men were involved. One is dead, Greg Swift is wounded and in the hospital, and Steve is in the Kenai Jail Facility. Talk to him and be his lawyer. See what you can find out about the case and what's been said to the troopers. Get Steve out on bail if it's possible."

"Who's paying?" asked Ben Little.

"Me, of course," was the irritated reply.

"OK, Gordon, I'll call and have him meet me in the attorney visiting room. This is going to take a lot of my time and it's going to be expensive."

"I expect as much, but I need to know what he told the troopers."

"I'll get on it right away and call you back when I learn anything," said the lawyer.

Gordon drove to his small log home overlooking the Kenai River near the Soldotna bridge. The house had not been occupied for many months and needed to be aired out and blinds opened. Gordon was tired and laid on the sofa to take a short nap and wait for the call from Ben.

Almost an hour later he was awakened by the telephone. "Gordon Tullis," he answered in a sleepy voice.

"Gordon, it's Ben. I just came from speaking with Steve Town. He said the troopers don't know anything. He and his partners were identified as the ones threatening your friend Darleen. He doesn't know how they found him, but it turned out to be a bad scene. They were arrested on the felony murder warrant and kidnapping charges when they took that liquor store manager away by force and killed him in Wasilla."

"I guess that's good news, but we need to get him out of jail on bail. See what you can do about that," ordered Gordon. "We also should find out what kind of shape Greg is in, at the hospital. This entire incident is turning into a problem for us. Darleen is frightened out of her wits, and I don't know if she'll be able to tough it out. If not, I'll find it necessary to replace her. I don't want to lose her because she is doing a great job. But she's scared and may be tempted to talk to the troopers. I can't have that."

"I don't want to know about any of that, Gordon."

"Just do your job and everything will work out," said Gordon.

"Anything else?" asked the lawyer.

"As a matter of fact, there is. These men leased an airplane and it's parked out there somewhere. We need to find it and have it sent back to the owner. I don't know where they have it parked, but someone in Nikiski should be able to find it."

"I have some contacts out there and I think I can find it without too much trouble. I'll ask Steve when I go back out to consult him about his bail hearing," commented Ben.

"Good, get back to me when you have something." With that comment he hung up the phone.

It was late in the afternoon and Tullis thought he should call Darleen. When they had talked earlier in the day, she seemed frightened and at a loss as what to do next. She needed reassuring and news of Ben Little coming on to represent Steve Town might be what it takes to cheer her up.

He dialed the number and she answered immediately. "Hold on a second while I go out to my car, and we can talk privately." She went silent for a couple of minutes before returning. "OK I can talk now. Do you have anything new you can tell me?" she asked.

"A couple of things, one is Ben Little is going to represent Steve in court. Steve will be arraigned tomorrow morning. They probably won't set bail at the arraignment, but there will be a bail hearing within a couple of weeks. I also asked Ben to go to the hospital and find out how Greg is doing. Have the troopers contacted you again?"

"No, not a word. I feel like they're guessing and hoped I would say something to confirm their suspicions, but I didn't."

"Just keep it that way. Don't talk to them at all. If they contact you, I want you to call Ben Little," Gordon gave her the telephone number. "Stay in town, but don't give them anything. Got it?"

"Yes, I have it. I have enough work to do here at the office to keep me busy for several days anyway."

"Good, stay at the office where they can see you and you should be just fine. As soon as I learn more about the shooting, I'll let you know what kind of plan I'm going to take. At this point I don't have enough information to make that decision."

Darleen relaxed a little, "OK. Gordon, call me when you decide. You know I'm with you all the way."

When she hung up the phone, she felt slightly relieved and walked back into the office.

"Is everything alright?" asked Susan.

"Yes, it's just fine. Just some personal business I needed to take care of. Is there anything I can help you with now?" asked Darleen.

"No, I'm almost caught up for today. That car in the shop has taken a lot of time and parts and it still has a couple of days work to do on it. Except for adding up the totals, it's slowed down the work crossing my desk. I just hope the car owner has a large balance in his checkbook," said Susan, snickering.

"Well, if you think you don't need me any more today, I'm going home and do some much-needed housework." Darleen, for once, was being honest with Susan.

Back in the trooper office, Bill Koogan and his men had finished their reports and made the phone calls to the jail and the court to speak with the DA about how to proceed. They learned there would be a bail hearing early next week. The DA, Walker, noted he was going to try to prevent a release on bail for any amount. He said his reasons for that approach was Steve Town would be a flight risk.

The next call was to the hospital to check on the wounded man Greg Swift. The nurse said she would have the doctor call them back as soon as possible. The four original Geezer Squad members, as well as the two new uniformed members, were drinking coffee in the conference room when the doctor called back.

"Trooper Koogan," answered Bill.

"Bill Koogan, this is Eric Winston from the emergency room. How the heck have you been? I didn't know you were back at work." Winston and Koogan had been acquainted for many years.

"Just temporary, Eric. How are you doing?"

"Busy, as usual. The nurse said you wanted information about the gunshot patient with the name of Greg Swift. Is that correct?" asked the doctor.

"Yes, it is, my men and I were involved in the exchange when he was shot. How is he doing, can you tell me?" Bill inquired.

"Yes, I can give you his medical status, but between you and me the prognosis isn't good. His wound was center chest and damaged his heart and left lung. In my opinion, even if he pulls through, he will be physically impaired and brain damaged from loss of blood to his upper extremity. I don't believe he'll make it, but if he does, he won't be able to speak again. Sorry I don't have better news, but those are the facts," answered Doctor Winston.

"We have a contract guard outside his door now, do we need to send a uniformed guard when he wakes up?" asked Koogan.

"That would be your call, Bill, but, like I said, I doubt he'll ever wake up. However, I'll keep an eye on him and if it looks as if he is coming around, I'll give you a call and you can make that decision yourself."

"Thanks Eric. I'm just trying to keep everyone safe. His two partners aren't a problem. One is dead and the other in jail. I'll be by to see you sometime soon." Bill hung up his phone and turned to the others.

"The doctor is a friend of mine, and he says the patients' outcome looks grim. He has a bad chest wound that caused a loss of blood to his brain and he may never regain consciousness or be cognizant again. Too bad, we may have learned something from him," explained Bill.

"We're not doing well with the witnesses in this case," commented Bob.

Glen Simms was next to comment, "I think Burt and I can help with that. Everyone on your list is high up the food chain in the drug business. There's one potential witness that might be tempted to talk."

"Who would that be?" asked Bob.

"Billy Forsythe," answered Burt. "He's a local scumbag and is on the run from the money man as we speak. If we can find him, we may be able to convince him to talk. All we need to do is find him and let him know we're better friends than those men we just killed and arrested. We've dealt with Billy in the past and he's a weak, spineless jerk that'll yield to pressure. The trick is to find him before another hitman does. Glen and I have several contacts in the drug business, some of them work for us. We may be able to find him."

"The captain has given us some latitude in our efforts and we're going after him, so sit back and relax, Team. The Geezer Squad is on it." The entire team laughed with Glen Simms.

CHAPTER TWENTY-NINE

Jake Vasilov was the undercover officer, looking like a criminal with scruffy beard, long hair, ratty attire, tasked with stopping at the little bar in Nikiski to inquire about the whereabouts of Billy Forsythe. Jake drove an old Volkswagen Bug with a headlight missing and fit the role he was playing very well. He parked in front of the bar and strolled inside.

The owner was tending bar, but since there were no customers, he was reading the newspaper and solving the daily crossword puzzle. He looked up when Jake entered. "Have a seat," he said to the new customer. "The one at the end of the bar is the most comfortable and right now it's open for you. What'll it be?" he asked.

"Draught beer," said Jake as he took the end stool.

"Where have you been? Asked the bartender as he drew the beer from the tap. "I haven't seen you in here in a long time."

Jake laughed, "I went to Fairbanks for a little vacation and got busted for a bar fight we had one night. I just got out and came back home," admitted Jake. "How have things been around here?"

"Quiet, except for two days ago,"

"What happened two days ago?" asked Vasilov.

"The troopers cornered some guys out on Halibouty Road and there was a big shootout. They killed one of the men and wounded another. I heard the third was in the Kenai Jail."

"Dang, I hadn't heard about that. What was the reason for arresting those guys?"

"I don't know all the details, but I heard they were wanted for the kidnapping and murder of a dealer in Soldotna. I never heard about that either. But then again, I live out here in Nikiski and it takes a while for news to get this far out the North Road." Both men laughed.

"Say, you just reminded me. Have you seen that Billy Forsythe around lately? He owes me a few bucks and I'd like to catch up with him," asked Jake Vasilov.

"He was in here a couple of days ago trying to get me to let him use my bar as a storefront for his drug sales. I ran him off. Haven't seen him since. He said he was going to go home when he left the bar."

Jake chuckled out loud, "Old Billy never was the brightest bulb in the chandelier," he said. "I guess I'll check out his house. He may be sleeping late."

"See ya later, Jake." Said the bartender as Jake stood to leave.

"If you see him before I do, tell him I'm looking for him." Jake waved goodbye as he walked out the door.

Outside, he sat in his VW for a while, thinking about where to look next and decided the house would be a good place to start. Ten minutes later he drove into the front yard. There was no indication Billy was at home, but Jake walked to the front door and knocked. There was no answer so he decided to take a walk around the property to see if Billy might be hiding in one of the outbuildings or somewhere on the large parcel of ground surrounding the house. He looked everywhere and wandered through the woods around the home. He found nothing to indicate anyone was living there at this time.

Using the trooper radio hidden in his VW, he called the office. "Dispatch, tell Trooper Simms I searched the property we talked about with negative results. I know of another property owned by this man's family. I'm going over there now to look around."

Further out the North Road, off to the left on a small lake and hidden in the spruce woods, there was a small log cabin with an outhouse, and a dock on the lake. There was no boat moored there and none could be seen on the property. Jake parked a short distance from the cabin and walked into the property. He could see foot tracks around the cabin as if someone was there recently. Jake kept low and walked around the cabin to learn if someone was inside the structure. He couldn't tell from the tracks if someone was still at the property and quietly stepped up onto the small back porch to check the door. It was locked.

He went back to the front and checked that door. It too was locked. Rather than trying the front door he called out, "Hey, Billy, are you in there?"

There was no answer, but Jake heard movement inside the cabin.

"Aw, come on Billy. I can hear you inside. I want a cup of coffee. Open the door, it's me, Jake."

A few seconds later the door opened a crack, and an eyeball could be seen looking out.

"Hey, Billy, what's the matter? Ain't nobody here but me."

A moment later the door cautiously opened, and Billy stepped out onto the porch. "C'mon inside Jake. I didn't know who it was."

Jake stepped out from behind a stack of firewood. "What's the matter, Billy? You seem awfully nervous."

"Yeah, I got some guys looking for me. I owe 'em some money and I can't pay 'em yet." His eyes darted around the area as he spoke. "Want some coffee?" he asked.

"Sure, I've been looking for you for a couple days to see if you got the money I'm owed. I guess by the way your speaking, you don't."

"Yeah, Jake, I'm sorry, but I've been running from these guys for a while and haven't had time to collect any cash. Don't get me wrong, I'm good for it. I just can't pay you now. I got instant coffee, is that OK?"

"Nah, Billy, forget it. Just let me know when you have the dough." With that he turned to walk back to his VW, then turned back again, "Say Billy. Did you know those men that were shot by the troopers?"

"Who were they?" he asked.

"I don't know for sure, but I heard they were hitmen from up around Wasilla and were down here to collect from someone who owed them a lot of money." He paused a moment, "Oh, my gosh, they weren't looking for you, were they?" asked Jake.

"I don't think so. I owe some money, but not enough to attract that kind of muscle. I'll get you your money in a couple of days. Let me know if you hear anything more about those hitmen."

Jake waved to him as he walked back up the drive to his VW. Inside the car he decided to back out and find a place to park where he could see if Billy left the property. In a secluded spot in the trees where he could sit and view the driveway to the cabin, he picked up the radio. He was about to key the mic when he decided to call Greg Simms on the cell phone.

"Trooper Glen Simms,"

"Glen, it's Jake Vasilov. I just had a conversation with Billy Forsythe. I shook him up a little, but he claimed he doesn't owe enough money to draw that kind of heat. I believe him. I think he may know who does fit the description, though. He didn't say who it was, but I made him nervous enough to want to talk with me the next time we meet. He's in an old hunting cabin out at Stickleback Lake. Give me a couple of days to get back with him."

"He may be the best lead we have right now. If you think you can turn him, I'll give you a few days to work on it. Is there anything new out on the North Road?" asked Greg.

"Not now. Everything seems peaceful. How about at the office?"

"Koogan is concentrating on Darleen North, but we think she's working for someone else. Except for financing local drug dealers, she doesn't fit the profile. We're keeping an eye on her. Stay in touch." Greg was disappointed his undercover man failed to come up with anything new.

In the jail, Steve Town and Nick North were in the same pre-trial dorm and became acquainted. Town knew North's wife was working for Tullis but said nothing to Nick. Being the intense individual he was, North had little use for men in the drug business. For the next two days they played cribbage and passed the time of day. The second day Steve Town asked North if he had ever heard of Gordon Tullis.

"No, can't say I have. Where's he from?" asked North.

"All over," replied Town. "He has a home in Wasilla, a home in Florida and one in Oklahoma. He's my boss and he's sent a lawyer to get me out on bail. I hope he's good."

"Good luck with that," said North. "Hey, you said this Tullis guy has a home in Oklahoma. Whereabouts in Oklahoma?"

"I don't remember, some small town outside of Okie City."

"That's where my wife's from, at least that area of the state. I wonder if they knew each other down there?" said Nick, thinking out loud.

"Wait a sec, Nick. Is your wife Darleen North?"

"Yeah, do you know her?" asked Nick.

"I don't know about in Oklahoma, but she knows him here. She's working for him, just like me."

"Oh hell, I've been the dumbest man in the world." With those words Nick hung his head in sadness. "I shot a man for nothing." It came out as a near whisper.

North sat a couple of minutes, saying nothing, before returning to his cell to be alone.

Town was still sitting at the table, playing solitaire when the floor officer came to get him. "You have an attorney visit, Town," said the female officer as she put the handcuffs and leg irons on him and escorted him to the attorney visiting room. Inside she removed the handcuffs and secured the leg iron to the wall ring. Once that was done, she escorted the lawyer to the small room containing a desk with two chairs, carpeted floor and good lighting. The door locked automatically when it closed, but only from the inside. When the lawyer finishes his business, he needs to use the telephone on the desk to call an officer to let him out of the small room.

While he waited to enter the visiting room, another officer inspected the briefcase he carried. Once security measures had been observed, Ben Little was admitted to the room.

Ben said nothing until the door had been secured and he was alone with the prisoner. "OK, Steve. I'm going to apply for bail and try to get you released. Gordon said he was going to put up the bail and have you released to him. I'd suggest you forget about jumping bail. Mr. Tullis would be much more dangerous to you than the troopers, if you get my meaning."

"I understand, and I don't plan to skip. I still have some work to finish for Mr. Tullis. I also have a good friend in the hospital I'd like to see."

This was the first chink in Steve Town's armor Ben had observed.

"Alright then, let's complete the bail request forms." They worked for more than an hour completing the request for bail forms. When they finished, Ben stood to stretch his back.

"OK, Steve, I'll take this to the office and have it all typed up and take it to the court. I'll let you know when the bail review hearing will be scheduled. Do I need to bring you a suit and tie?"

"Thanks, Ben. I don't want to go to court in an orange jump suit," replied Steve.

They discussed the sizes needed and Little called the guard to let him out of the visiting room. Another officer, the same female officer as before, came to take Town back to the pretrial dorm. Town was buoyed by the thought of getting out of confinement. He would still have to suffer the trial, but he could worry about that later. His thoughts went to curiosity as he wondered about the way Nick North had reacted to knowing Darleen North was acquainted with Gordon Tullis. Perhaps he could pursue that thought later when North came out of his cell to rejoin and mingle with the other prisoners.

It was almost dinner time when North came back to the common area and sat across the table from Town once again. He picked up the deck of cards and shuffled them as he looked into the Town's eyes.

"Is that lawyer of yours any good?" he asked.

"I don't know for sure, but he's going to try to get me out on bail."

"The next time you talk with him, ask him if he can get me out on bail. I have a public defender and he won't even try." Nick had a strange tone to his voice.

"I don't know what he can do, but I'll ask him to talk to you. Is there anything special you want me to ask him?"

"No," said Nick, "I just need to get out of here. The public defender said it could be six months or more before I get a court date. I don't want to sit in here that long. I have a business to run."

It was late in the day when the phone on Bill Koogan's desk rang, "Koogan," he answered.

"Bill this is Eric Winston at the hospital. I just wanted to advise you that our patient, your prisoner, just had a seizure and passed away. Time of death was fifteen minutes ago. Just thought you should know."

Bill exhaled in a loud manner, "I'm sorry to hear that, but you warned me. I'll be right over to relieve the guard. See you in a few minutes."

CHAPTER THIRTY

Bill drove to the hospital to meet with Dr. Winston and allow the guard to leave the hospital and go home. Eric Winston invited Koogan to his small office near the ER desk.

"Sorry we couldn't bring him around to make a statement, Bill. His wounds were just too severe. I really hate losing a patient, even if he's a criminal."

"I understand, Eric. I feel the same way. I just sent the guard home and all I need now is a written statement giving us the time of death and cause of death. Since he was in a doctors' care, we won't have to do an autopsy. You can release the body to the mortuary when you're ready. By the way did he ever make any statement at all?"

"No, he never regained consciousness."

Bill made a note in his notebook before turning back to Winston, "Has anyone been here to see him or called to ask about him?"

"I'll ask the people at the desk, but none I'm aware of," answered the doctor.

"OK, Eric, just send me a copy of the report when you finish writing it. Call me if anyone comes in to ask about him or calls to ask."

"I'll do that, Bill. See you later." With that he stood to return to his medical duties.

Bill had just returned to his office when John Ashley came in to tell him there was a telephone call for him. Bill picked up the phone and punched the flashing button.

"Trooper Koogan," he answered.

"Bill, this is Eric Winston at the hospital. I just had a visitor. It was the lawyer from Kenai, Ben Little. He was asking about one of my patients, Greg Swift. He wanted to know his condition and I told him I couldn't divulge that information. Little said he intended to represent
Swift if the troopers arrested him, as they had done with another of his clients. I told him he would have to get all that information from the troopers. I hope I did the right thing."

"You sure did, Eric, thanks. And thanks for calling me, also."

"Oh yes, one more thing, Bill. The nurse just reminded me there is a bag of personal items here and she asked what to do with the bag. I thought you might be interested in what is in the bag."

"I'm going to send you flowers, Eric. I'll be right over to get that bag. Leave it locked up until I get there just in case there is evidence inside."

Bill turned to John, "Come with me. I'm going back to the hospital to retrieve a bag of personal items belonging to Greg Swift. He's the patient who just passed away from gunshot wounds. Bring an evidence bag large enough to hold a hospital bag of clothing and personal items. We'll inventory it when we get back to the office. Let's go."

Bill drove his unmarked car with John riding in the right seat. Neither man spoke on the short trip to the hospital ER entrance. Together they walked inside to the registration desk and asked to see Dr. Winston. A minute later Winston opened the entry door to the ER treatment area.

"My nurse will take you to the lockers where we keep personal property. I have to get back to work. You've caused a major disruption in my schedule today."

"Thanks again, Eric. We'll talk later."

A young and pretty blonde nurse had been standing in the hallway. Dr. Winston motioned for her to come show the troopers where the bag was stored.

Ashley carried a large plastic evidence bag as the trio walked through a long hallway to a locked oak door. She had a key to open the door. Inside there were stacks of storage bins with locking doors on each front. The nurse found the number on the door of one of the bins noted in his hospital record and opened it with a key on her key chain. The bag inside was a large, white bag of personal items belonging to Swift. Even through the opaque bag they could see the blood from his clothing had covered one side on the inside of the bag.

John pulled the bag from the locker and placed it inside the evidence bag he had carried with him. She asked Bill to sign for the property and relocked the locker. John carried the bag as he walked back to the patrol car.

Outside the hospital, Bill turned to John and said, "It should be interesting to see just what he had in his pockets. We'll take the bag to the conference room and do an inventory."

Again, there was no conversation as they returned to the trooper headquarters. Once inside Bill ordered John to begin an inventory of the contents while he reported to the captain. He would rejoin John after speaking with the captain.

John and Bob had spread the damp clothing on the large table to air dry before returning it to the evidence bag once the inventory was finished. Each man had blue plastic gloves on their hands to handle the bloody garments. The shirt pockets contained one ball point pen, a small notepad, a pair of reading glasses and a bag of Skittles. The small items were placed in separate, smaller bags. The bloody shirt was left hanging on a hangar to dry to prevent molding. The shirt had damage on the left side of the buttons:

a single bullet hole.

A pair of combat style boots were inspected and bagged. White boot socks were folded neatly inside the boots, probably by a nurse. A 2-inch leather belt with a sturdy brass buckle was the next item out of the bag and inventoried.

The bloody cotton pants, Khaki in color, had a 34-inch waist and 31-inch inseam. This indicated Swift was somewhere around six feet tall.

With gloved hands, Bob emptied the pockets on the table. When the pockets were empty, they hung the pants to air dry along with the shirt.

The small pile on the table was topped by a leather wallet with a driver license issued to Gregory Swift by the State of Alaska. There were no photos in the wallet aside from the driver license photo. It contained $235.00 in cash. The last thing they found in the wallet was a corporate credit card in the name of Greg Swift.

These items were listed and bagged. In the other pocket was a large auto-opening, custom made pocketknife, with a blade nearly four inches long. Nothing else was found. No coins or change of any kind. These items were bagged too. All were tagged as evidence and placed in the evidence locker, except for the clothing which was hung to dry in a warm corner of the garage, which was always locked.

Bill returned as they were finishing the inventory. "Did you find anything interesting?" he asked.

"Not much," said Bob. "We hung the pants and shirt in the garage to dry the blood on them. The rest we placed in evidence. There is an inventory list in the locker, and we have one here. I found it interesting he had no metal coins in his pockets. I'm thinking he didn't want to rattle if he was running in a fight. These men are real pros. I would guess special forces of some kind."

"I think you're right, Bob," said Bill as he rubbed his chin. "I was just thinking about something Dr. Winston said. He said a lawyer had called to ask about Greg Swift. Since he had been Winston's patient, the hospital had forwarded the call to the Doc. Doc wouldn't give him any information and referred the lawyer to us. He may call here asking about Swift. We tell him nothing. The lawyer said he was representing the one we arrested and wanted to represent Swift also. I was just thinking about that and wondered if the lawyer, a guy named Ben Little from Kenai, was going to attempt bail for Steve Town?"

"Well, you know as well as me, the judge is required to set bail on everyone unless there are some extreme circumstances to prevent it," quoted John Ashley. "It's likely the judge will grant bail which he could set very high, making it less likely Town would skip. In my opinion someone else will put up the bail and Town will skip anyway."

Bill was again rubbing his jaw, "Randy, do you know what the mechanic did to disable the Cessna those three men parked in Nikiski?"

"Not specifically, but I think he took out some part in the magnetos."

"Is there some way we can talk to the mechanic?"

"I think I have his phone number in my notebook. Let me check." Reaching into his shirt pocket he found his notebook and placed it on the table. He wrote a number on one of the small pads on the table.

"Good," said Bill, "call him and ask if there is any way to start the engine without the parts."

"Don't worry Bill. I have a small plane and if there is any part of the magneto missing the plane won't start, guaranteed."

"That's good news. Now call your friend at the Nikiski airport and have him call us if anyone shows up to take the airplane." Bill leaned back in his chair, "This has been such a good day I think I'll buy lunch at Froso's."

"What time?" asked Bob.

"Thirty minutes," replied Bill. "I want to stop and have a word with Darleen North on the way."

Bill took his unmarked car and stopped at the repair shop. Susan was at her desk working diligently.

"Is Darleen around?" he asked as he entered the office.

"Oh, hello Trooper Koogan. No, she said she had a lot of housework to do and went home early. Is there something I can do for you?"

"No, I just wanted to talk with her a minute. I'll try to find her after I have lunch with my team."

As he drove the few blocks to the restaurant, he began to wonder why she would feel safe enough to go home and do household chores. This was very puzzling to the trooper.

In the restaurant a waitress brought menus and asked what each man wanted to drink. Before she could return with the orders Froso, the owner, came to the table to say hello.

"Well, hello. How are you all doing?" she said in a slight Greek accent.

"We are doing well, Froso. This is the only place no one will bother us. I think they look at us eating lunch like trying to take a moose bone away from a pit bull." Bill teased Froso and felt she was a true friend. She was not only very pretty she was a good friend.

No business was discussed at lunch, but good-natured banter was allowed. After lunch Bill paid the tab and told the other team members to go back to the office to wait. He was going to the North home to see Darleen North before returning to the office.

Her little white car was parked in front of the house. He stepped up on the front porch deck and rang the bell. Moments later Darleen answered.

"Trooper Koogan," she said in a surprised voice. "Come inside, would you like some iced tea?"

"Oh, no thank you, Darleen. We just finished lunch and I'm stuffed. I just wanted to check with you to see if you had received any other threats since these three men are out of service?"

"No, and I have been more relaxed. That's why I took this time to clean my house. I haven't done anything in here since I got home. I've been too worried and upset."

Bill let her finish before issuing a warning about complacency.

"I think the danger is over, Bill. Nick is in jail and so is the last of the enforcers you were looking for. I think I can relax a little bit now." Darleen seemed to be in a cheerful mood and without stress.

"OK, Darleen, it's your choice. I just came by to check on you to be sure."

"Thank you very much for your concerns, Bill, but I think the danger is over." She held out her hand for Bill to shake.

As he drove back to the office, he couldn't help but wonder why she would think the danger was over. He knew there could be other possible enforcers out there somewhere. When he returned to the office, he went to his small office to think about what had taken place. It puzzled him deeply. He was still in the little office when his desk phone rang.

"Trooper Koogan," he answered.

"Bill, this is Sergeant Lewis, at the pretrial facility."

"Oh, hi there, Don, what's up?" asked Bill.

"I'm not quite sure. I just thought you might be interested to know the lawyer representing Town just came in to see Nick North. It just seemed strange to me, and I thought I should pass this bit of information on to you."

"That is interesting, Don. Thanks for letting me know about it."

Bill noted the time and made a note in his notebook. When he finished, he went to the conference room to confer with the rest of his team. He called Glen and Burt asking them to join them. It was time for a brainstorming session.

CHAPTER THIRTY-ONE

"Got anything new for us, Glen?" asked Bill as the two uniformed officers entered.

"Not much," answered Glen Simms. "Our undercover man out there found Billy Forsyth and is still sitting in the car to see where he'll wander off to. What about your men?"

"I have a couple of things," said Bill. "First of all, a lawyer by the name of Ben Little has been out to see Steve Town. Of course, we don't know what they talked about, but I'm guessing it was about getting a bail hearing. The second thing was just reported to me by the jail. Lawyer Ben Little has just asked to see Nick North. Why would he want to see North?"

"It seems we are doing an awful lot of guessing in this case," said Burt Taylor. "But if I were to guess, I would say North was looking for some way to get bail too. We talked to the DA, and he said North wanted to know about bail, but the Public Defender refused to ask for a hearing. That would be my guess."

"The only one willing to put up bail for Town, in my opinion, would be the man who hired him in the first place. We still don't know for sure who that person is." This observation was made by Randy Craig.

Burt Taylor was the one to answer, "Our man in North Kenai found Billy Forsythe at an old hunting cabin on Stickleback Lake. He asked Billy about any threats. He said he owed some money, but not enough to justify a response that heavy. What if Billy is the one the enforcers are looking for. If our man found him, then the enforcers will be able to do it, too. There is only one of them left, but he has the skills to do the job himself. If Town gets bail, I think he'll find Billy and finish what they came to do. I don't know how Nick North fits into this, but as far as I know, he never knew these three hitmen until North met Town at the jail."

"So, you think Billy will be the next victim?" asked Bill.

"If our assumptions are correct," added Burt.

"Do we have any probable cause to pick up Billy?" asked Bill.

"No, we don't," answered Greg. "We suspect he's attempting to establish himself as the biggest dealer in North Kenai, but we have no real evidence to prove it."

"You may be on to something," offered Bob. "If Billy got in too deep with the financier and couldn't pay, he may be the one Town is gunning for. Billy may have figured this out and wants to find a way to pay his debt before it's too late. If that is the case, we need to keep a close eye on both Town and Billy Forsythe. We need to find out who hired Town and his partners and close his shop for good."

"OK, we should try to confirm some of our suspicions. Let's start with finding out if and when, there will be a bail hearing for Town. Do the same about Nick North. In my opinion, if North makes bail, he'll attempt to get even with his wife, Darleen," this came from Bill Koogan.

"That makes sense to me," said John. "This guy has an explosive personality, as we witnessed when we arrested him. I don't know if I'm the only one who suspects Darleen is fooling around with the man she's working for, but she's spent time with him at almost every home he owns, including here in Soldotna. I'll bet money she spent time with him in Oklahoma as well as Wasilla, recently."

"That may be the only reason he's wanting to try for bail. I think we should have the DA keep an eye on his calendar to watch for bail hearings for both Town and North," advised John.

"I think you could be right about this, John," stated Bill. "Glen, will you and Burt keep an eye on the court calendar for us?"

"We can do that. I think we can also keep an eye on Billy Forsythe to see if he begins to move around," said Burt.

"It's time everyone took some time off. Fishing season goes almost another month out in Bristol Bay. That means we're going to be here a while yet. Just stay in touch with me here at the office if you leave town or go fishing away from phone service." Bill knew his men were working long hours and were deep into solving this case. Sometimes those very things are a detriment to family life and Bill was determined to prevent that from happening, if possible.

Koogan finished writing his report and checking it for errors when he thought it was time for him to have a visit with Darleen North. He dialed the number for the repair shop and Susan answered. Hello, Susan, is Darleen there?"

"Sorry, but she said she had some housework to do and went home. Is there something I can do for you?"

"No, but thanks. I have a couple of things I need to speak with her about. Is everything alright there at the shop?"

"Yes, we're very busy, but no problems to complain about. The customers seem more pleased with the service than when Nick was here."

"That's good to hear, Susan. I'll be by to see you soon."

Bill hung up the phone and was about to dial her number when he had another thought. He could take a chance on her being at home and perhaps visit with her on a personal level without creating suspicion on her part. He stood and stretched his back before strolling to his unmarked car. Minutes later he drove into the drive and stopped in front of the deck, now covered with potted plants in full bloom. He stepped up onto the deck and rang the bell. He heard her footsteps coming to the door.

When the door opened, and she saw who was there, she smiled. "Trooper Koogan, please come inside. Would you like some iced tea or something?"

"Oh, no thanks, Darleen. I hadn't seen you for a few days and thought it was time to see how you are doing."

Again, she smiled, "I'm just fine, Bill. I've spent so much time at the office I left a lot of housework undone. I thought it was time for me to take the time to clean the house."

Bill returned her smile, "I'm curious, have you heard from Nick?"

"No, not a word. That's strange, too, because he was always calling me from the shop when he was working. Have you talked with him?" she asked.

"No, I haven't. The last time we tried to speak with him he refused to see us. I got word he was trying to hire a different lawyer, though."

"I feel sorry for him, Bill. He really is a nice man, but he gives everyone the impression he's a mean guy. He used to be fun and happy, but since he started the shop, he's changed. I hardly recognize him these days."

Bill smiled again, "The important thing right now is to keep you safe and comfortable. I'm sure it'll be rough for a while, but when it's all over and done, you'll be able to relax and reroute your life in another direction. Hang in there, Darleen."

"I thank you for being so kind to me, Bill. It just seems like it will never end." Her eyes were sad as she spoke.

Bill turned to make his exit, then turned back to her again. "Say, Darleen, there's a fella who owns a car lot over toward Kenai and I heard he owns a home in Oklahoma. Do you know him?"

"Oh, you must mean Gordon Tullis. Yes, he lives very close to where my family is living. The town is small, and I bump into him often when I'm visiting my family. Why, is he involved in something I should know about?"

"Nothing I'm aware of. I was just curious. I just learned he owns a home here on the river and I wondered if you knew him."

"Yes, I know him, not well, but I know him. We have lunch together on occasion."

"Well, thanks again. I should get back to the office. Call if you need anything." He stepped out onto the deck, into the sunshine, and turned back to wave goodbye to the lady in the doorway.

As Bill drove out of the driveway, Darleen thought she should call Gordy and let him know Bill had asked about him.

Gordon Tullis was a very busy man with so many irons in the fire it was difficult to know which one he was dealing with at any given time, even for Gordon. When his phone rang, he answered. It was Darleen.

"Hi Gordy, I just wanted to tell you Trooper Koogan was just at my house and he asked if I knew you. I told him I did. Of course, I didn't tell him we were working together."

"What kind of questions did he ask?" inquired Tullis.

"Nothing very important, just that he heard you owned a house in the same town as my folks are from and said he just learned you had a home here in Soldotna."

"That was all?" inquired Tullis.

"Yes, that was all. Like I said, nothing important."

"Darleen, those people don't ask about people unless they are looking for some specific information. You shouldn't be talking with him unless he has information you want to learn. Stay away from him from now on. I'll let you know when Steve is going to court. Until then I want you to keep a low profile. If we can get Steve out on bail, he can take care of your problem child in Nikiski, and we can get away from here for a while. I want you to be very careful."

"I look forward to getting away from here, Gordy. Maybe we can take a little time for ourselves when this is finished. I miss you." She hung up the phone and wondered if she had said anything to Koogan that would incriminate either Gordon or her.

Things were quiet at the trooper office for the next couple of days and Bill was able to catch up on his list of reports. He was in his small office when Burt Taylor knocked on his door.

"Come on in, Burt. Want some coffee?" asked Bill.

"Oh, no thanks, Bill. I just came to tell you a bail hearing was set for Monday on Steve Town and Thursday for Nick North. It looks like that lawyer, Little, has been very busy."

"Did the DA say anything about the outcome of the hearings? Or at least his best guess," asked Bill.

"Nope, he only said the judge would probably set bail for both men but make the amount so high they can't post it."

"Hmmm," said Bill, "Nick probably can't make it, but Town has someone backing him and he might. I think we should plan on Town getting out and going after his target in North Kenai. Is your undercover man still watching the cabin?"

"Not full time, but he reports that Billy Forsythe is still out there."

"I think I had better call a couple of my team back to help keep an eye on Billy," announced Bill.

"Jake could sure use a break, Bill. I think he would like to have the help. I'll let him know," said Burt as he turned to leave the office.

When he was gone Bill picked up his own phone to call Randy Craig and John Ashley. Randy was the first call.

"Randy, Bill Koogan, I need you to come to the office in the morning for a little stakeout duty. I'll call John to come in to spell you and there's an undercover man out there now. We suspect Steve Town may make bail on Monday. I think you can take the rest of the weekend off after I brief you regarding the surveillance. See you in the morning."

The next call was to John Ashley with the conversation going almost word for word like the one he had just completed with Randy. When he finished, he leaned back in his chair and stretched his aching back. It was time for him to take a few days off too, he thought.

He decided to keep this information private and not go to the auto shop to warn Susan. The trap had been baited and he wanted to keep any strange scent away from the bait. However, Bill decided it was going to be his job to keep Susan and Darleen safe from harm when Steve Town was released, assuming the judge did release him. Everything seemed to be a wild guess with peoples' lives at stake.

CHAPTER THIRTY-TWO

The weekend had been quiet. Jake Vasilov reported Billy Forsythe had only left the cabin one time to go to the grocery store. Jake was glad he was getting some relief with this stakeout. It had been a boring several days watching the cabin with only occasional sightings of Billy going outside to walk around the grounds.

On Monday Steve Town was taken to court for a bail hearing at 10am. The hearing lasted only about fifteen minutes with the judge having the last word.

"Having heard both sides, I have concluded that in accordance with state statutes, a bail amount should be set in this case. I set bail for the defendant Steve Town at $500 thousand dollars. Cash only."

With that short statement he stood, organized his papers, and left the courtroom,

Ben little turned to his client, "I'll call to see if it can be arranged. I'll get back to you as soon as I get an answer."

Town said nothing, but nodded understanding. A uniformed trooper transported him back to the pretrial facility to await his answer. It came an hour later when he was escorted to the lawyer visiting room to see Ben Little.

"I was able to get the court to take a cashiers' check for the bail. Get your stuff ready and get dressed to leave. I'll wait outside for you and I'll drive you to my office. Our boss has some instructions to pass on to you."

Town was escorted back to retrieve his few personal belongings, then escorted to the front booking area where he was given his personal clothing and other items taken from him during the booking process. He signed the paperwork facilitating his release and was escorted to the front entry where he was released.

Lawyer Ben Little was waiting in the parking lot across the street from the main gate to the jail. There wasn't much conversation on the short drive back Ben Little's office in town, where the men had a private conversation.

"Our boss wishes for you to complete your task as quickly as possible. We've learned the location of the target by having someone follow him from a grocery store in Nikiski. He's not the brightest individual and he's being sought by the troopers. The Boss wants you to take care of him then fly the plane back to Wasilla where he'll have a vehicle waiting at the airport. He'll contact you in a couple of days and arrange for your trip back to America where you can get lost for a while. Your payday will be in the vehicle. This is the key you'll need to enter the vehicle. Any questions?" asked Little.

"No, none. What about Greg?"

"I can't answer that. I tried to get information from the hospital, but they refused to answer any questions about his condition. If he is released, I'll do my best to get him bailed also, but at this point I don't know anything."

"OK, give me the location of where to find this person and I'll do the rest," said Town. "I'll need wheels to finish my work here."

"Behind my office is a green Chevy pickup. It's full of gas. You can leave it at the airport when you leave."

Steve Town stood to leave, "Thanks for getting me out. I probably won't see you again," and put out his hand to shake with the lawyer.

At a local pawn shop Town found a large belt knife and a smaller fixed blade knife suitable for concealment. He paid cash for the weapons and carried them to his pickup. Both knives were suitably sharp, but he wanted a slightly better edge on each. He stopped at a local hardware store to buy a good stone to hone the edges. Sitting in his pickup listening to country music, he spent more than two hours on the blades. He strapped the sheath for the large knife onto his belt while using some cardboard to make a holster he taped to the inside of his shirt in the center of his back. This would be his backup weapon if he needed one.

He had read the directions given for the location of his prey and found the home, Billy Forsythe's home, deserted. Frustrated, Town drove around the area to see if there was another hideout in the vicinity. He found none. Rather than waste more time he drove to the Nikiski Airport to check out the Cessna they had parked there. He did a basic walkaround to find the airplane was still undamaged and ready to fly. He went to the office and found Randy Craig at the desk.

"Hello there," said Town. "The Cessna over there," he pointed with his thumb, "My friends and I parked it there and I'm going to leave soon. I'd like to pay for the parking. Can you add up my storage bill so's I can pay you?"

"Sure, let me find the invoice with the rate and I'll add it up for you." Randy went to a file cabinet and found the file containing the rental agreement. "Ah, here it is. Give me a minute and I'll add it up." He pecked at the keys of an old adding machine and finally came to a total which he wrote on the paper. "Let me make a copy of this for you," said the busy Randy. He came back to the customer and handed him a copy of the totaled-up invoice.

Town looked at the invoice and said, "I think you should add on two more days for good measure. I have a couple of things to do before I can leave, and I want to be paid up if I decide to leave when no one is around the office."

"Sure thing, let me add two more days and I'll make you a new copy." More clicking of the calculator keys and another copy of the receipt was made.

"Will cash be alright with you?" asked Town.

"Yup, we still take U.S. Dollars. Give me your copy and I'll mark it paid."

Town counted out several hundred-dollar bills and placed them on the counter with an extra one for a tip.

"Thanks for keeping an eye on the plane for me," he said.

"Thank you, too. You can park here any time. By the way, do you need fuel before you leave?" asked Randy.

"No," replied Town, "I'm only going to Anchorage on my first leg home, but thanks for offering."

Randy watched from the office window as Steve Town walked to his truck. Luckily for the trooper, he didn't attempt to start the engine while he was inspecting the airplane.

When the truck drove away, he turned toward Nikiski as he left the dirt airstrip.

As soon as the pickup was out of sight, Randy called Bill Koogan. When he answered Randy related his dealings and conversation with Steve Town. "Do you want me to follow him, Boss?"

"No, I'll send Bob out to do that work. Just stay at the airstrip in case he decides to come back. Thanks for the call, Randy."

Bill decided he should go out to Nikiski to back up Bob in case of trouble. He contacted Bob and explained the situation and told him that he would be his backup. Next, he called Glen Simms.

"Glen, Town just did a preflight on the Cessna and told Randy he had some business to tend before leaving. Randy watched and he turned toward Nikiski. I just sent Bob out there. I'm leaving right now to join him. Is there a way you can contact your undercover officer to let him know what's going on?"

"Only if he's in his car alone. But I can try. If I reach him, I'll have him call you on your cell phone. You can explain the situation. I think he's still watching Billy at Stickleback Lake."

"Good, have him call me. I'm headed that direction now."

Twenty minutes later bill arrived in Nikiski to begin looking for Bob. He was about to call him on the radio when his phone jingled.

"This is Jake Vasilov. Is this Koogan?" asked the voice on the phone.

"Yes, it is. Are you still on lookout duty?" asked Bill.

"Yeah, I am. Do you know where this lake is located?"

"Not exactly, give me some directions. I'm in front of the fire station right now," Bill answered.

Jake gave him directions to the lake and the cabin. "I'm in my VW in a stand of spruce and willows on the small hill across the main road from his cabin. I hate to move for fear of being spotted."

"That's OK, I'll find a place down the road to park and watch for the green Chevy pickup our man is driving. I'll try to find a spot like yours where I can sit and watch. We can talk on the phone without much danger of being noticed. I'll let you know when I get into place."

"A quarter mile from here, in the direction of town, there's an old sideroad. There is a big rock at the entrance to the road. No one lives on that road these days. That might be a good place to watch the main road," Jake advised.

"Thanks, I'll watch for the place. I'll be in touch when I get set up. I have another man out here looking for the pickup. I'll let him know where I am in case we need another backup." Bill then hung up his phone and began the boring job of stakeout. He placed his notebook on the seat and made a note of the time and his location. It would be a long wait and a boring afternoon. Two hours later he called Bob on the trooper radio.

"Bob, I could use a cup of coffee. Can you get me one and bring it out here?"

"Sure, Bill, do you want a sandwich to go with it?"

"No thanks. Are you in the van or the unmarked car?" asked Bill.

"The unmarked car. Why?" he asked.

Bill gave him directions to the short sideroad where he was parked. "You can drive in and park behind my car. This spot is well hidden and above the road. I don't think they'll see us up here."

Half an hour later Bob arrived with the coffee in a quart thermos bottle. The two men sat in Bill's car and waited. It was after ten at night when a dark green Chevrolet eased its way down the main road. It stopped at the entrance to the cabin. A man stepped out of the pickup to look around. They waited as the driver, who both troopers recognized as Steve Town, walked down the edge of the short driveway to the cabin. Town walked to the back of the cabin and returned to the front, attempting to see through the window to the inside. There were no lights inside the cabin.

Town stood and watched the cabin for several minutes before stepping up onto the porch. Quietly he moved to the window to peer inside. He crept to the doorway and tried the door; it was apparently locked. Town took a large knife from his belt and inserted the tip of the blade into the edge of the door near the latching mechanism. With a quick twist of his wrist the door pushed open. There was a loud shout from inside the cabin as Town rushed inside.

Bob and Bill jumped from the patrol car and ran down the hill to where the cabin was located. Jake did the same from his vantage point. As they approached, they could hear sounds of a scuffle inside. Bill motioned for Jake to take a position between the pickup and the cabin.

Bill and Bob ran to the cabin porch, guns drawn. They could hear Billy pleading with his attacker. Bill took the lead and motioned for Bob to remain on the porch while he went inside and called out to Town.

"Drop the knife," shouted the trooper.

The order was ignored, and Billy continued to scream and struggle with his attacker.

Billy was much smaller than Town but was frightened and struggling furiously. He was making it difficult for Town to keep a hold on his prey and still put the knife into him. The distraction of the trooper shouting orders at him was enough to make him stop his attack on Billy and turn his attention to the trooper holding a gun. He turned loose of his victim to reach behind his head to get his second fighting knife. With a smooth swing he pulled the knife from his collar and threw it in the direction of Bill, who saw the motion and fired his weapon, striking Town in his left shoulder. The impact spun him slightly and he dropped the weapon he was holding with that hand. The knife he had thrown narrowly missed Bill and stuck in the door beside him. Bill rushed to the wounded man and snapped a handcuff on his good arm, taking him to the floor to grasp the wounded arm.

Bob heard the commotion inside the cabin and ran to the open door. Bill was on the floor struggling with handcuffing Town. Billy was attempting to get out of the cabin through a window at the rear of the room. Bob immediately gave Bill the assistance he needed to subdue Town.

Billy made it out the window and ran around the cabin toward the road where Jake Vasilov was waiting and ordered him to stop or be shot. Still frightened, Billy lost all sense of what he should do and fell to the ground, whimpering like a child.

"It looks like you broke your conditions of release, Steve. As soon as we get you bandaged at the hospital, we'll be taking you back to jail," said Bill in a calm tone.

He called out to Jake, "Jake, is everything alright out there?"

"Yes, just fine," replied Vasilov.

"I just called for some backup and help transporting these men. When the ambulance arrives, I'll send Bob with them to the hospital. I'll take young Billy here, to headquarters to make a statement. After all, he is a victim."

Jake was shaking his head, "You know, every time I get to liking a place, something like this happens and I wind up getting transferred."

An hour later Bob climbed into the ambulance to take his prisoner to the hospital for his shoulder wound, which looked very bad. The medics said they thought the shoulder joint was shattered.

Bill transported Billy to headquarters and took his statement. In the process he admitted he had been dealing drugs and expanding his business. This part of his statement would be the basis of his arrest.

CHAPTER THIRTY-THREE

Town was treated in the hospital emergency room where doctors determined his shoulder would need surgery to repair the damaged joint and tissue. Bill waited outside the operating room until the surgery was completed and Steve Town was taken to recovery. The surgeon met with Bill to give him a report and update.

"You made a good shot, Bill," said the doctor. "We stopped the bleeding and mended the torn tissue as best we could, but the bone was shattered. We were able to find a titanium shoulder joint to replace the damaged one, but it's not an exact size to match the broken one. He may have trouble with the new one for quite a while, but it'll heal. He'll be able to use it. It'll never be as strong as the original, but he will have use of the arm and shoulder."

"How soon can we move him to a cell at the pretrial?" asked Bill.

"I can't answer that right now, but it's going to be a while," explained the doctor. We can put him in the ICU while he heals and recovers. We can keep his room private there and your guard will be able to lock the door, if necessary."

"Thanks a lot Doc. This is a very dangerous man. We know he killed one man and was in the act of trying to kill another when he was shot. I'll recommend we keep two guards at the door, but it may not happen. I'll stay with him until you take him upstairs. I like the ICU idea though."

"I'll make a note for the nurses to be cautious when treating him," said Doctor Morton. "I'll check on you and him as often as I can. Is there anything I can get you before I leave?"

"It looks like it will be a long night, perhaps some black coffee to keep me awake. I don't know when my relief will get here."

"Well, if you need anything, just ask the nurse on duty. I don't expect him to awaken until morning, but we'll be checking on him and we'll monitor his vitals regularly. See you later, Bill."

It was early the following morning. Bill was still on duty outside the recovery room when two nurses came to take the patient to the ICU. He was heavily sedated and had not yet awake after surgery. Bill tagged along as the bed was loaded onto the elevator and taken to the second floor where the Intensive Care Unit was located.

The nurses kept a close eye on the patient as he was moved to the new room and plugged into monitoring devices. An oxygen canula was placed around his head to feed enriched air into his lungs. Bill watched from a spot near the door as the nurses performed their duties and checked all the equipment. Once finished, they returned to the front desk to address other patients. Bill would sit inside the room as long as Town was still sedated. It was time for breakfast when Bob Barratt came in to relieve him.

"Good morning, Bill. Did you have a good night?" asked Bob.

"Yes. Long, but good. He's still sedated and being monitored from the front desk. The nurses check on him quite often. I'm glad you're here. I'm getting a little sleepy. I think I'll go to the cafeteria and have some breakfast before I go home. Call me if you need anything. By the way, did you get Billy booked into the jail?"

"Yes, and I think he was happy to be in a safe place. Get some rest and we can talk later," said Bob, noting his boss looked very tired.

Bill went downstairs and ate an omelet in the hospital dining room. He drank only half his second cup of coffee when he realized he was extremely tired. The drive home seemed to take forever. When he arrived, he said hello to his wife and went directly to bed. He slept for nine solid hours.

After his shower and change of clothing he went to greet his wife. "Good morning, Honey," he said.

"Good morning to you, too. It was a long day, wasn't it Dear?"

"Yes, it was. I shot a suspect last night and had to sit with him at the hospital. I think I'm getting too old for this work," he commented as he sipped his first cup of coffee.

"Hopefully it will be over soon, and you can rest up."

"I hope so, too. We have a good team, but the crimes are getting more serious and more complicated all the time. I'll be happy to give it all back to someone else. I think this'll be the last time I volunteer." It was difficult for Bill to admit he wasn't as young or vibrant as he once was. He wondered if the other members of the Squad felt the same.

When he entered the office, he stopped to see the captain to let him know his report would be ready in about an hour. He also noted he'd go to the jail to speak with Billy Forsythe to see if he could learn who was financing his growing drug sales business.

It was late afternoon when he finally finished the paperwork and climbed into his patrol car to drive to the jail facility. He signed in and went into the secure portion of the booking area. He told the shift supervisor he wanted to speak with Billy Forsythe in the attorney visiting room. An officer went to the back to bring Billy out for the interview. He was chained to the wall as others had been and seemed to be relaxed in this surrounding.

"How are you doing, Billy," asked Bill.

"I'm OK, but I gotta tell ya, I'm in a dorm with Nick North. I don't want him to find out his wife was financing me. He's mean and would probably kill me."

"You're in the same dorm as Nick North?" asked a surprised Koogan.

"Yeah, and he said that guy Town had just been released on bail and he has a bail hearing tomorrow. I don't want to stay in the same dorm with North. He scares me."

"I'll see if I can get you moved," said Bill. "You just said Darleen North was putting up the money for your expanding business. Last night you didn't want to talk with anyone about that. What changed your mind?"

"Nick North. He scares me. If he knew I was doing business with his wife, he'd kill me in a minute. I don't want him to find out," Billy was speaking in a frightened tone. "Get me moved and I'll tell you anything you want to know," he said.

"Sit still and I'll see what I can do." Bill stood and picked up the telephone to be let out to speak with the shift supervisor. Minutes later he reentered the visiting room to tell Billy he was about to get a new room in segregation until after the bail hearing tomorrow. Billy gave a huge sigh of relief.

"Now, I want you to tell me how Darleen North works and how you got involved with her."

"It ain't a pretty story, but I'll tell you." Billy paused and asked, "Can I get a cigarette?"

"Sorry, Billy, there's no smoking in the jail these days. Now, what's the story about Darleen North?"

"If I tell you, will you tell the judge to go easy on me in court?"

"I'll tell the judge you cooperated with us, yes Billy. What he does next isn't up to me, so don't get your hopes up." Bill was being as honest as possible to this prisoner. "Is it OK if I record this conversation? It'll save some time and I won't have to take so many notes."

"Sure, I don't care. I'll tell you what I know, that's all." It sounded like Billy Forsythe was still very frightened.

Bill placed the recorder on the desk and asked Billy to state his full name and date of birth. He did this without further questions. Bill then began to ask questions.

"How did you get acquainted with Darleen North," he asked.

"Another guy from Nikiski and I were talking about selling dope, but we didn't have any money to buy any stuff. He said he knew a dealer in Anchorage who got backing from some rich guy. He never saw the rich guy, only an agent. The dealer told my friend he got backing from an agent and that there was one in Soldotna. My friend called to ask the name of the agent in this area, and he gave us a number to call. Anyway, we were finally contacted by Darleen North.

She said if we could show willingness to put up some collateral, she'd finance us. I put up my family's place to get her to back us. My partner backed out. I was glad, 'cause he didn't have anything in this deal, only I did. She gave me some cash. I bought some coke and hash and went out to find my own dealers. It was easy and I made some good money."

"I don't understand, Billy. How did you get so far in debt that they wanted to off you?" asked Bill.

"I thought I was a big deal and some of my dealers wanted more product. I let them hold off paying for a little while. That's when I learned you can't trust dealers to do what they say they will. I ran a tab for a couple of my dealers and borrowed more from Mrs. North. Pretty soon I was in so deep and couldn't pay. They sent some guys to see me and collect. I told them I couldn't pay right now, but I'd get the money real soon. The problem was I couldn't collect from the dealers that owed me the most money. Pretty soon I was getting real threats and you can see where that got me."

"Who threatened you?" asked Koogan. "Was it these same men?"

"Not the first time. When they first threatened me, it was a couple of goons out of Anchorage. They beat me up pretty good. That's when I started to hide out. Mrs. North kept trying to call me, but I wouldn't answer. That went on for a while and that's when they sent these three men after me. Believe me, I want to thank you for saving my buns and arresting me," explained Billy.

"It's my job to keep the public safe, even drug dealers. Tell me, did you ever find out who was backing Darleen North?"

"No. At first, I thought it was her husband, but it's not. I don't know who it is, but he's got a pile of money, all cash. In the beginning when I asked her for more money, she'd deliver it within the next day or two. It was always a pile of cash."

The interview went on for another hour with Bill asking the same questions in different ways. It was getting late in the day and Bill decided to end the interview for now.

"North's bail hearing is tomorrow. If he gets bailed you'll be able to go back to the dorm, but until then you'll be in segregation for your own safety. Is there anything else I can do for you, Billy?"

"Nah, I'm good. I just wanted to get out of the dorm with Nick North. Be sure to tell the judge I cooperated with you. Right, Trooper Koogan?"

"Yes, Billy. I'll talk to him. Thank you for being so helpful. Call me if you think of anything else."

Bill reached for the phone to call the officer to let him out and take

Billy to seg.

As he drove home, he thought the case would be closed fairly soon. He needed a strategy for arresting Darleen North. If Nick was allowed bail, given Nick's volatile personality, Darleen could be in grave danger. He'd have to see what tomorrow brings.

CHAPTER THIRTY-FOUR

The following morning, Bill was in his office finishing the report on his interview with Billy Forsythe when Glen Simms came to see him.

"I just had a call from the DA. He says the bail hearing for Nick North will be at 10:00 this morning."

"Thanks, I didn't know the time. I have some concerns for the safety of Darleen North if he makes bail. Nick has an explosive personality and may want to do harm to her. After all, he already murdered a police officer and has nothing to lose."

"Yes Bill, I think you're right about that. I'll call the DA and let him know this is one more reason to deny bail. I'll let you know how it goes," said Simms as he turned to go back to his office at the other end of the building.

Bill thought about it for a few minutes and decided to go to the courthouse to see for himself what the judge would do. What he did later would depend on what the judge said. Bill knew the judge would put restrictions on where North would be allowed to go and with whom he could have contact. That wasn't to say he'd abide by the parameters of his release.

Koogan sat at the back of the courtroom as the judge entered. North was accompanied by a prison transport officer and the court services trooper stationed inside the court building. The lawyer, Ben Little was seated next to North and was whispering into his ear. The courtroom became quiet as the judge entered.

"All rise," announced the clerk as the judge took his seat at the bench.

The judge studied the papers on his desk for a moment before looking down at the defendant and his lawyer. "I have a copy of the petition for bail, Mr. Little. Do you have anything to say as to why I should grant this request?"

Lawyer Little stood to speak, "Yes Your Honor, I have. Mr. North is a prominent local businessman with an automotive repair shop in Soldotna. He needs to go back to his business in to keep it successful and profitable. He needs the money he may earn to pay for his defense. His home is here, and his business is here. He's not a flight risk and plans to have a defense for the charges he is accused of."

The judge turned to Walker and asked, "What does the peoples attorney have to say?"

"Your Honor. Mr. North is noted for his explosive personality and the State contends this was one of the reasons he was arrested in the death of a Soldotna Police Officer. Even if he wasn't a flight risk, he's still a volatile, vengeful individual that poses a danger to his wife and others, if he's released." After making his statement, Walker took his seat at the prosecution table.

The judge made some notes in the file on his desk before speaking. "I have given both arguments much thought. This State says all prisoners are entitled to bail, under certain circumstances. I have reviewed this case and evaluated the risk and benefits of releasing Mr. North. It is my finding that Mr. North should be released to manage his business and his life. I set bail at $100,000.00." He stood, gathered his files, and left the courtroom.

Ben Little, whispered into the ear of Nick North. North nodded and stood to be taken back to the pretrial facility. Little watched as the transport officers took him away. Once North was taken away, Ben stepped up to talk with the court clerk.

As other spectators filed out of the courtroom Koogan followed and left the building. He drove directly to the auto repair shop to tell Susan and Darleen the outcome of the bail hearing. As he drove into the shop's parking area, he noted Darleen's Toyota wasn't there. He walked inside to speak with Susan. She was busy with her bookkeeping and only looked up when she heard the door.

"Good morning, Trooper Koogan," she said, smiling.

"And good morning to you, Susan. I don't see Darleen's car out there. Is she here?"

"No, she called to say she had some running to do this morning and wouldn't be in until later." She noted the worried look on the trooper's face. "Is something wrong?" she asked.

"I just came from the court. I stopped to tell the two of you the judge granted bail for Nick. I think his lawyer is getting the money arranged right now. I think he'll be released by this afternoon. I'm sorry, Susan. There was nothing I could do about it."

Susan began to cry, "Oh no. What am I going to do?" she sobbed. "I don't want to be around that man."

"I'm sorry, but that'll have to be your decision. If you'd like I can have a Soldotna officer stay around for a while if you don't feel safe." Bill reached out to pat her shoulder.

"I'm more afraid for Darleen. He might fire me, but he is sure to hurt her. I think I'll just leave and let the mechanic deal with Mr. North. I don't know what else to do."

"Do you know where Darleen is right now?" he asked.

"No, but she might be at home. I can call her and ask."

"No, I'd rather be the one to explain this to her. I'll call her myself.

Do you want me to have an officer hang around?"

"I guess not. I may leave and not come back. I just don't know right now." Tears were streaming down her cheeks.

"Don't hesitate to call me, Susan. I don't want you to be in danger."

Susan nodded and wiped her eyes dry with a tissue from a box on her desk. Bill walked to his car and called Darleen's cell phone. She was slow to answer but picked up on the fourth ring.

"Hello," she answered in a sleepy voice.

"Darleen, this is Trooper Koogan. Are you at home right now?"

"No, but I can be in a few minutes. Why?"

"I need to talk with you for a few minutes. It's important."

"OK, if it's important. I'll be home in ten minutes."

Bill looked at his watch. It was 11:35, making him wonder where she'd been napping. She sounded as if he'd awakened her. He drove slowly to the North residence to allow her time to get there and open the house. Her car was in the drive when he arrived. He parked behind it. She heard him drive up and was waiting near the door.

"Hello, Darleen," said Bill as he stepped up onto the front deck.

"Hello, Bill, what's this important news you have for me?"

"I just came from Kenai and the court hearing for Nick. The judge granted bail. I think his lawyer is getting the money right now. I stopped at your office, saw Susan, and gave her the message. She's very upset."

"Let's sit on the deck and enjoy the fresh air." She left the door open and stepped out onto the porch. She sat on one of the benches there and motioned for him to join her.

He sat beside her and continued to speak. "I thought you'd be worried about him coming home and I wanted to warn you. Susan was very frightened. She wants to quit and leave. I told her I couldn't help her with that decision. I'm more concerned about your safety, though. We both know how he functions when he's angry. I'm not sure it's safe for you to stay in the house. Do you have someplace safe you can go for a while?"

"Yes, I have a place to go. I'm afraid if I leave, he may just burn the place down. I don't want that."

"You know if you stay, he could burn the place down with you in it?" answered Bill. "I'd feel better if you could leave until we see how he's going to take the situation when he gets home. You know, having the shop open and all."

"You make a good point I suppose, but I don't think he'll ever harm me. He loves me too much to do that."

"I've seen his explosive personality in action. I don't think he can control himself when he gets angry. You know him better that I, but I could never trust his behavior when he's in a rage. It's your call, Darleen. Are you confident enough that he won't harm you?" asked Bill.

"I understand why you feel that way Bill, but he and I have been married for a long time and he's never laid a hand on me. I've seen him in a rage, but he's never attempted to harm me. So, the answer is yes, I am confident he'll never hurt me."

"All I can say is I've warned you. Please keep your cell phone with you case you're wrong. I'll respond immediately if you call." Bill stood to leave and smiled at her. "Good luck to you, Darleen."

He drove back to the office to report to the captain. Captain Phil Bradshaw was in his office waiting for him.

"North just posted bail and is being released as we speak."

"I warned both ladies, Cap. Susan is frightened and said she may just walk out and never come back. Darleen on the other hand, said she was staying and that he'd never do harm to her. I tried to talk her into being more cautious, but she said she's staying in the house and waiting for him to come home. I couldn't talk her into getting out."

"You've done everything you are supposed to do. I hope she's right in her thinking because we're about to find out. You might want to call SPD and ask them to stand by in case there's trouble at the auto shop."

In his office he called Chief Bud Griffin. "Hey, Bud, this is Bill Koogan. Nick North just bailed out and could be headed over to his shop. I'm going to be out near his home in case he decides to go there and beat up on his wife. We just don't know what he has in mind. With his history I don't think it's going to be very good."

"Thanks for the heads up, Bill. I'll have a couple of officers hang around there to see if he shows up and does anything bad." Griffin called two officers at the station doing reports. He explained the situation and asked them to patrol the area near the auto repair shop owned by Nick North. He cautioned them about approaching North without backup.

Half an hour later, the officers reported that North had just been dropped off at the shop and had gone inside. They could see him speaking to the girl at the front desk. There didn't seem to be any problems.

Inside the office, North walked calmly to the desk of his receptionist, Susan, who was still doing accounting chores. She was frightened as he approached her desk but held her composure.

"Hello, Mr. North," was all she could think of to say.

"Hello, Susan. Is my wife around?" he asked.

"No, Sir, she went home to do some housework."

"I see my old truck is out back. Hand me the keys, will you?"

Susan reached into the center drawer of her desk for the keys to the pickup and handed them to Nick. "Is everything OK, Mr. North?" she asked.

"Yes, I just have to tie up some loose ends. By the way, I see you found someone to pick up the slack while I was gone."

"I called the same mechanic you used a lot. He's been doing a great job while you were away," she said, being careful not to incite her boss.

"Are we still making a little money?" he asked.

"Yes, in fact we're showing a slight increase in profits."

"Maybe we should keep him on for a while, then," offered Nick.

"Are you going to be back in the shop now?" she asked.

"I'm not sure just what I'm going to do. If I do stay it may drive off any business we have left. People get scared when the owner of a shop gets arrested. Looks like you and the new mechanic are taking good care of the office. I'd like you to continue to run it for a while. I still have a trial coming up and I don't know how that'll turn out. My lawyer says I have a fair chance of getting off on the murder charge. Seems the troopers made some mistakes in gathering evidence and it could taint their case."

"Are you going to be in town the entire time, Mr. North?"

"I plan to be, but a lot depends on Darleen. I'm going to the house to see her now. Would you call her and tell her I'm on my way to see her?"

With the truck keys in hand, he walked toward the rear door of the shop.

Immediately Susan dialed Darleen's cell phone.

"Hi Susan, what's up?"

"Nick was just here and got the keys to his truck. He said he was going to come see you," explained Susan in a tense voice.

"Is he calm or angry?" asked Darleen.

"Actually, he seemed really calm. He acted like he had no fight left in him."

"Trooper Koogan said he was going to keep an eye on you. I hope he does." said Susan.

"Don't you worry, Susan. Everything will be just fine. Now I'm going to make some coffee for when he gets here. I'll call you later and let you know what he plans to do next."

Susan's next call was to Koogan. "Mr. North just left the office and was going to see Mrs. North. He seemed calm and everything, but he still scares me," she reported to Bill.

"It's OK, Susan, I'll drive out there and check on her."

Bill called out to Randy in the next office. "Come with me, Randy. North is headed to his house to see Darleen. I think we should drive out there to be sure it stays peaceful." The men left the office together in Bill's unmarked patrol car.

CHAPTER THIRTY-FIVE

Bill was driving with Randy in the passenger seat as they drove to the home of Mr. and Mrs. North. "Why is it the only people who think Nick North is dangerous, is us?" asked Randy.

"I don't know, Randy. I haven't known him very long, but I think he's a very dangerous man. I hope I'm wrong, but I think he's going to be pleasant at first and work up to another fit of rage. I don't want to interrupt his homecoming, but I agree with you, he could get very dangerous very quickly. When we get there, we need to stay in the car and wait to see how it's going. I'll park near the entry to his driveway and listen for any loud voices or shouts. I'll walk down the drive to see if his pickup is there. If it is, we'll wait out here. If she screams, we should hear her. If they start shouting at each other, we should hear that. I just hope we don't hear gunshots."

When they arrived at the end of the driveway, Bill parked in the same spot Lee Woods had parked the evening he was murdered.

"Wait here. I'll go see if Nick is there," said Koogan.

He stepped out of the patrol car and walked down the driveway until he could see the back of Nick's truck. He turned to walk back to the patrol car and climbed inside, rolling the side window down to listen for any loud voices from the house. The troopers sat quietly for almost an hour when they heard Nick's pickup truck start.

Bill started his car and moved on up the road to avoid being seen by North as he backed out of the drive. When he had gone, Bill turned around and drove quickly to the North home. When they reached the house, he opened his door to move into the house to check on Darleen.
As he stepped out of the car, the front door of the house opened and Darleen appeared on the front porch, looking neat and tidy and apparently unharmed.

"Are you alright?" asked Bill as he neared the deck.

Darleen snickered, "Oh, yes, Bill, I'm fine. How long have you been out here?"

"I got word he was on his way here and decided to play it safe and sit out front to be sure you were safe."

"I appreciate your concerns, but I told you it would be safe for me."

"Just the same, keep your phone with you in case he suddenly stops being nice. Call me if you need anything." He waved and walked back to his car.

He backed out of the drive and returned to the office. He made notes in his notebook on the times he and Randy had been watching the drive and the time they returned to the office. He was still very uneasy about Nick being in the neighborhood.

As soon as Bill and Randy had gone, Darleen called Gordon Tullis.

"He was just here," said Darleen.

"Did he make any threats?" asked Tullis.

"No, but interestingly, as soon as he drove away Trooper Koogan drove in to check on me."

"Hmmm. I don't like that trooper hanging around. What are you going to do now?" he asked.

"I should go back to the office for a while. I need to find out what Nick said to Susan and see if she knows what he intends to do about the business. I think I'd like to keep it going. It makes a good amount of income for me and is a good front for our other endeavors. With Susan there, I'm able to stay gone most of the time."

"Where's Nick going to stay until the trial?" asked Tullis.

"He wanted to stay here, but I told him it wouldn't look good to the customers if he did. He said he's going to rent an apartment in Kenai. He doesn't have a cell phone yet, but that's on his list of things to do."

"I don't like him popping in and out like that," complained Gordon.

"I agree and that's exactly what I told Nick. I told him I didn't like him coming to the house or the shop. I told him it was bad for business, and he should stay away."

"Steve Town has disappeared, or I'd have him take care of the problem. If Nick becomes a nuisance, I'll have someone take care of it."

"I would rather not do that, Gordy. I think the court will take him out of circulation when they take him to trial." She paused a few seconds before continuing, "I had a phone call this morning to say Billy Forsythe was arrested and is in jail. My informant doesn't know what happened to Steve Town, but he said there had been a shooting at a cabin and someone was killed by troopers.

"This just keeps getting better all the time. I wonder what else can go wrong," Tullis said, almost in a whisper. "OK, I'll send for another enforcer to take over for Steve Town. We need to get this taken care of as quickly as possible. I may get Billy Forsythe bailed out, since I can't send a man to take care of him in the jail. We can't have Billy bragging about how he cheated us out of a lot of money. From now on, I want you to do a lot more research before bankrolling another druggie. This is the second time you let them take us to the cleaners. There won't be a third. If you get my meaning."

"I'm sorry, Gordy, I didn't find out he was a user until after he was into us for a lot. Had I not listened to someone who knew him and was a good customer of ours, I never would have allowed it to happen. I'll make it up to you somehow." Darleen had just learned how dangerous her affair with Gordon Tullis had become.

Tullis continued to bark orders, "Go back to the auto shop office and stay there. You need to be seen by the public as well as the police. I'll take care of Billy while you're keeping your head down. I'll be calling you soon."

Darleen hung up and pondered what to do next. Gordon would be checking to see if she had gone to the office. She decided to comply with his wishes rather than incur his ire. She reached into the pantry to get a six pack of bottled tea for the office refrigerator and walked to her car. At the office she sat at her desk, found the newspaper, and began to read. She finished the rest of the afternoon by reading and working the crossword. She had greeted Susan when she entered. She had very little conversation with her the rest of the day. At closing time, she let Susan lock up the shop as she drove back to her house.

Bill Koogan was about to leave the office to go home when his cell phone jingled. It was Billy Forsythe.

"Hello, Billy. How are things going for you?"

"I'm back in the pretrial dorm again. Thanks for keeping me away from Nick. That guy you shot, is he going to be coming back to this dorm?" asked a worried Billy.

"Not right away, he had his shoulder operated on and a metal joint installed. I expect he will be in the hospital for another four or five days. After that I don't know. I'll try to get him sent to the Anchorage jail until his trial. By that time your case should have been decided. I have an appointment with the DA for lunch tomorrow. I intend to talk with him about your case then."

"Trooper Koogan, I haven't done much with my life so far, but you've taught me there must be a better way to live. When I get out, I'm going to get a job and stick with it. I know I'll have to pay for the things I've done, but I don't ever want to go through this again. I wanted you to know I'm grateful to you for giving me the chance to start over."

Bill felt a bit of satisfaction as he drove home. The following morning his first stop was the ICU wing of the hospital to check on his officers and the patient. John Ashley was on duty, posted at the door.

"Good morning, Boss. How is it going this morning?" he asked.

"I haven't been to the office yet. I just wanted to stop and check on you and the patient. How's he doing?"

"They've kept him sedated most of the time. He was in a great deal of pain most of the day yesterday and last night. The doctor was in a while ago and said they're going to try to get him awake today and start therapy. He also said he won't be in any shape to give me any trouble for at least two more days," reported Ashley.

"What time does your relief come on?"

"Randy should be here any time now. Randy is never late."

"Can I get you anything?" asked Bill.

"Nope. I'm going home when Randy gets here. I'll brief him. Thanks for checking, though."

Bill walked to the bed and checked on Steve Town. He was sleeping soundly, his shoulder bandaged and in a stabilizing brace.

Bill stopped to check on the official condition of the patient while passing the front desk. The nurse assured him Steve Town would be bedridden for at least two more days before the therapist goes to work. Koogan wasn't sure Town would stay down that long.

At the office he stopped to see the captain and give him a report on the condition of the patient. The captain had news for Bill.

"I spoke with the colonel this morning. He called to let me know the Bristol Bay fiasco has been resolved. The season will be over soon, and the troopers will be coming home. I'm going to ask you and the team stay on for a few days to give the men a few days with their families before returning to work. They've been away from family for almost two months without a day off. They need the time. Can you and your team hang on for another week or so?" asked Captain Bradshaw.

"We'll manage, Sir," replied Bill. "We still have a few loose ends to tie up on the cases we're working. I really don't know if we can get it all done before we're terminated, but we'll do our best."

"I know you will, Bill. You and your team have done an outstanding job while you were here. I give you my thanks." Captain Bradshaw was pleased he had chosen these men to take the task of investigations and do it so very well.

Bill was at his desk when the phone rang. It was the air taxi operator from Nikiski.

"Say, trooper. That Cessna you had us disable is still parked out here. What do you want us to do with it?"

"I've been so busy I forgot all about it. Have they replaced the parts taken from the magnetos?"

"No, but I can call him to come out and fix it."

"Let me ask the captain what he wants to do. I'll get back to you as quick as I can."

"Sure thing, Trooper. Call me back when you get an answer." The air taxi owner hung up the phone and Bill dialed the captain's office. He explained what was happening in Nikiski and asked for advice.

Bill called back to talk with the man who had called him from the Nikiski airport. "Hi, there. This is Trooper Koogan. I have a couple of questions for you."

"OK, what do you want to know?" he asked.

"Is the Cessna in the way and keeping you from doing business on the other side of the runway?"

"No, Sir, it's not in the way. I just feel I'm responsible for the plane while it's here. I don't want it vandalized with me responsible."

"I understand, what if we draw up an agreement for you to rent us a space to store the plane and we pay the rental fee. We can add a paragraph stating you aren't liable for vandalism, and if there are other damages, like a plane strikes it or someone driving on the parking area hits it, you won't be held responsible. Is that good enough?" asked Bill.

"Yeah, that sounds good to me. You type it up an bring me a copy and we can both sign it. Thanks a lot Trooper," Bill just nodded into the phone and hung up.

Later that same afternoon he read the typewritten sheets and gave them to Randy Craig to deliver after signing two copies of the documents.

It was early evening when Gordon Tullis called Darleen North. "Hello, Darleen," he said when she answered.

"Oh, hi, Gordy. Have you learned anything new?" she asked.

"Not really, but I think we should have you pack a bag and the two of us leave town for a while. I have a man coming to complete Steve's job. I don't want to be around when it goes down. This is costing me a lot of money and I don't want to be here when it happens. This will be a total cleanup where Town and his men failed. I'll pick you up in an hour and we can drive to Wasilla. We'll have a late dinner in Anchorage before going to my place. Call Susan and tell her she will have to run the business until you get back. We won't know when that will be. We may have to go to Oklahoma to visit your folks. We'll talk about all that later."

"Oh, Gordy, that sounds wonderful to me. I'll be ready in an hour.

CHAPTER THIRTY-SIX

Midmorning the following day Bill got a call from Billy Forsythe. "I just had a visit from that lawyer, Ben Little. He said he wants me to hire him and he wants to get me bailed out. I don't know why he wants to do that. Do you?"

"No, not really. He may be wanting to get you out of jail so the people who sent Steve Town after you can get to you again. I don't know that for sure, but it would be my guess."

"Is that Steve guy out of the hospital?" asked Billy.

"No, he's going to be laid up for a long time with an artificial shoulder joint. I don't think he'll be the one chasing after you. The other two men with him are already dead. I still haven't learned who hired them. But if he has enough money to hire them and to back a lawyer to get Steve and you both out of jail, he has a lot of money and can afford another enforcer. You should be careful about being bailed out."

"I guess I had better stay in jail for now," replied Billy.

"How did you get involved with them anyway?" asked Bill.

"I already told you. I was looking to expand my sales network and needed cash to buy more stuff. My friend said he knew someone who could help. That someone turned out to be Darleen North. My friend talked her into loaning me money and vouched for me with her. I guess I wanted to be a big shot and let some new clients have product on credit. They used the stuff and didn't pay me. It just kept happening and I got in so deep they sent those goons to get me. I was really dumb. I know that now. I thought I was gonna get rich in the business like some of those others."

"One other thing, Billy. Do you know who her backer is? I mean his name or how to get in touch with him?" asked Bill.

Billy thought about the question for a moment before giving an answer. "Sorry, Trooper Koogan, all I know is that he has an office somewhere north of Anchorage; Palmer or Wasilla, somewhere up there."

"You said Wasilla?" replied an astounded Koogan.

"Yeah, she used to go up there sometimes and my friend in Nikiski found out about it. That's all I know about what she does."

"Thanks for the call, Billy. Stay safe." With that he hung up and thought for a moment. Picking up the phone again he dialed the auto repair shop.

Susan answered. "Hi Susan, is Darleen in the office today?" he asked.

"I'm sorry, Trooper Koogan, she called me last evening and said she was leaving town for a couple of days. She didn't say where or why, she just said she was going."

"Do you think she went alone or was she traveling with someone else?" he asked.

"I have no idea, but I don't think she was driving. I think she was going with someone else."

"Thanks, Susan. I'll check her house and see if her car is there. Call me if you need anything."

Bill called Bob Barratt to his office. When he arrived, Bill told him of his suspicions of another man, possibly her financial backer, taking her to the Anchorage area. You have friends in Wasilla, Bob. Can you call one of them and see if Darleen North is at Gordon Tullis' home in Wasilla. If she's there we may have just discovered her financial backer. If he is, we may have to do something to keep the two of them from leaving the state. He has homes in Florida and Oklahoma. They may try to get there. If these three hitmen work for Tullis, he may have just lost his enforcers and feels threatened enough to leave town."

"You know, Boss," said Bob, "All this makes perfect sense. If he came down here to check on her and her business dealings, and if the three enforcers we shot were working for him, then he may want to leave town until he can regroup. I'll call someone I know in Wasilla and ask him to check it out."

"Thanks, Bob, let him know this is a priority." Bob nodded understanding and went to his office to call.

An hour later he returned to let the boss know Gordon Tullis' car was at his home in Wasilla and it looked like he had company.

"What do you say we get in my car and drive up there and have a talk with Mr. Tullis and see for ourselves if Mrs. North is there with him. If she's there I think we'd have enough circumstantial evidence to arrest them both. Money laundering alone would justify an arrest."

"Instead of driving, we could use the Cessna parked in Nikiski. It'd save us a lot of travel time. I can have my old buddy get us a car in Wasilla and if we make an arrest, we can call the local troopers to take custody of them." Bob said, enthusiastically.

"Dang, Bob, you're beginning to think like a real trooper. Call the mechanic and have him repair the airplane as soon as possible. I'll check in with the captain and we can hit the road." Bill was excited about the possibility of closing this case while they were still on the payroll.

An hour later Bob was making a walk-around at the airplane to see if all the parts were still together and that the fuel tanks had enough fuel to reach Wasilla airport. Satisfied the craft was flight worthy he asked Bill to get in and buckle his seatbelt. Bob untied the tiedown ropes, climbed into the right seat, closed the door, and turned to Bill. "Hang on, here we go!"

The airplane itself was a work of art with all new digital navigation equipment and GPS map on the panel. The takeoff was smooth. The airplane felt strong. Bob was used to flying smaller Piper aircraft but had flown Cessnas like this one many times. Once off the ground he pointed the nose to the north and crossed Cook Inlet to fly the west shoreline to Wasilla, located just north of the Knik River, which flows into Knik Arm, east of Anchorage. At cruising altitude, he checked with Anchorage Center to advise he was passing to the north. Cruising at an airspeed of 165 miles per hour they were in a pattern above Wasilla airport within three quarters of an hour. Bob landed smoothly and taxied to the transient parking area, where a car and driver were waiting.

Bob climbed out to greet his friend Dave Winslow, who was waiting near the car. "Good to see you, Dave," Bob called out.

"Good to see you, too, Bob. What's up?" Dave asked.

"An investigation we're conducting. Do you know where Gordon Tullis has a house here in town?" asked Bob.

"Sure, I'll show you where he lives and then you can drop me off at the station." Dave paused a second, "Say, is it true you and your team are known as the Geezer Squad?"

"So, you heard about that all the way up here, eh?"

"Nothing gets past us professionals. You know that Bob."

"Say, Dave. Do you have time to follow us to the Tullis home? We don't anticipate trouble, but you know how these things go; unpredictable. We could use you for a backup if we need it."

"Just let me tell my boss and then I'll lead you there," answered Dave.

Dave was driving and changed course to go to the station. "You can come inside with me if you want. I just need to tell my sergeant what I'm doing. You fellas can take this car and I'll take my patrol car."

"Give the Sarge our best, but we'll wait out here," said Bob as he gave a short salute to his friend.

Bob and Bill followed Dave to the home of Gordon Tullis. It was a large, modern home on well-manicured grounds. It looked to be about three to four acres surrounded by trees and shrubs. Bob drove up the drive and stopped in front of the garage doors. The men walked up the short flight of steps to the front entry deck and rang the bell. They waited for several minutes and rang it again. They could hear the TV inside and knew there was someone home. They rang the bell again and began knocking on the door. Finally, they heard footsteps approaching the door from inside.

The door opened and a large man in a gym suit held it open. "Yes," he said, "What can I do for you?"

Bill flashed his trooper ID and asked, "I beg your pardon, but are you home alone?"

"No, I have a friend here with me. What is it you want?" he asked.

"Are you Gordon Tullis?" asked Bill, ignoring the question.

"Yes, I'm Gordon Tullis. What can I do for you?"

"May we come inside? We have some questions we want to ask you. It won't take long," asked Bill.

"Very well, but I'm a very busy man and don't have a lot of time to waste," was Gordon's reply.

"Thank you, Sir," said Bill as he and Bob entered the house, "you said there was someone here with you. May I ask who that would be?"

"Just a friend spending a couple of days with me." Gordon was beginning to worry about inviting them inside.

"Would that be Mrs. Darleen North?" asked Bill.

"As a matter of fact, it is. Her husband is out on bail, and she needed a place to go and not have to be in her home when he came to call.

"Would you be so good as to ask her to join us?"

"I see no need for her to be embarrassed by you," replied an indignant Gordon Tullis.

"Just the same I would like to speak with her, too, since she's here and we're asking questions. By the way, this is an official visit. So please ask her to join us."

Tullis was about to say something when Darleen appeared in the room. "Trooper Koogan, what a pleasant surprise to see you. How did you find me?" she announced as she crossed the room.

"I think you know why we're here, Darleen. We have information that you're financing drug businesses on the Kenai Peninsula, and we'd like to ask you a few questions." He turned to Tullis and continued, "We have other information that she's working for you, Mr. Tullis. Would you like to explain it to us?"

"I don't have to explain anything to you and neither does Mrs. North. Now excuse me, I'm calling my lawyer," said an angry Gordon Tullis.

"Go ahead and call your lawyer. Advise him you have just been arrested on charges of money laundering, which is a federal charge. We are also arresting Mrs. North on the same charge. Make your call, then put your hands behind your back." Bill turned to Bob.

"Trooper Barratt, please secure Mrs. North's hands. We don't want any misunderstanding."

Bob stepped over to grasp the wrist of Darleen.

"Gordon! Are you going to allow this?" she shouted.

"Do as they say for now, Darleen. I'll have my lawyer meet us at the jail. We won't be there long."

Tullis finished dialing the telephone and asked the lawyer to meet them at the jail. He then turned to Koogan and asked, "Which facility will we be booked into?"

"I think the Palmer holding facility. You'll be processed by troopers but will probably be moved to another facility after booking. I hope you understand. You and Darleen will be processed separately."

Bob had both Darleen's hands handcuffed. He seated her on a nearby chair. Gordon finished the conversation with his lawyer and volunteered his wrists to be secured.

Bob keyed his radio and asked Dave to join them and to bring backup for transportation of the prisoners.

When a van and two more troopers arrived, Gordon Tullis was loaded into it. Darleen was placed in the rear seat of Dave's patrol car for the ride to Palmer.

The booking process took a little more than an hour, during which time the lawyer for Tullis arrived and waited in the visiting room until booking was completed. Tullis had said nothing to anyone except to give his personal information during the booking process. He was clearly impatient with the officers doing the booking. When they were done Tullis was placed in a visiting room to speak with his attorney, Grayson Smith, a well-known local criminal attorney.

Darleen was booked and placed in a holding cell to await transport to a facility with accommodations for female prisoners.

When Tullis asked to be let out of the visiting room, he told the booking officer his lawyer had advised him to comply with whatever they asked. He also said the lawyer would be contacting the judge to ask for immediate bail. It was plain to the Booking Officer that the judge would not be granting bail until the arraignment tomorrow in the Palmer court.

"I guess we need to go back to Soldotna and file our reports. The judge will need them tomorrow." Bill spoke to Bob.

Late afternoon found the two officers working on the information to be filed with the court. There were a lot of questions to be asked and answered before they could go home for the day.

CHAPTER THIRTY-SEVEN

The following morning there were two men posted in the room with Steve Town as he was being revived from his drug induced coma. Doctors had said he would be too weak to be combative, but John and Randy both knew the capabilities of this man and didn't want to take any chances of his being combative.

In the office, Bill Koogan called the transport officer at the pretrial facility and asked if they could bring Billy Forsythe to the trooper office for an interview. He asked that they do it discreetly. The transport officer said he could be discreet and would have it done within an hour. Bill told him the interview would take about an hour or perhaps a little more.

The officer in the pretrial module told Billy he had to appear in court today and was to come with them to the booking area where a transport officer was waiting.

Billy asked repeatedly, nervously, what court date did he have?

He shouted, "I don't have any court date! I don't know anything about any court hearing!"

Billy demanded, "I want to talk with my lawyer!" The pleas were ignored, as the transport officer placed him in chains and cuffs for transport.

In the transport van, the officer explained to Billy he didn't have a court appearance but was being taken to the trooper office for an interview. The story of a court date was to distract snitches who might be in the same mod. It was for his own safety. Fifteen minutes later he was led into a garage entrance at the trooper headquarters to insure his anonymity. He was met there by Trooper Bill Koogan.

"Sorry for the ruse, Billy. I just wanted to get you to this interview without anyone knowing."

"It's OK, Trooper Koogan, I understand. I don't want anyone else shooting at me. I guess I should thank you," said Billy in a quiet tone.

Bill asked the officer to remove the chains from the prisoner and to come back in an hour. The officer complied and went back to his van to leave the building.

Bill and Billy walked down the hallway to the conference room where Bob was waiting. A video camera was set up for the meeting.

"Want some coffee or a soda, Billy?" asked Bill.

"Sure, I'd like a Coke. Haven't had one in a while."

Bob walked down the hallway to the front of the building to retrieve the bottle of soda. When he returned and handed the bottle to Billy, the result was a complete change in his demeanor. Billy relaxed and leaned back in his chair. He took a long drink of the liquid and hissed "Aahhh."

"Ok, Billy. We're going to video this interview for legal reasons. We'll be using it as evidence in the indictment and trial of the people who hired the men who came to get you. I want you to tell the truth and if you don't know an answer to a question, just say so. Don't guess at anything. Do you understand?"

"Sure, I understand. I have one question before we start."

"What's your question, Billy?"

"Did you arrest Darleen?" asked Billy.

"Yes, we did, Billy. Both her and the man she worked for. The man who supplied the cash she gave you. Both are in jail and will be indicted on federal money laundering charges. Those charges will keep them from hiring anyone else to come after you, at least for now. We, as the State of Alaska, are attempting to acquire evidence of murder, extortion, drug sales and any other charges we can find. Your testimony will be crucial to our investigation. We're going to want names, dates, places, verifiable instances of money transactions and other illegal acts you may have been a privy to." Bill had given his speech and now asked Billy, "Are you ready to start?"

"I guess so," he said as he set the empty bottle on the table.

"OK, then, here we go. Bob, turn on the camera and recorder," ordered Bill.

Bob started the machines and returned to the upper end of the table where the camera could view all the men.

Bill Koogan began the interview, "I'm Trooper Bill Koogan. With me is Trooper Bob Barratt and we are here to interview a person we arrested following the shooting and altercation that took place in North Kenai on the date listed on the filing papers." Bill turned to Billy, "Would you please give me your name and date of birth," he asked.

Billy gave his name and date of birth.

The interview had progressed for almost an hour, and it revealed many names of local drug dealers and users. At one point Billy asked about the chances of Steve Town coming after him again. Bill assured him Town was in no condition to make any more threats and would return to jail for non-compliance of conditions of bail on murder charges, as well as the assault on Billy.

The final question of the day for Billy was asked by Bob, "Billy, you've already stated you received cash money from Darleen North, and she knew this money was to be used to buy drugs for you to sell. My question is, did she know you were buying drugs with this money prior to her loan to you?"

"Oh, yeah, she knew. She even asked what kinds of drugs I intended to buy and sell, and who the dealer was that I was going to buy from. I already told you those names, but she wanted to know. She seemed to know them. She was happy enough with my dealers. She gave me the cash. We never signed any papers or anything, but she made it clear what would happen if I didn't pay on time. I was sure I could do it and she gave me the money in cash. All this took place out near the helipad on the road to the Nikiski docks."

Bob and Bill looked at each other and nodded agreement.

"OK, Billy," said Bill, "I think that about does it for now."

Bob stepped to the head of the table to turn off the recording device

"Is there anything we can do for you, Billy?" asked Bill. "If not, I'll call the transport officer to come and take you back to the jail."

"Nah, but thanks for the Coke. But I want to tell you both that I meant what I said about getting myself straight. You guys have been straight with me, and I don't want to go through this ever again."

Bill stood and shook Billy's hand, "I'll let the DA know how much you've cooperated with us and see if he can get you a break at sentencing. Thanks for your help, Billy."

Bob brought him another Coke while they waited for the transport officer to take him back to the jail.

Once he was on his way to the jail, Bill and Bob returned to the conference room to begin translating the interview to a written report. They decided it was time to call Walker at the DA's office. When they finally reached him, they explained what had happened over the past several days.

"I know some of it, I had a call from the U.S. Attorney in Anchorage. He was asking me about the arrest of two suspects for money laundering. He said you were the arresting officers, and they were arrested on Federal charges. He said he had nothing to take to the arraignment and wanted to know what he should do. I told him you'd get him a report before arraignment. I hope I told him the truth." Walker was in a good mood, probably because it was the federal attorney's problem and not his.

"That's what we're calling you about," said Bill. "I have a report here and I want to know if you want a copy of it. We also have a new report coming that lists more State charges with evidence taken from an interview we just now finished. There'll be several other arrests made following this. We have names, places, and amounts of drugs being exchanged. We also know that Gordon Tullis, the man arrested on money laundering charges, is the force behind the murder of that liquor store manager from Soldotna. The kidnapping took place in Soldotna, but the murder took place in Wasilla."

"It sounds like you boys have been busy. How soon will I see the report on this?" asked Walker.

"As soon as we can get it typed up. There's a lengthy interview, so it'll take at least until tomorrow." Bill paused a moment and continued. "I want to tell you; the team and I have had fun working with you this time. It looks like we'll finish here by the first of the week and the regular officers will be back in the office."

"It's been a pleasure working with you again, Bill. Tell your crew thanks for the good work. Get me that written report and I'll get busy on the warrants. See ya, Bill."

After hanging up, he turned to Bob, "OK. Let's get all this together and over to the girls on the other side to start putting it together."

"I'm making copies of the tapes right now. I'll take it all over there in a few minutes." Now it was Bob hesitating, "You know, Bill. I can't remember when I've had more fun on the job than I've had this time. We had a great team and a good boss in you. It makes me glad I'm retired and don't have to do it for another ten or fifteen years. But it's been fun."

"I feel the same way, Bob. I have one thing to do before we disband, though. I want to have a dinner with all the team and their wives. All this after we finish our duty and out of uniform."

"I'll make the arrangements when we finish the tour. We still have two men at the hospital guarding a very dangerous man. I'm hoping we can get the court to revoke Town's bail and we can give the guard duty back to Corrections. It won't make him any less dangerous, but they'll be responsible, not us. I think we'll be relieved by the end of the week, anyway."

Bob stood and walked to the end of the table to check on the electronic equipment. "This has finished making our copy. I'll mark the tapes and take the copy to be copied into the report. Why don't you go and report to the captain and I'll meet you here when we both finish. We should go to the hospital and see how John and Randy are doing."

"Good idea, Bob. See you back here in a few minutes."

A short time later the two officers were in Bill's car driving to the hospital. They entered through the main entry and checked in with the receptionists at the desk. They gave no details but said they were here to see a patient. In the lobby they found the stairway to the second floor where the ICU was located. The front door to the unit was locked. They spoke into the intercom for entry. The door buzzed and opened. The nurse at the desk met them and took them to another secured room and unlocked the door. Inside they could see the patient was awake, obviously uncomfortable, and Randy standing near the door while John sat near the bed reading an Outdoor Life magazine.

"The doctor will be here soon to explain the patient's condition. He's doing as well as can be expected after shoulder replacement. Call me if you want out of the room." With that she turned and went back through the exit door.

John watched her go before commenting, "Hail, Hail, the gang's all here."

"How are you doing, guys?" asked Bill.

"We're doing fine, Boss. Ol' Steve here is doing fine, too."

The door opened again, and the doctor entered. "Well, it looks like this patient has quite a fan club," he said while still looking at the patient. "How are you feeling, Mr. Town?"

"Like I need to get out of here," replied Town in a tired voice.

"Well, let's take a look at that arm and see how it's doing." The doctor peeled back the bandage and looked at the incision site. "Roll onto your good side for me."

Town complied, wincing as he moved.

"It's looking good. Lie back down, now. I think you'll be able to leave the hospital in a couple of days."

The doctor turned to the others in the room as he stood, 'I'm guessing you're all troopers, correct?"

"Yes, that's correct, doctor. Did you mean what you said about him being able to leave in a couple of days?" asked Bill.

"Yes, he'll have to go to therapy sessions a couple of times a week, but will be able to leave the hospital," the doctor replied.

"Thanks, doc, that's good news." Bill then turned to Town, "Isn't it Steve?"

Town only grunted and closed his eyes.

"Let us know when he can be picked up and we'll make the arrangements," said Bill.

When the doctor had gone Bill turned to his men, "We'll likely be done the first of the week. Thanks for making this recall a good experience. You did a great job, men." Bill wanted to say more but was reluctant to do so in front of the patient. "I'll call the DA to see what they want done with him. I'll get back to you as soon as I find out. Stay alert, guys. Do you need anything?"

The answer was no. Bill left the hospital with Bob, returning to the office where Bill called Walker to explain the pending release of Town. Walker said he would check with the judge and get right back to them.

When the answer came, it was to return Steve Town to Corrections. His bail had been revoked.

CHAPTER THIRTY-EIGHT

Friday morning seemed much different this week. It was their last week as contract troopers and Bill Koogan had very mixed feelings about it.

He'd selected these men because each had a different personality and different skills. For that reason, the small team was able to do an outstanding, thorough job.

The murder of Lee Woods had taken away any time to be bored or distracted and gave the Squad a real purpose for being there every day.

The captain gave Bill the task of evaluating each man's performance while under contract with the State. He sat at his desk, daydreaming, while thinking about how well they had performed overall.

He couldn't think of any instance in which they'd failed any assigned task. They not only completed their tasks but did so without flaw. After thinking about it for a long while, he decided to give every man an outstanding evaluation.

There was a blank form to be filled out for each one. He had just begun the task when the three men came into the office. Bill put the forms away and joined them at the coffee pot. They gathered in the conference room to plan the last day of duty.

"Say, Boss. If you had it to do over again, I'll bet you'd have picked a different team," commented John Ashley. The others laughed and agreed with him.

"I'd pick the same bunch. I've learned from this experience that the threat of DO IT OR BE SHOT works very well with you guys." Now the entire team was laughing.

When the joking was over, Bill made a serious statement. "With all sincerity, I want you all to know I'm very proud of the way this Squad performed. I know it was partly because you were here voluntarily and not just for the paycheck. I also know I picked the right men for the job. I give you my deepest thanks for what each of you brought to the team."

"I've worked for worse bosses," said Bob Barratt. He then added, "Oh wait a minute, that was you, too." The entire table erupted in loud laughter.

"What about you, Randy? Did you have as much fun as the rest of us?" asked Bill.

"I guess if this is true confessions, I'd have to say this is the best team I've ever worked with. Every man here, including you Bill, did his job in an exceptional manner. Never passing the buck, never attempting to avoid doing any task. It's made this little stint a very memorable time for me."

"Thanks for the kind words, Randy. We feel the same about you and the way you performed."

Bill took a last swallow of coffee and gave one of the last orders he would give here. "Clean up the office and empty the file cabinets. I have some paperwork to do. And, I want to have a farewell dinner at Froso's tomorrow evening. Six o'clock, bring your appetite and your wives."

He returned to his small office to finish work on the personnel evaluations. He knew the captain would be writing his today and would call him to the office to read and sign it. The others would get to read theirs, one by one, in the captain's office too.

As things began to wind down, he called the DA. "Hi there, Walker. I like using your private number. I can talk with you any time I want."

Walker chuckled, "Thanks for interrupting my day, Bill. I suppose you want to know about the Fed arraignment?"

"Good guess, how did it go?"

"Held over for trial with no bail, as he was deemed a flight risk. Are you happy now?" asked Walker.

"Yes, I am. Today is our last day as troopers and I wanted to say so long and thank you for being so helpful for us here at the Geezer Squad."

"I'm going to be sorry to see you go, Bill. You and your team did an outstanding job. Thanks," said a grateful Walker.

He sat in his small office for a long while after finishing the evaluations, going over the list of things he should do before leaving the office. Each man, including himself, would be asked to come to the office on Monday to turn in the uniforms and gear belonging to the State.

While here, each would be invited to the captain's office to read and sign their evaluation reports. It was all a formality. He was glad the tour was ending. He was also sad to be leaving a job he loved.

Finally, he decided he had no other duties to perform, and would take his own vehicle to make reservations for dinner tomorrow night. Then he would go to the Soldotna Police Department to invite Chief Bud Griffin to the dinner, too.

Froso, the restaurant owner is a beautiful and very personable lady. She takes every customer as a friend. No free lunch, but she makes everyone feel at home in her place. The food is always good and the service excellent, but Bill and his crew would get extra care at this dinner.

Bill took Froso aside and explained what he had in mind. She agreed to go along with it. She'd have the banquet room ready tomorrow evening. Six o'clock. The guests would be ordering from the menu.

With all the details worked out, Bill drove to the station to invite Griffin to the dinner.

The chief came to the lobby to escort Bill to his office. He offered coffee, but Bill turned it down. "What can I do for you today, Bill?" asked Bud.

"I don't know if you're aware. Today is our last day on duty with the troopers. We'll come to the office on Monday to turn in our State gear and we'll be done. I came here to ask you and your wife to join us for dinner at Froso's tomorrow evening at six. Will you be there?" asked Bill.

"I'd be delighted. When you leave, I'll call my wife and tell her to get prettied up for the occasion. I'm honored, Bill, thanks."

Bill stood to leave, "Good, I'll see you tomorrow evening.'

On his way home he reviewed the past weeks and decided there was nothing left to do. He was satisfied with what he'd done and was proud of the Squad's performance. His wife would be glad he was home for good. Bill had to admit he was glad it had ended, too.

The following evening, Bill and his wife dressed in evening attire and drove to the restaurant for the gathering. Some of the guests were already in the banquet room with glasses of wine in front of them. The next to arrive was Bud Griffin and his young wife. They were shaking hands when the last couple came into the room. It was John Ashley and his wife.

Everyone was seated around the table when Froso came to ask what they'd like to drink. Bill ordered several bottles of wine, a kind for every taste: Red, White, Dry, and Sweet. She made certain there were no empty bottles, replacing them with full chilled ones.

At the appropriate time, Froso and another waitress came to take the orders. More wine was delivered during the meal. It was a very pleasant event. No one drank too much. Everyone joined the conversations.

When the main courses were finished and the tables cleared, Bill invited everyone to the desert bar for pie and ice cream. Froso asked Bud Griffin and his wife what they'd like, and she would get it for them. They opted for pie and ice cream. She brought it to them so they didn't have to stand in line or wait.

While they waited for her to return, the rest of the banquet guests formed a line and exited the restaurant through the door at the other end of the main dining room. '

When Froso returned with their deserts, she handed Bud an envelope with his name on it. He opened the envelope to find a card saying "THANK YOU".

Inside the card was the tab for the entire meal and wine. The message inside read:

Thank you for dinner
THE GEEZER SQUAD

"He said he'd get even," Chief Griffin laughed so hard he had tears in his eyes.